DESIRE IN DEADWOOD

LYNN ELDRIDGE

WOLFPACK
PUBLISHING
— EST 2013 —

Desire in Deadwood

Paperback Edition

© Copyright 2022 (As Revised) Lynn Eldridge

Wolfpack Publishing

5130 S. Fort Apache Rd. 215-380

Las Vegas, NV 89148

wolfpackpublishing.com

Paperback ISBN 978-1-63977-239-1

DESIRE IN DEADWOOD

To My Family
You make all of my dreams come true.

The course of true love never did run smooth.
    —William Shakespeare

CHAPTER 1

Deadwood, Dakota Territory
August 1876

ACES AND EIGHTS. THE DEAD MAN'S HAND.

"Damn you, take that!" yelled the crooked nose man as he squeezed the trigger.

The blast knocked his feet out from under him. Brilliant lights flashed before his eyes as his head slammed against the wooden floor. He blinked hard, seeing the revolver swaying four feet above him. Shouts surrounded him as blackness obliterated the agony.

Shivers of pain up his right leg roused him. Had he missed something? Like a few hours or with any luck, only seconds. Why was he spread-eagled on the floor? He tried to sit up, but searing torture knifed through his right foot. He raised his head and looked down his vest, shirt, and chaps to his booted feet. Blood was pooling under his right boot. As his head fell back against the floor he eyed the elderly gentleman, with a drooping mustache, looming over him.

"Wild Bill Hickok's just been shot!"

Was the older man calling him Wild Bill Hickok or someone else? The name Bill Hickok sounded familiar. He couldn't think. The fire in his foot clouded his concentration. Grunting, he took another stab at sitting up, but again the pain stopped him.

"I've been shot," he mumbled.

"Sure 'nough." The aged man scratched his bald head making wisps of gray hair, over his ears, bob. On one good leg and one peg leg, he took off at an amazingly fast trot. "Hickok's reflexes were so fast his gun was halfway outa his holster!"

Feeling for a gun, he found he had two, both holstered. Then he heard a man cry out in pain.

"The bullet that hit Hickok is buried in my wrist!"

"Cap'n William Massie's been hit, too!" someone hollered.

The name William Massie wasn't familiar. Besides, the pain burning into him was in his heel, not his wrist. What was going on?

"What happened?"

"O'course, the town crier'd stick his nose in where it don't belong!" the peg-legged man said.

Bursting through swinging doors a tousle-haired, gangly young man huffed, gawking this way and that before wailing, "I'm just doin' my part to report the news, that's all."

"Awright, awright! Fer now, you can tell yer newspaper boss that Hickok, the riverboat cap'n and a stranger got shot. Also, tell Mr. Merrick that the others playin' five card draw, Carl Mann and Charles Rich, ain't been hit. Now scat!"

Mann and Rich rang no bells. Was this utter confusion and intense pain hell? Had he been bad enough in life to go to hell?

"Well, stranger, fell into some trouble, didn't you?" came a soft drawl, southern maybe.

He rolled his head sideways toward a gingham skirt partially covered by a worn apron. His eyes took in a tiny waist and full breasts. Pink lips treated him to a sunny smile of concern. She had the most alluring eyes he'd ever seen. The deep green of a lush forest, a sparkle in those eyes mesmerized. The eyes of an adventuress in the face of an angel.

Was he in trouble? Yes, he'd gotten himself into big, damn trouble with a capital T.

"Burns like the devil?" the angel-face asked.

Was that a golden halo around this angel's head? He squinted. No, it was her hair piled atop her head. Wonder how long her hair...

"Did you bite your tongue off when you got shot?"

"No," he replied, his ears ringing now. "Where am I?" *Who am I?*

"Deadwood."

"I'm dead?"

"You're in the Number Ten Saloon in the Black Hills."

Pulling up a chair she angled it toward him, grasped his arm, and tugged. Gritting his teeth against the pain, he managed to sit up. Then wrapping both of her delicate hands around his right arm, she pulled harder. Delicate, yes, but stronger than she looked. With her help, he stood on his left foot and dropped into the chair.

Frowning, he barked, "Are you trying to make this worse?"

"Oh, stop that bellyaching."

He squinted. "Do I know you?"

"No. I'm Tansy." Did she just cringe? "Who are you?"

"Not all right, that's who, Ta..Tan..?" Trouble with a capital T? Damn the pain! "Who?"

"My name is Jigger Crown," she replied. That's not what she had just said, and Jigger didn't sound like a real name to him. "I run the saloon next door. I've only been in town since last—"

"Listen, lady, I don't care what you do or how long you've been here. Why're you telling me your life story when I'm bleeding like a stuck pig?" he asked, pointing at his foot.

Hands going to her hips she said, "I've been told I have an entertaining bedside manner and was just trying to get your mind off your pain. Since you're set on dwelling on it, I may as well tell you there's no exit hole in your boot. I figure the bullet's lodged on the inside of your heel, below your ankle."

"What did I do to get myself into this mess?" he asked himself.

"Doesn't take much. Deadwoods soaked in blood, whiskey, and corruption. Men die every day over jumped mine claims or poker bets or women or..." She stopped when he held up his hand.

Who was this breathtakingly chatterbox?

"Anyway," she went on, "I heard that Mr. Hickok shot you when he tried to pull his gun out of his holster. I was next door at the time, but I wouldn't doubt it. Everybody knows Wild Bill, the Prince of Pistoleers, had somewhat of a reputation for shooting the wrong man."

"If he'd had that first chamber in his gun empty, for safety's sake, I wouldn't be bleeding," he said, now fully conscious that he wasn't dead or Hickok.

"Yes, well," she placed her hand to his forehead and

continued, "my father was a doctor and I've done some nursing in my time, so I thought I could help out here today."

He sensed blood oozing out of his body and blinked as things threatened to go dark again. His foot throbbed like a thousand poisonous snakes had bitten him all at once. But the angel's palm and fingers were soft, cool, and comforting against his pounding forehead.

"Gimpy says you're lucky to be alive. The gunman snapped his revolver at you and several others. But after the first shot through the back of Mr. Hickok's head, the gun misfired."

"Gimpy?" he tried to rally. "Who the hell is Gimpy?"

"The man who made sure you were alive by tapping your right foot." So, that's what had roused him from the blackness of oblivion. The angel withdrew her hand. "You're chilled. You probably have a concussion. Let's get you into bed so that I can see to you."

If she got him into bed, he'd see to her. Straining to remain coherent he asked, "Isn't there a doctor in this godforsaken hellhole?"

"Doc Pierce is busy now. I'll get one of Doc Young-blood's rejuvenizes for you later." When she smiled down at him, he imagined pulling her to him for a kiss. "I don't expect you'll die in my hands."

Die in her hands? Wouldn't be the worst way to go. Was she saying something else?

"Tansies can be poisonous to..." He was drifting in and out. "But for healing..." The ringing in his ears roared and he lost track again. "...slender stem, yellow button of a flower...eases headaches, dizziness, and weakness." What? "...called tansy tea."

Why did she just bite her lower lip? He reached for

his foot, but the floor rushed toward him, and he was out again.

A FEMALE VOICE, singing unfamiliar words, Spanish he thought. As he opened his eyes, he hoped getting shot had been a bad dream. No, the pain in his foot was still there. Feather pillows were propping him up in a short, wide bed, and flowers strewn before him looked like a meadow sprinkled in yellow. No, not a meadow, but a scroll or a painting. What kind of flowers were they? Hell, his head hurt.

Curtains, ruffled by a warm breeze, drew his attention to an open window. Seeing the top of a pine tree, he knew he was on the second floor of a building. Footsteps shuffling down a wooden boardwalk and the clamor of agitated male voices drifted up to him.

Grimacing at the pain in his foot he felt the sheets stuck to his back. Bare back. Was he naked? He glanced down the black hair on his chest to the white sheet below his navel. Underneath no gun belt, chaps, or pants. Suddenly, the door opened, and he felt the pillows slip sideways.

"You were shot in the foot." The angel smiled, noticing his concern. "Everything else is just fine."

So, she was a sassy little spitfire who'd seen how much of him?

"You and your property are up above my saloon now. Your pants were bloody and torn and you don't need your vest and shirt or chaps in bed, so that's why you're naked."

If being bare assed wasn't bad enough, his foot hurt so much he thought he might black out again. Have to stay awake to figure out what's going on, he thought.

"I went downstairs for some red-eye," the blond angel with emerald, green eyes said, indicating the cheap, saloon fare bottle of whiskey in her hand. Closing the door she warned, "You'll surely need it when I go after that bullet, Mr. Rivers."

"What did you ca—? How do you know my name?"

CHAPTER 2

"After Gimpy cut off your britches, I looked through your belongings. Your pants and vest pockets were weighted down with double eagles. I guess money won't be a problem for you."

Double eagles were twenty-dollar gold pieces with a liberty head on one side and an eagle on the reverse. He also remembered that five hundred dollars seemed to be the amount he usually carried.

"I know who you are because your peace officer's badge with your name on the back was also in your pocket. What I can't figure out is why the badge was in your pocket with your money, instead of pinned on your leather vest."

"Because...because that information is confidential. Let me have my badge."

"You can have it later."

As she leaned over and readjusted the pillows under his head, the neck of her cotton frock gaped slightly away from her body. A soap fresh scent wafted pleasantly up his nose as the swell of her ample breasts hastened his heartbeat. She had cheeks the color of peaches and skin like honey dripped over creamy oatmeal. Desire hummed in his loins as he groaned at the conglomeration of swirling emotions.

"I know you're hurting, Mr. Rivers," she said. "Gimpy went looking for the town doctors to purchase chloroform. But Deadwood has a population of forty-eight hundred people these days. So, as I feared the chloroform's been used up on the men feuding over jumped mine claims or poker bets or well, you know. There's no morphine or laudanum, either." With a shake of her head, she warned, "You asked if I was trying to make this worse and well, this *is* going to get worse before it gets better."

But making it better at the moment was watching her bosom jiggle as she gave his pillows a final pat. He couldn't remember the last time he'd seen a woman this close up. But his heated reaction to her suggested it had been a while since he'd bedded one. She stood up straight as a wayward strand of long golden hair slipped out of the bun on her head. It curled around her graceful neck and slid between her breasts. Oh yeah, he wanted this angel of mercy even if she was a chatterbox.

Her appealing drawl, he decided, sounded more Texan than deep South. Her frock was thin, meant to deal with summertime heat. But the Dakota Territory was known for its cold, not its warmth. She turned and walked to the foot of the bed. The dress outlined her hips and her bottom swayed. She faced him again and he quickly looked her in the eye. Her arched brow raised telling him she knew his eyes had been fixed on her rounded fanny.

Her appraising look made him even hotter.

"You must be six three or four because your feet are

hanging way over the end of the bed," she said with a sweep of her hand. "This bed has two mattresses, one on top of the other, and I know it's comfortable. But Gimpy had to bring up my piano bench and put it at the end of the mattresses to accommodate your height."

"Six four." How did he know that? "Two hundred, twenty pounds."

"Yes, you're a big one. Big boned, big hands, broad shoulders, muscular chest, long legs and..." A blush stained her cheeks as her voice trailed off, "and...such."

He had a peace officer's badge. So, if he were asked for an official description of her, he'd say she was a beautiful green-eyed blonde, about five feet five and a hundred pounds lighter than he was. Privately he'd make note of her sunny smile, small bones, slender figure, and a full bosom that strained against the bodice of her worn frock.

Despite a familiar warmth coiling in his lower body, he recklessly let his gaze linger on her breasts as she placed an extra pillow under the injured heel. Fierce pain shot through him. But the crease of ivory cleavage distracted him, and he licked his lips. He fought the conflict of a rising desire in his loins and the stabbing pain in his heel by closing his eyes.

"Are you still with me, Mr. Rivers?"

"Yeah," he groaned. "Just call me by my first name."

"Only if you won't call me any foul names when I dig that bullet out of your foot. Deal?"

"Deal." He opened his eyes despite the agony and lifted his head. His right foot was already turning black and blue. It was swollen and oozing a steady stream of bright red blood. "Dammit," he muttered and sank back on the pillow. Bathed in sweat and sick to his stomach, he said. "Pour some whiskey over it before gangrene sets in and then give me the bottle."

"Yes, I planned to."

Whiskey sloshed over the wound, shocking his senses with a crucifying torture making him hope he would die on the spot.

"Sonofa—" He cut himself off. Then a second onslaught of whiskey burned him like liquid fire. "God —" With iron will he locked his jaw. Grasping the sheets, he balled his hands into fists.

Moving to his side she took his left hand and eased his fist open, placing the whiskey bottle in his grip as she slid a soft hand under his neck. "You have gorgeous hair," she said smoothly, unruffled by his yelling, his wound, or the shootings which had caused both. Her composure was proof she'd done some nursing. "The silver streak at your right temple is a fascinating contrast to the rest of your coal black hair. It's like a slice of moonlight at midnight. I bet when you untie that rawhide strip at the back your long hair spreads across your broad shoulders like fine silk, doesn't it?"

"Hell, no!" he choked and glared up at her. With his free hand, he wiped the sweat off his burning brow. "I don't have silk hair."

"Were you born with that streak?"

"I was struck by lightning!" That wasn't true, but he was in such pain he didn't care. "Just get on with fixing my foot or you'll be damn good 'n sorry!"

"Hush," she murmured. "Your first name tells me you were born with that streak."

He didn't understand. But if he asked her to explain, he'd tip his hand about his splintered memory. He'd wager her hair felt as soft as fine silk. Liking the length and the light color, he followed the wayward, curling strand from around her neck to her tempting bosom.

"Drink the red-eye. Mayhap you'll be less ornery."

"Listen, lady, I was tipping whiskey bottles while you were still in diapers. Let go of me."

"You're the one acting like a baby." She pulled her hand from under his neck and crossed her arms under her breasts.

Ignoring her comment, he swigged the whiskey. It burned his throat in a good way. Just to prove he could and to dull the pain, he downed half of what was left then covered his eyes with his right arm.

"Dig the bullet out," he grumbled.

"Please, Jigger?"

"Please, ma'am."

"I see we're our own man." There was a definite smirk in her soft drawl. "Slip this between your teeth and bear down when the pain gets too bad."

Smelling pine, he clenched his jaw refusing to let her slip the wood between his teeth. She laid the piece of pine on his bare chest. He smacked the wood away and gulped more whiskey.

Dear God, why am I unshaven, naked, dripping sweat and blood, and about to make a trip into the depths of hell? Just then cold steel touched the fevered flesh of his heel and he braced himself as the blade pushed deep.

"Christ Almighty!" he roared.

"Hold still!" she yelled right back.

Through a haze of pain, he could make out this angel nurse on the piano bench at the end of the bed, his foot between her knees. All he had to do was stretch and his toes would touch that ivory cleavage. Instead, he tipped the whiskey to his lips and drained the bottle. Any other time, the foulest oaths he could spew would have bounced off the walls of this bedroom. He threw the empty whiskey bottle at the door.

"Bolton Rivers!" the angel shouted as glass shattered.

Bolton? Yeah, Bolt sounded familiar.

In a far corner of his mind, a smiling man said he was born during a lightning storm. A gentle lady whispered that when his guardian angel kissed him, she'd left behind a lock of blond hair. It had since turned silver. Then the snarling, scarred faces of desperate men replaced the tenderhearted people, swearing the silver streak in his hair was the mark of the devil.

Bolt arched his back away from the sheet as the pain intensified. Rather than break his word and curse, he laughed. Loudly. He squeezed his eyes shut and howled with laughter. It distracted him some. But he was living second by second, wondering if he could possibly survive another full minute of this hell. Then for a moment, the cutting stopped. Flattening his hands to the sheet over his stomach, he tried to catch his breath.

"Do ya need help, Jigger?" Sounded like Gimpy.

Bolt didn't open his eyes when a new female voice spoke.

"Mi Dios, he is atractivo...attractive," she whispered with a Spanish accent. "He looks as strong as a...as a..."

"A wild stallion," the angel said. "I'm glad you're back Gimpy. Lupe, thank you for coming with Gimpy to help. I think Mr. Rivers has lost consciousness again. The two of you hold his legs because if he wakes up, he'll buck like a bronco when I pull out that bullet."

Feeling two sets of hands clamp down on him, one set on one leg and one on the other, Bolt slit open his eyes. Gimpy, on his right, was studying his foot as a young Mexican woman stared at the sheet over his hips. The knife dug in again and he laughed.

"I don't know if he's still awake or not, but I jist seen his eyes roll up in his head like winder shades," Gimpy said.

"I'll bet this man can work magic on a woman." Lupe tugged the sheet from under Bolt's hands. "I'll have a peek."

"Lupe, you certainly will not!" the angel snapped. "He needs us to work our magic now."

There was a disgruntled female sigh and then Lupe's hands clamped down on his thigh and calf.

"Like you asked, Jigger," Gimpy began, "I went back to the Number Ten Saloon to see if anybody came to Deadwood with Mr. Rivers."

"And?" she asked.

"Nobody knowed," Gimpy whispered. "But his name struck fear on the faces of gunmen I thought was the baddest of the bad."

"Ooh!" Lupe tittered. "Who is Señor Rivers?"

Bolt gritted his teeth against the pain and held his breath. He needed to hear the answer.

"Dear Lord, help me," the angel prayed. "The bullet drove scraps of leather from his boot so far into his heel that I know, unconscious or not, trying to get the bullet and leather out is killing him."

Bullet...killing...Bolt had just entered where? The Number 10 Saloon? As he strode in back of a man playing five card draw, he'd noted the poker player held two black aces and a pair of black eights.

Another man who'd come through the rear door was now within three feet of the poker player. Too late to intervene, Bolt saw the man fire a gun at the back of the seated man's head. In that split second, the card player was a dead man.

"Gimpy!" Lupe squealed. "Who is this big bad

hombre, who laughs when a bullet's being dug out of his foot?"

A branding iron heated by the fires of hell burrowed into his gunshot wound.

"Rivers is the infamous and notorious..." Gimpy replied as Bolton Rivers passed out cold.

CHAPTER 3

Tansy pressed a cool cloth to Bolton's forehead, relieved the sheets were no longer damp from his fevered sweat. When his eyelids fluttered, she seated herself in a chair beside the bed.

"Bolton, we could talk about the mother doe that was slaughtered by the horrible giant with frizzy red hair. You've been mumbling," she explained as his brow furrowed. "It touches my heart that you found a home for the doe's orphaned fawn."

"That giant orphaned people, too," Bolton rasped, as he forced his eyelids open.

Since meeting him, this man's eyes had been filled with pain. Today, Tansy found herself thinking their color rivaled the deepest blue of the sky above Deadwood's Black Hills.

"So, you are with me," Tansy said to the most magnificent man she had ever laid eyes on, guessing he was less than ten years older than she. "Who orphaned what people?"

Bolton's strong, square jaw clenched. In a husky voice, he finally whispered, "I'm not sure."

"Memories can be as slippery as a bunch of wet puppies." Placing the cool cloth on his forehead, Tansy folded her hands in her lap. "Your fever broke during the night."

"I take it you got the bullet out?"

"Yes, three days ago. And we figured out which horse was yours. Gimpy took him to Red Clark's Livery for food and shelter. What's his name?"

"Silverheels," he replied, rubbing his temple.

"Silverheels? But he's all black except for the white star on his forehead."

"Yeah," he muttered. "I was thinking of Tom's horse."

"Tom?" she asked, trying to make sense of this handsome man's train of thought.

"Tom Smith, the United States Marshal who put the lid on Abilene, Kansas back in seventy. And he did it without firearms until..."

"Until...what?"

"Until he quit being the marshal."

Bolton closed his eyes. Tansy suddenly felt adrift and gave herself a mental shake. Something in Bolton's manner, along with his badge, said he had seen a side of life that would make her shudder.

"Why did he quit being the marshal?"

"Seems like there was an ax murder," Bolton replied, opening his eyes. "They...he...I think people were killed and I can't remember how or why!" He smacked the bed with his fist. "Blazes!"

Tansy jumped. "You've surely suffered a concussion and you lost a lot of blood. I didn't mean to upset you. All you should do is rest now."

She looked down at him, promising herself she wouldn't get lost again in his hypnotic sapphire gaze. But his eyes had the same controlling glint as a lone wolf once had when he stared her down and stole one of her chickens.

"Ma'am?"

"Yes?" She hoped he'd forgotten her real name.

"I want to thank you. I'm in your debt. Name your price."

"You're welcome and you owe me nothing," Tansy murmured. It was one thing to deal with Bolton Rivers when he was a cranky, delirious patient and quite another as a virile, lucid man. "I always do my best to heal anyone in need of my nursing."

He tossed the cloth from his forehead and took her hand just as a knock sounded on the door. She squeezed his hand gently, then stood up.

"Stop!" he barked. "Where's my gun belt?"

"You don't need it."

"Where is it?"

"Right there," she replied, pointing to where his holster hung, loaded with two pearl handled revolvers, over a chair. "I'm sure it's Gimpy or Lupe."

"Always ask who's at the door before you open it."

"You're edgy, but that must come with your claim to fame."

"My claim to—" He tried to sit up. "Hell," he groaned at the pain in his foot. "Give me my guns before you open that door."

"What are you doing in there with my *novio*, Jigger?" came a female voice from outside.

"You see?" Tansy smiled. "It's Lupe. Novio means sweetheart." She turned the doorknob. "He's not your *novio*. You don't even know him and besides, I'm only talking to him, Lupe."

"Women never do what you tell 'em," Bolton said when she opened the door without giving him his gun belt.

Tansy couldn't imagine many if any, women not doing what this man told them. Lupe, all eyes, and grin, entered. Bolton yanked the sheet up the slim trail of masculine fur decorating his washboard stomach, past his broad chest, to his sun bronzed neck.

"Aww," Lupe pouted.

"He must have been awake when you said you were going to peek under the sheet the other day, Lupe," Tansy said with a soft laugh.

Lupe tossed her long black braid over the puffed sleeve on her shoulder and swayed toward the bed. "You sat with him when he was sick. Now that he's awake, I'll feed him."

"I can feed myself, thank you," Bolton said.

Bolton looked Lupe up and down and Tansy wondered if he found her brown eyes, black hair, and light olive skin attractive. Certainly, a man as handsome as Bolton Rivers had known his share of women.

"Jigger? Lupe?" Gimpy called at the door. "Is he awake?"

"Sí," Lupe purred, going to Bolton's bedside.

"Come in, Gimpy," Tansy said, motioning him into the bedroom.

"Ain't ya skeered to be near him now that he's back with the livin'?" The wizened man darted a skittish sideways glance at Bolton and stammered, "Ya—ya know he could turn on ya in a heartbeat, Jigger. He's—" Gimpy choked. "He's Bolt Rivers! Heck-fire, he's—"

"He knows who he is and what he does," Tansy interrupted and turned to Bolton.

"Let him speak his mind," Bolton said. His dark blue

eyes narrowed, as wary as those of a cornered animal. "I want to hear what he has to say."

"I'm sure it's nothing you haven't heard before," Tansy replied. "We aren't here to pass judgment, are we, Gimpy?"

"It's fer sure I ain't never heared you say nothin' bad 'bout nobody, Jigger," Gimpy said. "But, in this here case," fear quivered Gimpy's voice as he ducked his head respectively at Bolton, "beggin' yer pardon, Mr. Rivers, but yer a..."

"A human being who saved a fawn once," Tansy interrupted.

"Don't tell my secrets," Bolton said.

When Bolton winked at her, Tansy's pulse raced. This unpredictable male radiated strength and power and stirred her senses even when flat on his back.

"I just love a man with a secret past!" Lupe said. "Will you tell me yours, Señor Rivers?"

Bolton scowled.

"Gimpy, why don't you go see if you can get one of Doc Youngblood's rejuvenizes for our patient?" Tansy said.

"I don't need a rejuvenizer."

"Fine," Tansy replied. "I have to wait on customers, but I'll fix your supper first."

"Wait!" Bolton called out as Tansy turned toward the door. "Is Bill Hickok dead?"

"Yes, he died instantly," Tansy said. "A man known as Crooked Nose Jack McCall shot him."

Bolton sighed. "It was suicide for a man with Hickok's gunfighter reputation to sit with his back to the door."

Inching out of the room, Gimpy glanced at Bolton's guns. "He's speakin' from experience, Jigger."

"Now, Gimpy," Tansy said gently with a shake of her head. "Other men in our saloon have said the same thing." Looking at Bolton, she explained, "They say Mr. Hickok tried twice to get Mr. Rich to trade places with him at the card table. But Mr. Rich refused. Mr. Hickok was buried on Boot Hill and Preacher Smith said a few words over him. Most of the town attended the funeral."

"Do people think Hickok came to Deadwood alone?" Bolton asked.

"Did you come with him?" Lupe asked, wide-eyed.

A muscle flexed in Bolton's jaw. The thickened, black stubble of beard gave him an even darker and more menacing edge than when Tansy had first met him.

"Lupe, Mr. Hickok came to town with his friend, Colorado Charlie Utter," Tansy answered.

"Did they get Hickok's killer?" Bolton asked.

"Yes, a large crowd found him hiding in the back of a butcher shop. He was tried by a miners' court in the McDaniels/Langrishe Theater."

"Why'd McCall shoot him?"

Gimpy piped up. "Hickok done beat ol' Crooked Nose McCall in cards and offered him money for breakfast. Guess McCall was embarrassed."

"But Jack McCall said it was revenge for Mr. Hickok shooting his brother in Abilene," Tansy added, figuring the peace officer in Bolton needed answers. "It's rumored some skullduggery took place because they found McCall not guilty."

"Blood money buys things," Bolton said.

Tansy shivered. What would she have done had someone burst into the bedroom and shot her patient while he was unarmed and unconscious? She picked up Bolton's gun belt and put it next to him on the bed.

Gimpy finished the story. "A man named California

Joe said Deadwood air might be bad for McCall's health, so Crooked Nose Jack left town."

Shooing Gimpy and Lupe out of the room ahead of her then, Tansy said over her shoulder. "Lupe will be right back with your supper."

She left the room without a backward glance at the sexy rogue in her bed. Lupe all but skipped down the hall ahead of her. Tansy drew in a deep breath and walked alongside Gimpy.

With that ebony hair shot through with the slate streak, those midnight blue eyes, and that muscle packed body, he was a lot of man to deal with for more than a few minutes at a time. On the other hand, if she had looked at him a moment longer, she was afraid she could not have left him at all.

What? Where had that come from? Never before had she thought about a man that way!

Yes, Bolton Rivers was potentially lethal. He emitted savage danger and his reputation confirmed that he could be ruthless and untamed. Yet, as he lay helpless, sprawled across her bed, he was terrifyingly appealing. Stop it! What was wrong with her?

"He'd as soon shoot ya as look at ya, Jigger," Gimpy said.

"You might not think so if you'd heard what he said when he was delirious. He's a dreamer, Gimpy." Pushing her own fears of Bolton Rivers aside, she added softly, "A beautiful dreamer."

"You call him a dreamer, but he catches killers, Jigger!"

"I know. But mayhap he won't take me for one."

CHAPTER 4

So, his name was Bolt Rivers and he had secrets.

Did everyone know what those secrets were except for him? Lupe was back and humming a tune, but he was only half listening as he finished his soup. He handed Lupe the empty bowl. He'd refused the tea she'd also brought, saying he'd stick with whiskey. Lupe had told him Jigger said he had to drink her homemade brew because, among other things, it helped to keep away fevers, cured sores, and dulled rheumatism, so it might even ease his foot pain. He wasn't about to drink out of the dainty cup offered, so he'd had her pour the tea into a half empty bottle of red-eye. It was an awful mixture.

Why was Lupe still here? He wanted the angel back. Whenever her pink lips parted in the sunniest smiles, he'd ever seen he glimpsed straight white teeth. If he undid the bun on her head, would it deepen the peach blush of her soft cheeks? He imagined her flaxen hair spilling down all around her creamy skin. Her creamy naked...

"Jigger took me in when no one else would!" Lupe blurted out, interrupting his thoughts.

"What do you mean?"

"I'm a mixed breed. My padre was white and my madre was Mexican. We came to the Black Hills to pan for gold. One day on Whitewood Creek, a big black bear came out of nowhere and was on us before we knew it. I was close enough to see that it had an eye missing." Lupe lowered her head and sniffled. "It killed my folks and I got away, just barely." She raised her head and shivered. "Other people have seen that same bear since and it's killed some of them!"

Lupe's recollection blended with Bolt's own foggy memories of people being killed...maybe along a stream or a river.

"After I found my way into the gulch," Lupe continued, "I stopped at Deadwood Dolly's Doves and Dance Hall in the badlands. I begged Deadwood Dolly for a singing job. Said she didn't take in riffraff, but that Jigger Crown did. Dolly meant Gimpy. Jigger saved me. I'd never leave her. Neither would Gimpy."

"That's a shame about your folks. You're a survivor. That's good," Bolt said, moved by the girl's story and devotion to her savior and boss. "What's Gimpy holding against me, Lupe?"

Sitting taller, Lupe said, "Don't you know?"

Bolt shrugged and frowned. "People have different prejudices."

"Sí." Lupe sighed. "But just when Gimpy was about to tell your infamous, notorious," her dark eyes grew wide, "secret the other day, Jigger shushed him." She touched a finger to his forehead. "I can do more than sing and serve drinks. I—I'm sure I could make that frown go away."

"No, Lupe." When he brushed her hand from his forehead, her smile faltered. "But thanks."

"Jigger can barely afford my room and board," Lupe fretted. "I'm fourteen; old enough to be an upstairs girl who could earn her keep and not be a burden. But Jigger said no."

Bolt took a sip from the red-eye bottle.

"Since you'd be my first, I wouldn't ask you to pay." Her youthful voice shook. "Just teach me."

"Hell no!" Bolt almost choked on the whiskey tea. "You're a kid, Lupe!"

"Bueno." She stood and made her way to the door. "Maybe when your foot is better, *novio*."

As the door closed behind her, Bolt flung an arm over his eyes. He'd find out about himself from the angel later tonight. So far, he'd only admitted to a memory lapse about people being orphaned and to an ax murder. An ax murder? Preservation instincts warned him against admitting the full extent of his confusion.

Hearing the piano, which Lupe had said her boss played, Bolt's thoughts turned to the angel.

What had he first called her? Ta..Tan? He looked at what he'd figured out was a painting of flowers on a canvas without a frame. *Slender stem, yellow button of a flower.* Slender, with full breasts and a rounded fanny. Yellow buttons, like her blond halo hair. She was as delicate as a flower and smelled just as fresh. A flower somehow connected to tea. Why hadn't he asked Lupe the name of her homemade brew? What was the blonde's real name and how had she wound up in this Dakota Territory gulch?

Damn! He should have listened to her life story when he'd had the chance. It was late and he made the mistake of closing his eyes. The next thing he heard were chirping birds outside his window.

"Dammit," he muttered, irritated that he'd fallen asleep.

"Well, good morning to you, too," the angel said from a rocking chair near the window.

"What are you doing over there?"

"Darning the bullet hole in your sock."

Wrapping the sheet around his waist, Bolt struggled to a sitting position.

"No, Bolton. Lie down."

"I'm getting out of this bed today unless you wanna crawl into it with me."

"You cannot do anything, yet, but rest," she replied.

"Don't bet on it." He swung his good foot to the floor.

"Bolton! Whatever it is you want to do, let me do it for you," she said, jumping out of the rocker.

"I need to get rid of the soup and that foul whiskey tea...what's the name of that tea?"

"Uh...I don't know."

"Yes, you do." Sensing a fib, his eyes narrowed. "Blazes!" Bolt yelped, touching his bandaged foot to the floor. "Why does it still hurt so bad?"

"Well," she drawled, stopping at the end of the bed. "Because."

"Because part of my foot is gone?"

"No." Shaking her head, she came around the bed and placed her hand on his shoulder. Her touch was instantly soothing. "I'm afraid the pain means I didn't get all the boot leather out," she explained and stood back. "I dug out several pieces along with the bullet."

"If you didn't get it all out, we'll know soon enough because it won't heal." A wave of disappointment had swept over him the moment her hand left his shoulder.

"I know you're speaking in part from experience." A blush heightened the peach of her cheeks. "I saw some old scars on your shoulder and ribs."

Bolt concentrated, sweeping cobwebs off the events in his past. "The shoulder scar came from a bullet wound in...uh...Colorado City and I took a Missouri toothpick in the ribs around...St. Louis." When she tilted her head, he said, "A Missouri toothpick is a knife."

"You lead a perilous life," she whispered. "Gimpy brought Doc Pierce by when you were asleep. He said we need to ward off red streaks at all costs. Red streaks mean septicemia; a blood infection according to my father, Dr. Wiley."

He recognized her now familiar cringe.

"If you'll show me to the room where you keep the tub, I need to...to wash up."

"The bathtubs at the other end of the hall. You'd never make it."

What the hell, he could hold it. With a grin, he clamped his hands around her small waist. "So, you're gonna crawl into bed with me?" He lay back across the bed, pulling her to him. Her breasts pressed against his bare chest and her legs slipped between his thighs. Naked under the sheet, he groaned. He thought he felt her heart pounding, but maybe it was only his own.

"I'm quite certain I will never crawl into bed with you."

This was a woman, not a kid, and not an upstairs girl...or was she? Bolt's grin faded. "Why haven't you slapped me?"

"I'm a healer. You don't need to lose what ground you've gained in a fight with me, Bolton."

"Take a nap with me. That would be the best medicine," he said, wanting to ease further into the bed and roll over on top of her. In preparing to do so, he pressed both feet to the floor and lightning exploded in his right foot. He caught sight of the flower painting again. Trouble with a capital T. "Tansies!" He remembered. "Tansy tea." What else had she said? "Tansies are poisonous!"

"I said tansies are poisonous to intestinal worms!" she said, rolling off him and out of bed.

"Worms?" He must have missed that part. "Well now, I don't have that problem, *Tansy Wiley*."

He saw the adventuress as her green eyes took on a wild look and her body tensed, ready to run.

"You figured out my given name!"

"Yeah," he said, managing to sit up on the side of the bed.

"My father used flowers and herbs in his doctoring. So, he and my mother named me Tansy because of the tansy's many healing qualities. Mama painted those tansies for me." She pointed to the unframed canvas and then glared at her own finger. "I don't know why I'm telling you all of this! Stop staring me down like a wolf about to steal my chicken!"

He smothered a grin. "You have chickens, chatterbox?"

"Right out back!" Smacking her hands to her hips she said, "Stop asking me personal questions!"

Bolt chuckled for the first time in a long time. It felt so good to tease her. "You'd better be trying to heal me and not planning to poison me."

"I don't poison people! I promise I will heal you." Her eyes glittered with determination. "Now if you'll excuse me, I'll fix you a hot bath," she said as a knock sounded on the door.

"Go away!" Bolt barked. No one dared open the door,

so Tansy hurried to it. She had her hand on the knob when Bolt said, "Stop!" Tansy twirled to face him. "Lupe was here singing your praises and I'll bet Gimpy's come to warn me off. I see no parents. I see no wedding band. Yet, you introduced yourself to me as Jigger *Crown*. I hear a southern kinda drawl out of place in Dakota Territory. So, the peace officer in me wants to know why the daughter of a doctor is all alone and running a saloon in a town soaked in blood, whiskey, and corruption."

Tansy saw the glint of battle in his sapphire blue eyes. With a cool, collected air she didn't feel she opened the door and let Gimpy in. She'd been so careful about her past until now, she thought as she closed the door behind her. What came over her in Bolton Rivers' presence that made her blurt out the truth to questions he asked?

It could not be a coincidence that this dangerous rogue was here in Deadwood. People didn't venture into this *godforsaken hellhole* without a reason. He was the law and worse. Much worse.

For the first time since fleeing Texarkana, Tansy was deathly afraid.

CHAPTER 5

"Weren't no sawbones around to come see 'bout me that day, so I'da bled to death if Jigger'd been too squeamish to finish the job," Gimpy said, rapping his wooden peg with his knuckles.

Still irritated over the scene with Tansy, Bolt grabbed his pants from Gimpy. Wielding his Bowie knife, he sliced open a couple inches of the right seam near the ankle to accommodate his bandaged foot.

"Finish what job?" Bolt asked.

"Takin' my foot off. I was in Jigger's saloon when that ugly cuss wouldn't pay fer the two bottles of red-eye he swallered up. I kicked him and," Gimpy grimaced, "he took my foot near clean off with a hatchet."

A hatchet. Bolt's memories were stuck to the bottom of a river. Why wouldn't they surface?

"Sit." Bolt motioned to the chair near his bed. "That's too bad about your foot."

"Jigger sewed me up with a curved needle and silk thread. Her papa learned her nursin'."

"Yes, so she said. Why does she go by Jigger?"

"On accounta that's her name!" Gimpy snorted with a laugh. "I'd say it's a right perfect one fer a barkeep who says the red-eye is too strong to serve more'n a jiggerful at a time. The customers don't like that none, but she's so purdy they come here anyway."

Pretty? Stunningly beautiful, Bolt thought.

"When I tried to get my job back in the mines the bosses poked fun at me sayin' my peg would sink into the red clay and I couldn't pull it out. That's when Jigger gave me room 'n board. I love Jigger like the child I never had. As fer Lupe, she woulda ended up a soiled dove if Jigger ain't a took her in."

"You mean at Deadwood Dolly's?"

"Been to the badlands, huh?"

"Where's her family?"

"They were in Texarkana. Her mama died when she was little. She won't say when her papa died jist that he's gone now. With nothin' to keep her there, Jigger come here to the Black Hills."

Bolt shook his head. "That's a long way for a woman to travel by herself. And why Deadwood, for God's sake?" Gimpy only shrugged. "There's not even a stagecoach into this gulch. It's like trying to reach the end of the world to get here. There's more to her story than meets the eye." Bolt knew in his gut there was more to his own story, too.

"She's here and that's all that matters to me and Lupe and ever'body who's lucky 'nough to cross her sweet path."

AT THAT VERY MOMENT, Tansy was wishing Bolton Rivers had never darkened her doorstep. She should have been suspicious the moment Gimpy told her what his profession was. Being too trusting had once again proven her downfall. She closed her father's doctor's bag and snapped her carpetbag shut.

"I DIDN'T MEAN ANY DISRESPECT," Bolt said as he made an effort to stand.

Gimpy nodded and fetched the stick he'd propped against a chest of drawers. "I brung ya this walkin' stick, Mr. Rivers," he said, handing Bolt a tall, sturdy tree limb with a padded, shorter limb nailed on top of it. "Jigger told me 'xactly how tall ya was and I whittled this fer ya jist like I whittled me this here peg."

"Thank you, Mr.—?"

"Goe. Jist call me Gimpy. It's my given name."

Gimpy smiled under his gray mustache. Bolt wondered if that mustache was to hide a couple of missing teeth.

"All right. But I want you to call me Bolt instead of Mr. Rivers."

"I might if ya was to swear ya ain't here to hurt Jigger and that ya won't ask me no more questions 'bout her."

Bolt nodded. "Tell me what you've heard about me then, Gimpy."

Gimpy shook his head. "Jigger ain't allowin' me to do that, neither. But in case yer awondering 'bout my name, I was borned with a club foot and my pa was borned with a sense of humor," Gimpy said cackling, at peace with his lot in life.

Bolt motioned to the silver streak in his hair. "My father had a sense of humor, too." And his mother had been as lovely as she was kind.

"That ugly cuss I kicked in the shin swore he'd done me a favor by riddin' me of my club foot. I'm the only man in Deadwood with a peg leg. Jigger says it's my claim to fame."

What is my supposed claim to fame, Bolt wondered?

"Now that I have a walking stick, I can make it down the hall. Earlier, when I said I needed to wash up, somebody wouldn't let me out of bed."

Gimpy's wrinkled face flushed. "I never knowed Jigger to...to...forget it."

Bolt kept his word and didn't ask. Not knowing the layout of the saloon's second floor, he allowed Gimpy to accompany him down the hall to camouflage the fact he had the walking stick. Sure, enough they passed a wide staircase where he glanced down to a room full of men before continuing on to the hot bath. With a nod, Gimpy opened the washroom door and returned to the saloon.

TANSY SWIPED tears off her cheeks and told herself to turn her wishbone into a backbone. Though Deadwood was too cold for her in the winter, she'd felt safe here. Now that Bolton Rivers was after her, she was safe no more and had to run. At least it was Sunday, the perfect day to hitch a ride out of the gulch with the wagon train. Most people who left the Black Hills went south to Cheyenne to make connections elsewhere. Going south was dangerous for her, but since she couldn't afford a horse, she had to go wherever the wagon train was headed. In an ox-pulled wagon it took a week to reach Cheyenne, walking took fifteen days. In Cheyenne, she would talk her way onto a stagecoach or sneak aboard the Union Pacific train and get as far away as possible from the man who captured killers.

.   .   .

"I JUST GOT out of the tub and I'm naked, but you're welcome to come in, ma'am," Bolt said, hearing the timid knock and grinning.

"It's Lupe, SeñorSeñor Rivers," she said, not opening the door. "I'm looking for Jigger."

"I haven't seen her for a while. Is there a problem?"

"It's just not like her to stay away from the saloon this long when we're so busy."

"I've heard the noise. Gimpy says there are twenty-six saloons in Deadwood. Why is this one suddenly so busy?"

"Because on Sunday the mines are shut down. Most of the miners in the Hills come to Main Street with their gold dust to get food and supplies or spend money in the saloons and dance halls. Our saloon is so busy because of the men like Jigger. If you see her, will you tell her we need her downstairs?"

"Yeah," Bolt growled, knowing something was up.

HEART POUNDING, Tansy peeked around the doorjamb of her bedroom but seeing Lupe, she ducked back. She'd given up this room to Bolton because it had the biggest bed. Up here on the second floor, besides the wash-room, hers and Lupe's rooms, there was another smaller bedroom. But she hadn't used it because she'd dozed in the rocking chair to keep an eye on her patient.

Gimpy preferred having the room downstairs near the kitchen.

When Bolton was asleep, she had slipped clothes and things she needed out of her room. Today, she'd needed to get her father's doctor bag and stuff whatever she could into her carpetbag.

Lupe's footsteps said she was hurrying down the staircase to the increasingly rowdy saloon.

Tansy knew everybody was probably on the lookout for her now. She planned to get away through the extra bedroom because that's where they kept a ladder in case of fire. But it was next to the washroom. Making matters worse, the staircase lay between her and freedom. Where the stairs met the second floor hallway, she could be seen from the saloon. But there was no avoiding that dangerous part of her only escape route. Spurred by the mental picture of descending the ladder and running down Main Street to the wagon trains, she took another peek around the doorjamb.

Lupe was gone and seeing no one else, Tansy crept out of her room. For the first time, the hallway looked really long. But she knew all the squeaks in the floor and could avoid them. Slipping down the hallway she didn't make a sound. She ducked her head to the side as she darted across the staircase opening. No one called out her name. She'd made it with ease. Now all she had to do was sneak into the bedroom next to the washroom. Finally reaching the bedroom door she grasped the knob a little too fast and it rattled.

The scrape of a stick across the washroom floor made her stomach flip flop.

"Goin' somewhere?"

Before she could scream, Bolton Rivers clamped his hand over her mouth. He dragged her back into the washroom and knocked the door shut with his walking stick, riveting her spine to his hard chest.

"Let me go!"

"You'll behave if I do." It was not a request.

He let her go and she whirled to face him. He wore only his pants.

"Explain this adventure," he said, pointing to her bags.

"Who are you to tell me what to explain? I told you not to ask me personal questions. This is my saloon and my town!"

"And this town isn't big enough for both of us?" he asked with a lazy grin and leaned against the door. "I swear I've heard that one before."

"I don't doubt it!"

Tansy was awestruck by the oh-so-gorgeous half naked man, realizing this was the first time she'd seen him standing. He indeed looked six feet four, two hundred twenty pounds. His upper body rippled with muscles as he combed back his thick black hair back with his fingers. He'd shaved his beard, leaving his bronze skin smooth.

A muscle in Bolton's jaw worked and his slashing brows furrowed. Tansy swallowed hard, wondering how she was going to get out of this. Bolton's handsome face had become a grim mask of chiseled strength. But it was the predatory glint in his wild, wolf-like stare that pushed her attention down to his bare chest. The black hair on his chest fascinated her. Following the narrowing trail of hair down his flat stomach to his navel, she noticed his pants were only half buttoned.

"Your changing expressions say you can't decide if you want me to button my pants or take 'em off."

"I was just wondering where you got pants at all since Gimpy and I cut your others off!"

"I gave Gimpy a double eagle and he got them for me today."

As he buttoned his pants relief briefly surged through Tansy, then an unfamiliar disappointment dropped over her like a heavy tarp.

"What about those bags, Jigger?"

Other than when he'd guessed her given name, had he ever called her Tansy? No. Regret unexpectedly knifed her in the heart.

"Deadwood stinks!"

"I took a bath. Deadwood smells fine now."

"I don't care! I'm sick and tired of this muddy old gulch!"

Bolt had a sudden memory flash of men coming into this gulch from the north. Tying ropes to trees they lowered wagons down the sides of hills. Another fleeting picture hinted of a southern road into town.

"Tell me the truth about why you're leaving," he demanded, leaning more heavily against the door, and sliding the walking stick under his arm.

"I'm leaving because of you!"

"Because of me?"

"I know who you are, why you're here and I'm scared to death of you!"

"You called me a baby the other day." Bolt reached out and placed his hand on her shoulder. "And now you're so afraid of me you're running away? Why?"

"You know why!" she replied. "Most of the very gunmen who've made Deadwood one of the wildest and wickedest towns on the frontier have already run like rabbits because you're here!"

"Settle down," Bolt said, squeezing her shoulder.

"You and I both know he sent you after me."

"He?" Bolt's gut tightened. Why had his stomach just tied itself in a knot? The feeling was unfamiliar. "He who?"

"Don't play the fool with me!" she said and dropped her bags next to the chair. Draped over the back of the chair was his gun belt. Smacking his hand off her shoulder, defiance, and fear mingled in her green eyes. "I won't go back to him, and you can't make me!"

"Oh, I imagine I could," Bolt said as if he knew to whom and what she referred.

She turned and swayed toward the small window, then to the big oblong bathtub and back to the window again. Two hairpins slid out of the loose bun on her head and several long, blond curls bounced halfway down her slender back as she paced back and forth.

"Not that I don't enjoy your sashaying while you try to figure out a way past me, but this being my first time up you're making me dizzy." Bolt hooked the chair with his crutch and pulled it to him. With a groan, he sat down in the chair, his walking stick clattering to the floor.

"Let me help you back to your room," she said, softening as she came toward him.

"No." He held up his hand to stop her. "Gimpy won't answer any more of my questions about you so why don't you tell me why you're hiding behind the name Jigger Crown? Pick up your story where you met the man you don't want me to take you back to."

"You already know, or you wouldn't be here."

"Then persuade me not to take you back to him."

CHAPTER 6

"If you don't talk, you don't leave this room," Bolt said.

The beautiful blonde paced away from him again and stared out the window. When she finally spoke, it was as if she were in another place in another time...very far away.

"He pretends to be sweet as molasses, but in truth, he's meaner than a hyena who's had the laugh kicked out of him."

"Who is he?"

"The big toad in a little puddle at the junction of the Texas and Pacific Railways," she whispered. "It's a place called Texarkana and was just getting settled when I left a little over a year ago. But I imagine you already know that."

"Keep talking."

"He's got a lot of money and owns a lot of people." She faced him and folded her arms under her breasts before continuing. "Like the killer he yanked out of jail, who now wears a sheriff's badge on his chest. A badge much like the one I found in your pocket!"

"Uh-huh. What's this big toad's name?"

"I don't know what game you're playing, but I don't have time to play along." She fixed a withering stare on him. "If I scream, I just might get a couple of cowboys up here to help me."

"Probably." Bolt braced his left elbow on his right wrist and rubbed his index finger across his chin. "But playing a damsel in distress isn't your style." He was calling her bluff and she tapped her foot in agitation. "Is it?"

"No!" she hissed. "And besides if most of the gunmen have run, it wouldn't be fair to ask a couple of cowpokes to tangle with the likes of you!"

"You stay and tangle with me," he began with a grin despite the fact his heel had started throbbing, "until my foot is better."

"I have to leave while your foot is still too wounded for you to follow me."

"You'd go without a word to Gimpy or Lupe?"

"I left them letters, saying I'd send for them. Some-day." Her voice trailed off. "I hope."

"But you'd say nothing to the stranger in your bed?" Anger tinged Bolt's voice. He drew his right foot closer and brought his right ankle to rest on his left knee. "The man you *promised* to heal?"

"You said you owed me and to name my price," she replied. "My price is for you to allow me to leave! Today!"

Bolt clenched his jaw and gritted, "You said I owed you nothing. Is your word worthless?"

"No!" she snapped. "I will admit your foot needs more attention before it can be stitched."

"You'll need to stay until then." She was all woman, alluring, sensual, and baffling as hell. "What's the toad's name?"

"Lewis Rance. Whip, as people in Texarkana call him, because he's never without his bullwhip."

Bolt saw her suddenly glance at his gun belt. "If you were going to shoot your way out of this, you'd have grabbed at those guns the second you dropped your bags."

"Oh really?"

"Really," he replied, squeezing his ankle as if that could block the pain in his heel. "How does this Lewis Rance make his money?"

"He owns a cattle ranch. The railroad needed land and paid him a lot of money for some of his acreage. His claim to fame is being the richest cattle baron in Texarkana."

"So, you figured to sink your claws into a rich old man, changed your mind for some reason, and ran away?"

"No! Rance is forty-four, twice my age, but that isn't old."

Twenty-two, eight years younger than I am, Bolt thought. "You married him, didn't you? Your real last name is Rance, not Crown. Talk about a secret, lady. That's a blistering one. Hell, you were on top of me in bed, but married!"

"You pulled me into bed!" she said, pointing at him. "And no, Rance isn't the man I married."

"But you *are* married?"

"My husband has nothing to do with you," she whispered as footsteps sounded in the hall.

Something not quite jealously turned in Bolt's gut.

"Señor?" Lupe called outside the door.

Tansy pressed a finger to her lips. Bolt knew what Lupe wanted. But he wanted it with the woman before him and he couldn't have it since she was married.

"Lupe, did you find your boss?" he asked.

"Jigger isn't back yet, novio," Lupe purred. "It's a perfect time for us."

"No, Lupe," Bolt said, grinning at a wide-eyed Tansy.

"Bueno." Lupe sighed and her footsteps receded.

"Well, Mrs. Whoever the Hell You Are, get on with it," he said.

"Rance was kicked in the stomach by a horse and my father made a house call on him." Grasping a couple of loose locks of her long hair she twined them around the bun on her head making her breasts jiggle. "I went along that day to help Papa. When Mrs. Rance fell ill two days later, Rance sent for me and asked if I could stay on a while to nurse them back to health."

"Such a wealthy cattle baron has no hired help?"

"Oh yes. He has a cook and countless ranch hands. But they had other duties. I was happy to stay on and help them both." With a self-depreciating laugh, she said, "I have a pattern of helping the wrong people."

"I'll be sure to tell Gimpy and Lupe you said that," he said, shaking his head

"Please don't," she replied, her soft drawl shaky. "I didn't mean Gimpy and Lupe."

"Continue."

"Rance's wife died about the time he was up and around. He said he didn't want me to leave and asked my father for my hand in marriage. At my request, Papa refused him."

"Refused? Why?"

"Because I despised him! Lewis Rance is an awful man!" She shook her head. "He's cruel and demanding to the people who work for him. He was cold and uncaring toward his wife. When she died, instead of mourning, he started pressuring me to marry him! If his poor character isn't bad enough, he has sparse, light hair and I prefer bla—" She cut herself off with a cough.

"You weren't attracted to him."

"Not in the least!"

Bolt almost grinned. "What else?"

"Shortly after I returned home, a couple of Mexican henchmen of Rance's showed up with a Missouri toothpick!"

She'd learned that term from Bolt. He found that endearing while at the same time steeling himself for what she'd say next.

"And?" he asked.

"And one of the men held me back while the other man, Sanchez, stabbed my father in the stomach. My father fought back, and Sanchez lost his index finger in the struggle. Then Sanchez stabbed Papa in the heart."

Bolt remained calm as her chin quivered just slightly. She hugged herself and it took all of Bolt's willpower not to pull this lost little girl onto his lap.

"I'm sorry your father was murdered," he said.

"He died in my arms. Both men ran and I told Sheriff Mullins. He placed me in," she frowned, "protective custody."

"You didn't know Rance owned the sheriff."

"Protective custody turned out to be Rance's house. Built like a fortress with railroad money. I was guarded twenty-four hours a day. Rance tried to convince me that he had nothing to do with my father's death." She shivered. "He proceeded to what he called 'woo me' which was browbeating and pressuring me day after horrible day to accept his proposal."

"But you still refused?" he asked, and she nodded. "What did he have to say about that?"

"I don't know."

"That's your reply when you don't want to answer me." He had looked at the peace officer's badge in his pocket. United States Marshals didn't track down innocent people. He wished he understood her, recalled everything about himself and what her running had to do with him. "Blazes! How did you get away from Rance?"

His aggravation must have startled her because Bolt heard a gasp escape her lips. Even so, she raised her chin and stood her ground.

"I accepted Rance's proposal," she replied. "He was so elated; he lifted the guard immediately. I quietly walked out of his prison that very night and sneaked onto a train."

"You're lucky he didn't wire ahead and have the train searched."

"I thought of that," she said. "I got off that train and hid on another. Then I left that train and walked until I managed to slip onto The Big Horn, a steamer that travels up the Missouri River. After that, I hitched on with a wagon train into Deadwood."

This adventuress was as smart and courageous as she was beautiful and compassionate.

"What then?" Bolt asked.

"The day I arrived I married Clyde Crown. Clyde was seventy-five years old and—"

"Stop!" Bolt held up both hands. "How the hell could you marry a total stranger the day you arrived?"

"I answered a mail order bride advertisement placed by Clyde Crown in a local Texas newspaper."

Cocking his head to the side, Bolt asked, "Did he say he was seventy-five in the newspaper?"

"Yes, anyway that's how I came to be in the Black Hills. Finding it so inaccessible was a bonus. Clyde passed away six months later, and I inherited a saloon I didn't know how to run. For the past six months, since Clyde's heart attack, I've been trying to figure out how to pay Gimpy and Lupe a wage along with their room and board. But I'm always broke. And just when I thought things couldn't possibly get any worse," she pointed her finger at him, "you show up!"

"Well," Bolt blew out a sigh. "That's a hell of a life story, even for a chatterbox to spit out." He crooked a finger. "Come here."

"So, you can handcuff me?"

"There's an idea."

"Did I persuade you not to take me back?"

"Did you tell me the whole story?"

She didn't answer and didn't come to him. Bolt recognized a standoff when he saw one. Grabbing the walking stick, he used it to stand up.

"I'm feeling down-right poorly," he said. She stepped forward then and laid her hand to his forehead. He caught her slender wrist and yanked her closer. "Let's go back to the bedroom, Tansy."

The sound of her real name on Bolton's lips replayed in her head and weakened her entire body.

"All right?" he asked, releasing her

For an answer, she slipped her arm around his naked waist. Bolton draped his left arm around her shoulders, molding her to his side. Strength radiated from this muscular man. Never before had Tansy experienced a sensation so all consuming. Standing next to him like this was as overwhelming as the man himself. Together they faced the door as Gimpy's unique gait sounded in the hallway.

"Bolt?" Gimpy called. "Need help getting back to yer room?"

"No, thanks."

"Bolt?" Tansy mouthed his name as Gimpy walked away. First, he'd charmed Lupe and now Gimpy. "I haven't confided in Gimpy and Lupe, because they aren't strong enough to shoulder my burdens," she whispered.

"But I am, even as I lean on you?"

"You know you are," she replied. Bolton's lips spread into a smile, showing his straight, white teeth. When he winked conspiratorially, Tansy's heart pounded. "Gimpy and Lupe don't realize I'm hiding here in Deadwood. They only know me as Jigger Crown. Help me keep it that way."

Gimpy was trotting back. "You seen Jigger?"

"Jiggers with me."

"In-in the t-tub?" Gimpy sputtered.

With the tub at his back, Bolton's grin was hot and cocky. "Coming clean in the tub with me is what she had in mind."

"That's not true, Gimpy!"

Tansy immediately yanked her arm from around Bolton's waist, but his arm still circled her shoulders. He lost his grip on the walking stick and, not putting weight on his right foot, he sailed back into the big oblong tub, taking her with him. He cursed in pain as they hit the water. Tansy landed on top of him and when she grasped the sides of the tub, Bolton's knuckles were under her palms. Muscles rippling, he brought them both to a sitting position. Shoving the hair out of her face, Tansy straddled his hips as his long legs hung over the end of the tub. Quickly, she glanced at his right foot. The bandages were dry, but spots of bright red blood showed through the white strips now. Looking into his blue eyes, she stiffened her backbone as his jaw clenched.

"Would you let me go if I gave you my saloon?" she asked.

"Just tell me what your past has to do with my *infamous, notorious* claim to fame!"

CHAPTER 7

"YOU'RE A BOUNTY HUNTER!"

The instant the words left Tansy's mouth; Bolton's large hands gripped her waist so tightly she could hardly breathe. As if she might hold down this wild stallion of a man, Tansy touched her fingertips to his naked chest. The water had washed his long thick hair around his broad shoulders, and she had the crazy urge to comb his hair back with her fingers. Without warning, Bolton brought her up and out of the water. Scrambling over the edge of the tub she stood on wobbly legs.

This man was masterful. He was powerful. He was frightening. And he was climbing out of the tub.

"Is ever'thing awright in there?" Gimpy asked outside the door.

A growl rumbled in Bolton's throat as the water from his drenched pants soaked his bandaged foot. Tansy knew the soapy water was burning his heel as the strips of sheet turned a pinkish red.

"Bolton, I didn't mean to make you lose your balance," she said and picked up his walking stick.

"Forget it," he grumbled. "I should have known I couldn't lean on you."

Ignoring the walking stick, he yanked his gun belt off the chair and flung it over this shoulder. The guns, the muscles, and the man were so intimidating Tansy wanted to back away. She didn't.

"I don't know how much Lewis Rance offered to pay you for me," she lifted her chin and kept her voice steady, "but my saloon is yours in exchange for my freedom."

"Hell, you just told me it's a losing proposition."

She looked up at the man towering over her. "At least don't hurt my friends because of me."

Bolton's steely blue glare was noncommittal, his expression both seductive and threatening. With his gun belt over his shoulder, he squared his broad shoulders and yanked open the door.

"Well-sir!" a befuddled Gimpy said, gaping at their soaked states.

Bolton stepped around Gimpy and strode down the hall. When he passed the stairs, where he could be seen by the men in the crowded saloon, he yelled over his shoulder.

"Come on, Jigger!"

As he disappeared into her room, Tansy and Gimpy stared at the trail of blood on the floor.

"That had to hurt like the dickens, but he done it with no trace of a limp," Gimpy said.

"Blazes!"

Tansy jumped as Bolton's shout split the air and then raced down the hall. Coming to his doorway, she faced him. This man was commanding, even when propping himself against the wardrobe. His guns lay on the bed and two letters were in his hand. He wiped sweat off his brow and glowered at her.

"Can Gimpy and Lupe read?" he demanded, scowling at the names written on the letters.

"No, but Dolly can read the letters for them. Bolton, sit down and let me look at your foot."

He stood where he was. "Deadwood Dolly?"

"Yes." An unfamiliar pang hit Tansy as she wondered how he knew about the badland's madam. "Dolly's around thirty...about your age?"

"Yeah. So?"

"So, Dolly's very pretty." Tansy saw Bolton's black brows draw into a frown, but continued, "I'll bet she'd take you in if—"

"Where's my letter?" he asked.

"Your bandage is wet from your bath. Let me take it off." She started toward him, but he held up a hand stopping her within arm's reach.

"I asked where my letter is."

"You don't honestly think I'd tell the man who is hunting me where I'm going, do you?"

Was he hunting her? Is that why he was in the Black Hills? Bolt didn't know. Damn, when was his life going to make sense again? When his memory returned in full? When would that be? Tomorrow? Never?

Tansy suddenly made a frantic swipe for the letters. He crumpled them in one hand and caught her delicate wrist with his other hand. He then twirled her around to face Gimpy who had just appeared in the doorway with her bags.

"Get in here, Gimpy," Bolt ordered.

"Yes, sir, Mr. Rivers!" Gimpy quaked, inching forward.

"Next to that black Stetson on the chest of drawers is my money. Take four double eagles and my good boot and go buy me a new pair. Also, get me another pair of pants and a couple of shirts."

"I can buy all that with a gold eagle left over."

"Keep the rest for your trouble."

"Thank you, sir," Gimpy said, flabbergasted at being given ten dollars. He set Tansy's bags down and took the money. "I'll be back faster'n a kicked mule." With that, he was gone.

Bolt released Tansy and glared at the letters. "Dolly would send Lupe and Gimpy packing along with these letters."

That strange new pang knifed Tansy again. That was probably true about Dolly. But how did he know it? She wanted off the subject of Deadwood Dolly.

Bolton ripped the letters in half and grumbled, "Help me get my pants off."

"Dear Lord." She looked down at the puddle of blood on the floor. With trembling fingers, she unfastened the top button of the pants molded to his muscular body.

"Why are you shaking? Surely, you did this for Crown and," Bolt paused and gritted, "Rance. Hell, apparently you even did it for me, when I was unconscious."

"I did not do this for Clyde. And Rance? No! Never!" She swallowed. "Only you."

Silence permeated the room for a long moment as Tansy's fingers lingered at the second button.

"Tansy." He placed his finger under his chin and tipped up her head. "Just pretend I'm unconscious." He smiled. "Or a seventy-five year old man."

"Even when you were unconscious, compared to Clyde Crown, you pack a cannon to his derringer!" she said incredulously.

Bolt chuckled. Realizing what she'd blurted out, Tansy blushed as he caressed her soft cheek with his thumb.

"That was one helluva compliment," he said with a grin. Locking his gaze on her emerald green eyes, he ran his thumb over her full pink lips. He wanted to taste her mouth on his and tugged her closer. "Every man likes to believe a woman thinks he has a battle gun to get them through the wars in life."

Before he could lower his mouth to hers, she backed out of his grasp. "I think you can get your own pants off." She walked to the door and grabbed up her carpetbag. "I'll change into a dry dress and come back to see about your foot when you're in bed."

Bolt looked at her carpetbag before meeting her gaze. "If I *were* hunting you and you left me with my foot like this, you would not want to deal with me when I caught you."

From where Tansy sat playing the piano the following evening, she saw the girlish adoration burning in Lupe's eyes as she peered up the staircase, obviously singing to Bolton.

Since he'd arrived, Lupe would sing and then hurry upstairs to check on their patient. Tonight, as usual, after they'd entertained the customers, Lupe bee-lined across the crowded saloon. Skirting around men and tables she scooted into the kitchen.

Tansy joined Gimpy behind the bar and helped him serve up the red-eye whiskey and Gold Nugget Beer. With a sandwich on a tray, Lupe emerged from the kitchen. Saddened by her folks' deaths when she'd asked

Tansy for help, Lupe had never been animated and cheerful.

That is until Bolton Rivers had come along.

"I'm taking supper to my novio." Lupe smiled as she picked up an empty tin mug.

A dozen thirsty prospectors, gamblers, cowboys, drifters, and other strangers stood before Tansy at the bar. As they smiled, nodded, and vied for her attention, they were a blur.

In a whisper, Lupe asked, "Isn't Señor Rivers something, Jigger?"

Bolton Rivers was as terrifying as Lewis Whip Rance, as gentle as Clyde Crown, and more attractive than any man she'd ever seen, anywhere at any time. Yes, he was something.

Still speaking in a hushed tone, Lupe added, "He said he doesn't want banditos thinking he was hurt bad." Lupe filled the tin mug with beer as Gimpy joined them. "Señor Rivers said if anybody asks about him to let them spec...spec—" she struggled with a word she'd apparently learned from Bolton, "speculate on why he's upstairs."

"That's onaccounta Bolt's life hangs on his reputation of getting' the drop on the other man first," Gimpy said quietly. "And he always does accordin' to rumors 'round Deadwood."

"Of course, he does!" Lupe agreed. "Jigger, do you think Señor Rivers was tracking any of the desperados who left town pronto?"

"Well," Tansy stalled, knowing Bolton wasn't after them. "Anything's possible."

"Mi Dios!" Lupe gasped. "There he is."

At the top of the stairs stood the most captivatingly handsome man on earth. He wore the black Stetson and evidently a rawhide strip held back his black hair. His face was lean, sun bronzed, and chiseled in determination. Tansy's heart thumped as his sapphire gaze found her.

Rippling muscles shaped the fabric of his causal blue shirt as rigid thighs balked at the restraint of his snug pants. He wore no vest today, but his gun belt rode low around his tapered waist.

"Gimpy, he's not using his walking stick," Tansy pointed out with worry.

"He'll strangle you if ya try to help him in front of all these men," Gimpy warned.

"Dear Lord, he has on his new boots. How'd he get a boot on his bad foot? Why is he doing this?"

Heads turned as he descended the staircase moving with no trace of a limp. He reached the bottom of the stairs and looked over at a table where a couple of customers, sat staring at him. He took only one step toward their table before the two men scattered like so many chickens. Bolton now had his pick of seats at the table in the corner nearest to the staircase.

"He's a gunfighter, all right," Gimpy noted."Did you see how put his back to the wall?"

"Gunfighter, not gunman?" Lupe asked.

"Gunfighters are usually on the side of the law," Gimpy explained. "I'm giving Bolt that much since he's a United States Marshal from New York. But I think most ever'body else is speculatin' since he's a bounty hunter he's a gunman."

"How do you know he's from New York?" Tansy asked in astonishment.

"I talk to him," Gimpy replied innocently.

Lupe headed for Bolton's table carrying the tray. She

sat down at his table and when he had finished his supper Lupe returned to the bar with his empty plate and mug.

"He wants you, Jigger, a deck of cards and a bottle of our best red wine," Lupe said glumly.

CHAPTER 8

TANSY GRABBED UP A BOTTLE, A DECK OF CARDS AND headed in Bolton's direction. The brim of his Stetson shadowed an unreadable expression. She was almost to his table when three intoxicated customers stumbled into the saloon. The drunkest man grabbed her arm. She was accustomed to dealing with men who over-celebrated after a good week in the mines. But this man with his rotting teeth, foul odor, and filthy clothing was particularly offensive.

"Let go, please," Tansy said politely, but his grip tightened. Then as the two men with him looked past her to Bolton, their faces turned ashen. Bolton's rakish brow was merely cocked in regards to the man who had a hold of her. "Let go and I'll give you a drink on the house."

"Yer gonna gimme a kiss 'n lot more!" the man said loudly, for all to hear.

"That's not on the menu."

Several customers glanced at Bolton, pushed back their chairs, and left the saloon. Bolton now had his left hand on the gun strapped to this hip.

"For God's sake let her go, Crazy Earl!" one of the men with him pleaded, his eyes on Bolton. "Let's get on up to Deadwood Dolly's and wake snakes."

"Why cain't I raise a ruckus right here?" Crazy Earl asked, his fingers digging into Tansy's arm as he gawked at his companions.

"Cuz nobody can outshoot Rivers," the other man warned, watching Bolton.

Crazy Earl yanked Tansy against him, and Bolton drew his gun. Behind her, Tansy heard chairs scraping the floor. A fleeing customer bumped into Crazy Earl causing his grip on Tansy to loosen. Quickly, she jerked her arm free and dashed to Bolton's table.

"You can holster your gun now," she said as she placed the cards and bottle on his table.

But Bolt kept the gun trained on Crazy Earl who was approaching them. How dare he put his grimy hands on Tansy? Bolt knew he'd just been recognized by another outlaw as the would-be ruckus-raiser abruptly turned and fled through the swinging doors. Of the two men with him, one tipped his hat at Bolt and the other gave him a respectful nod before they rushed out.

Bolt surveyed the room as he'd done countless times, instinctively looking for wanted men. The remaining customers ducked their heads, drank their whiskey and beer, or studied their poker hands. But none made direct eye contact with him. Convinced all was calm again, Bolt holstered his gun and turned his attention to Tansy. Dressed in a faded frock her sparkling emerald gaze enchanted him.

"Bolton, you shouldn't be down here nor have your boots on," Tansy scolded under her breath.

"Why shouldn't I?"

"We agreed yesterday that I shouldn't wrap your foot

so air could get to it. And now you've got your foot shoved in a boot."

"You could chatter a man's ear clean off. Maybe it's you and not me, these men fear," Bolt teased, but she was not amused. "Sit down."

Tansy pulled out a chair and sat at his left side. "Why are you in this rowdy saloon in your weakened state?"

Bolt felt in his element. Excitement, a full stomach, and a woman's company. Yeah, this was the kind of summer night he liked, and Tansy was the woman he wanted to spend it with. Tonight, her long blond hair cascaded in curls nearly to her tiny waist. He glanced around the room and saw no one studying him. Funny how some habits, like sitting with his back to the wall, hand going to his gun, and surveying his surroundings returned like a second nature. That was second nature for a marshal and for a bounty hunter if that's who he was. Shoving his memory loss to the back of his mind he grasped a lock of Tansy's hair. It was as silky as he'd thought it would be.

"If you think I'm going to stay cooped up in that room, you're crazier than Crazy Earl."

"Bolton," she sighed his name and he imagined how that might sound in bed. "You're going to have a boot full of blood."

"Maybe." Frowning, he picked up the bottle. "You brought whiskey. I asked for wine."

"In Deadwood, the restaurants at the IXL Hotel and Grand Central Hotel serve wine; but saloons serve whiskey and beer."

Bolt took a drink. "You serve the usual saloon rot gut."

She nodded as if she knew that. "I made it out of

Texarkana with my tansy painting and my tea. Want some tansy tea for your whiskey?"

"Hell, no." He chuckled and then sobered. "Listen, if you don't want people to know your real name, don't say it in public." She nodded at his advice. "And speaking of my foot, it's not healing."

"Let's go upstairs and I'll have a look," she said.

"Later."

The Crown Saloon had stirred to life again keeping Lupe and Gimpy busy.

"Later might be too late."

"What's that supposed to mean, Jigger?" he asked.

"Bolton." Tansy touched his left arm. "By coming down here, you're giving people fair warning you're well enough to be a threat, aren't you?"

"Is that what bounty hunters do?"

"Are you admitting you are one?"

"Why don't you go play the piano for me?"

"That's what Clyde used to say."

Bolt studied Tansy until she looked away. Her eyes were deeper green than the stems on tansies and her lips matched the muted red of her dress. She was fresh air and sunshine. He knew Clyde Crown had surely thought himself a lucky man the day she arrived.

"Was Clyde Crown a nice man?" Bolt asked.

"Very," Tansy murmured. "I miss him."

Bolt felt a jab of pain. He wasn't sure if it had come from his foot or chest. "What do you miss most about Crown?"

"Playing the piano for him," she replied. "Clyde's mail order bride advertisement requested a woman who could sing or play the piano." Tansy sighed and glanced at the piano. "When I got here that piano, a kindly husband, and a place to hide were waiting for me."

"You've been here a year. Crown's been dead for six months. I see no baby and you're not with child." He wondered what else Crown expected from her besides playing the piano.

"I'd like nothing better than to have a baby to love." Bowing her head, Tansy stared at her lap. "But under the circumstances," her voice broke, she stood and continued softly, "it's for the best that I don't have one. I'll play Clyde's favorite song for you and ask Lupe to sing along."

With a variety of emotions running through him, Bolt let her walk away. Since the piano bench was upstairs, she pulled a chair up to the piano. He recognized "Little Brown Jug" and apparently it was a favorite because gamblers, merchants, prospectors, cowboys, miners, and drunks sang along with Lupe and cheered Jigger's name when she finished playing.

Lupe made a point of visiting with Bolt while Tansy stopped at every table but his.

"Does she always visit like this, Lupe?"

"No, she does not."

"Let me know if you find out what she's up to."

Lupe nodded and went back to waiting on customers as Tansy talked to a man on the far side of the room. Gimpy smiled at Bolt from behind the bar a time or two. Gimpy had told him how Tansy had dozed night after night in the rocking chair while he'd been so sick. Bolt felt guilty about that. Earlier, Tansy had seemed genuinely concerned about him, and yet she'd grown progressively distant. Damn, he wanted her in bed with him tonight.

He was more than ready to go back upstairs because his foot was throbbing against the inside of his *boot*.

Picturing the ladder in the small bedroom, Tansy's fair warning to him echoed in his head.

I have to leave while your foot is still too wounded for you to follow me.

Tansy was at that same customer's table. Lupe joined them and when Tansy nodded at something the man said, Lupe took hold of her arm. After a moment, Lupe pivoted and ran to where Gimpy stood washing glasses behind the bar. Lupe whispered something in his ear and Gimpy's shoulders sagged.

Tansy turned and avoiding eye contact with Bolt, crossed the saloon. At the staircase, she paused to give a sunny smile to Gimpy and Lupe. Lupe shook her head. Tears swam in Gimpy's eyes.

"Goodnight, Bolton," Tansy called over her shoulder from the bottom stair.

Later might be too late.

Tansy Wiley was an adventuress who knew how to disappear. If he let her walk away this time, he'd never see her again. Climbing the stairs, she never looked back.

"Señor Rivers!" Lupe skidded up to Bolt's table. "Jigger says she has to leave town. She shushed me when I tried to tell the prospector who you are."

The prospector was just pushing through the swinging doors.

"Gimpy's speculating she's going with him because of you. We don't know who you think she is or what you think she's done, but she's the best amigo I've ever had. She can be your best amigo, too." Lupe gripped his arm and pleaded, "Don't make her run away. Por favor!"

Bolt glanced from Lupe's tearstained face to the staircase.

Beautiful Tansy had vanished.

CHAPTER 9

"Hurry, Mr. Larson!" Tansy said, scrambling into the ox cart in front of the Pioneer Drug Store. As the prospector took his time untethering the ox, Tansy glanced from side to side for any sign of Bolton. "Do hurry, please!" she said again.

The Pioneer Drug Store was dark, but lights from several saloons cast a glow down Main Street.

The prospector hoisted himself into the cart and scratched his sunbaked forehead. He lifted one side of his upper lip, displaying a mouthful of tobacco stained teeth.

"We oughtn'ta be aleavin' at night," he said, shaking his head. "Comin' into the gulch from the north I hadta lower this here cart in with ropes. Won't hafta do that goin' south, but it ain't easy travelin' in the dark."

"You told me you were sick of worthless claims and ready to leave the Dakota Territory," she reminded him.

"I didn't mean this dern minute. I meant in the mornin.' At night, the Injuns'll murder us!"

"No. The Lakota generally attack at dawn," she replied.

"What'll keep 'em from attackin' at dawn? Maybe we oughta wait for that wagon train aleavin' in the mornin' for Cheyenne. I don't want no damn Sioux scalpin' me."

"Don't talk about the Lakota people that way. I don't believe their warriors would be attacking anyone if they hadn't been lied to. The Black Hills were promised to them. But since General Custer and his men found that gold at French Creek, our government hasn't stood behind the treaty."

She breathed deeply in an effort to calm down, suddenly noticing how awful Larson smelled. She thought back about Bolton's clean scent when he'd pinned her against him after his bath.

"I'm ashamed of the way white men have treated the Lakota people," she added.

"Well, if yer done with yer preachin', let me say my piece," the prospector said, sneering.

Tansy shivered, wondering if she would be safe with this man on the long trip to Wyoming.

"In case you ain't heared, on June twenty-fifth, them Sioux yer mewlin' over, along with the Cheyenne," as if to show his contempt, Larson spat a stream of tobacco juice onto the ground, "slaughtered General Custer and his Seventh Calvary. And here yer defendin' them redskins responsible for that massacre."

"I heard about Little Bighorn. I feel terrible about what happened to our Army." Wrenching anxieties born of sadness for all the men killed in battle mixed with her own desperation. Fear churned in Tansy's stomach as she thought of being ambushed by anyone Indians or prospector. She eyed Larson warily. "I hate war."

"You hate Custer! Yer a dern Injun lover. Get outa my wagon!"

"No!" She had to keep out of Lewis Rance's reach. "Please, Mr. Larson, my life depends on getting out of Deadwood. I promise not to say another word."

He scowled and spat tobacco. "Well..."

"She's a chatterbox," came a deep voice from the drug store shadows. "She'll talk your ears clean off."

"Who said that?" Larson asked.

Tansy knew and grabbed the ox's reins. "Go!" she commanded to the unresponsive ox.

"Get her, Gimpy," the deep voice ordered.

With an ear to ear grin, Gimpy trotted out of the shadows. "Howdy, Jigger!"

"Gimpy, I have to leave. Please help me."

"I'm tryin' ta help ya," Gimpy said firmly, tugging her out of the cart.

"Hold on!" the prospector demanded, glaring at Tansy. "What about the dollar you promised me?"

"Yes." Tansy dug into her pocket.

"Forget it." Bolton grabbed Tansy's hand and hauled her into the shadows with him. "Get outa here Larson, or I'll turn you in for that dead or alive bounty on your hide back in Missouri," Bolton said.

"Nobody's lookin' for me in Missouri."

"That's your word against mine. You look like Jesse James to me." Bolton stepped into the light and said with a snarl, "Especially if I drag you in dead."

"I ain't Jesse James!" Larson said just before dawning showed on his face "Yer Rivers, the—the bounty hunter ever'body's skeered of!" The man quickly flung Tansy's bags to the ground. "I'm aleavin' Deadwood tonight, sir!"

"Tonight, or in the morning. Makes no difference to me," Bolton replied.

"Tonight!" Larson slapped the reins to the ox's back, glancing over his shoulder warily as the ox moseyed south on Main Street.

Bolt glared down at Tansy. She was trembling with what he figured was both fear and fury as she yanked her hand out of his.

"If you're set on taking me to Rance, you can just put a bullet in my head here and now. I will never go back to him alive!"

"Returning runaways doesn't ring any bells with me." Noting her vehemence he said calmly, "Turning in outlaws on wanted posters is more likely."

"Blood money buys things," Tansy said, throwing Bolt's words back at him. "Returning a runaway would be a lot easier *money* than turning in an outlaw like Jesse James."

"Uh-huh," Bolt said and grabbed up both of her bags with one hand. "I saw your broken ladder on the ground under the window. What happened?"

"I don't know!"

"Clyde Crown's," Gimpy said. "Too old and rickety for her."

"Yeah." Bolt cocked his brow at Tansy who rolled her eyes.

Bolt shifted his weight. His foot was on fire and sweat beaded on his brow. Taking Tansy's arm, Bolt motioned toward the Crown Saloon. "Let's go." Gimpy took her other arm. "She's gonna look at my foot to see if I've got blood poisoning because of her poor doctoring."

"Poor doctoring?" Tansy said.

"Damn poor," Bolt replied, showing a slight smile. With his first step down the plank walk, pain exploded in his heel. "Blazes!"

"What's the matter?" Tansy asked, a worried look on her face.

"Nothing," Bolt replied, determined not to limp. But another crucifying step and he had to stop. Tansy took her bags from him and handed one to Gimpy. Then she draped Bolt's arm around her slender shoulders. "No," he grumbled. "I can't lean on you."

"I promise you can," Tansy said with conviction and slipped her arm around his waist. "But to hide the fact that you are, we'll act as if we've all had too much to drink."

"Good idee," Gimpy agreed and swung Bolt's other arm around his shoulders.

Muscles rippled under Tansy's arm and palm. Bolton felt big and heavy, and the short walk would take forever. Gimpy sang "Little Brown Jug" and if passersby came too close Tansy could be heard singing right along with him. When the lights of the Crown Saloon finally loomed in front of them, Tansy looked up at Bolton. The brim of his Stetson couldn't mask the torture clouding his handsome features.

"Almost there," Tansy whispered.

"What happened to my novio?" Lupe cried, opening a swinging door to the now closed saloon.

They stumbled into the empty establishment. "Lock up, Lupe, and then run upstairs and get Bolton's walking stick!" Tansy said.

They had Bolton to the stairs as Lupe came back. But it took all three of them a good ten minutes to get Bolton to the second floor.

Lupe ran down the hallway ahead of them and lit a lamp. Tansy and Gimpy slowly followed, helping Bolton into the softly lit bedroom. He sat down hard on the bed and Tansy took off his gun belt, placing it on the bedside table. Gimpy took the Stetson and handed it to Lupe who laid it on the chest of drawers, brim up. Tansy could see the pain in Bolton's blue eyes just before they closed. He fell back, his head sinking into the feather pillows. She had to make good on her promise to heal this man.

Tansy went to the end of the bed and took off his left boot. Bolton didn't move a muscle.

"I'm afeared fer ya to take off his right boot," Gimpy said in a tight voice.

"Me, too," Tansy admitted. As she cupped her hands to the boot's heel, Bolton groaned. "You two hold him down. If his foot's swollen, we're in for a tussle."

Gimpy positioned himself on the left side of the bed as Lupe moved to the right. The moment Tansy tugged on the boot heel; Bolton jerked himself into a half-sitting position. No recognition showed in his untrusting sapphire eyes as he grabbed at his boot.

"Dammit to hell!" he yelled.

"We have to get this boot off!" Tansy said.

Placing their hands to his shoulders, Gimpy and Lupe struggled to control the powerful man. Bolton swatted at them as if they were bothersome flies.

"Señor Rivers, let us take off your boot!" Lupe said, beginning to cry.

"I'll do it!" Bolton roared and clawed his pant leg up to the top of his boot.

"Bolt, lay yerself down," Gimpy said in a stern voice.

Bolton threw off all sets of hands and yanked on his boot. When it wouldn't budge, he let loose a string of curses.

"Bolton!" Tansy shouted over his oaths. "I need to do my job!"

He focused on her now. "I can't do my job, whatever the hell it is if I lose my foot."

"Cooperate or I'll amputate your foot, leave town and let you bleed to death!"

"I don't want anybody holding me down."

With that, Bolton dropped back on the bed and grabbed the posts of the headboard. Gimpy and Lupe backed up and Tansy pulled on the boot again.

"Mi Dios." Lupe crossed herself.

"Try again," Gimpy said, tugging on his mustache.

"Get it the hell off!" Bolton bellowed.

The hoarseness in his voice tore Tansy's heart in half. She gritted her teeth and yanked with all her might. Bolton's body tensed and his muscles flexed as he gripped the headboard.

"That boot didn't budge," Gimpy said anxiously. "Let's cut the blamed thing off!"

"We can't cut into the heel with his foot so swollen and that's the part that's stuck." She was afraid and wasn't sure what to do. "I'll pull harder this time."

As Tansy yanked, Bolton arched raising his back off the bed. She felt his body shudder and then the boot slipped a little.

"Yer getting' it, Jigger!" Gimpy said.

Bolton didn't utter a sound, his back flattened to the bed and Tansy pulled again.

"One more time should do it, Señor Rivers," Lupe promised.

Tansy's next effort separated the boot from the man. On the inside of his heel was a raw, bloody hole. She dropped the boot and then there was a second, heavier thud.

"Lupe fainted, but she ain't in no pain," Gimpy said. "Let's leave her be fer now."

"I promise I'll do my very best doctoring, Bolton," Tansy said, seeing his eyelids open to half-mast. Gratitude and trust shone in his blue eyes before they closed. When his strong hands slid down the bedposts, Tansy said, "Bolton has lost consciousness. Gimpy, there's fresh water in that bowl on the dresser, please get it and then help Lupe."

When Gimpy brought the water Tansy washed the blood off Bolton's oozing foot. When his foot suddenly stopped bleeding, she saw the problem, leather scraps.

"Lupe's wakin' up," Gimpy said and helped her to sit up against the wall. He then came back to Tansy's side and looked at Bolton's foot. "Them red streaks comin' off that wound looks bad."

"They weren't there yesterday," Tansy said.

"Gangrene?"

"No. His skin isn't cold, his heels had a blood supply, and the wound doesn't smell. Nature's been easing those leather scraps loose toward the opening. Shame on me for almost leaving him like this."

"Is he gonna lose his foot, Jigger?" Gimpy asked.

CHAPTER 10

"HE'LL LOSE MORE THAN HIS FOOT IF I CAN'T GET THIS infection out and stop the poison from spreading," Tansy said. "Gimpy, you look so tired. Please go rest."

"No, ma'am!" he replied, pulling up a chair and sitting next to her. "Not 'til I'm sure you can save Bolt and his foot. He's too young and proud to wind up with a peg like mine."

"I don't believe he'd want to live if he lost his foot," Lupe said weakly.

"All right. No more talk about Bolton losing his foot," Tansy said with determination. "He's going to live. Gimpy, get my doctor's bag from downstairs."

"I'll get it," Lupe said, leaving a bit unsteadily.

Tansy and Gimpy lit more lamps and Lupe quickly returned. Tansy's promise to heal Bolton lay on her heart. She would settle for nothing less. Papa would have delivered such an outcome. So must she.

With tweezers in hand, Tansy removed the first scrap of boot leather. She frowned as if it were a live enemy. She then turned to Gimpy and dropped the poisonous scrap into a cloth in Gimpy's hand. With gentle determination, she went after the next sliver and then the next.

As suddenly as the blood had stopped, damned-up infection drained unhindered. When Tansy was satisfied every drop was out, she cleansed the wound. Although she knew she had succeeded in retrieving all the leather from Bolton's foot, digging for the leather had left a hole twice the size of the original gunshot wound. But, for the first time, she felt confident it would heal.

"Looks better now, Jigger," Gimpy said. "Don't it?"

"Yes." Tansy wiped her damp brow and nodded. "Gimpy, can you mix that meal and herb poultice like I did when your leg was injured?"

"Be back quicker'n a starvin' dawg!"

"You look tired enough to just fall over," Lupe said. "What can I do to help?"

"Tear a clean sheet into strips." Tansy leaned over Bolton's foot and, with her curved need and thread, closed the wound for the first time. When Gimpy returned, Tansy applied the meal and herb poultice to Bolton's heel before bandaging the entire foot. "If we can keep him off this foot, it will heal this time," she said, looking at her work.

"We?" Gimpy's bushy gray eyebrows lifted. "That mean you ain't leavin' us, Jigger?"

BOLT WAS SWIMMING AWAY from the shore. New York City. The East River or maybe the Hudson. As he looked toward the bank and saw her. With thick, tall trees as a backdrop, a young woman with dark hair was sitting beside his parents on a patchwork quilt next to a picnic basket. She was smiling as she glanced over at his mother and father. Noticing that they were focused on him, she turned and blew him a kiss. He waved, then swam farther out.

It was the summer of 1866. The War Between the States was over and thankfully the North had prevailed. The future looked bright. The sun warmed his face, clouds were in the blue sky, and he had very few cares to worry him. Life was good.

The brunette's family had moved next door to his when they were both ten. At nineteen, he'd proposed. He couldn't remember her name. Maybe it started with an E.

At twenty, he was ready to settle into marriage. He loved her, his parents, and his friends. His best friend, Tom Smith, had recommended him for a job he loved with the New York City Police Department.

Next week he would be married in a big church wedding. Even Tom had come back to be his best man. Yes, he was glad to be alive.

Suddenly her scream floated across the water, and he looked to the shore.

Please God, let this be a nightmare! From the direction of the forest, a man with a hatchet bore down on his father who glanced up from his pocket watch. Bolt yelled as the blast from a shipyard blew its lunch-time whistle. His father fell.

Bolt tore through the river arm over arm, packing every ounce of energy into pulling himself through the water at top speed. The current fought against him.

As his mother leaned over his father the murderer turned on her. His mother was killed instantly. His fiancée was running.

The monster with the hatchet was a giant, six foot eight at least, with frizzy red hair sticking out from his head and face. The giant ripped her dress bodice as she slapped and kicked. But the killer flung her to the ground, putting beefy hands to his britches.

"Help!" the young woman screamed, scrambling to her feet.

"Run to me!" Bolt yelled, but instead, she darted toward the trees. "No! Run to me!"

The giant spotted him and their eyes locked. Turning, the giant caught her and raised the hatchet. Bolt was near enough the shore that the higher ground slipped out of view.

Shots! When his feet finally touched mud, Bolt sloshed out of the river and tore up the bank. He barreled into a man holding a gun.

"Bolt!" Tom Smith grabbed his shoulder and turned him toward the river. Tom's black hair fell across his furrowed brow. A tear streaked his handsome face and settled on his thick mustache. "I was on my way to the picnic when I heard screams."

"Let—" Bolt gulped air, "me—" the hard swim had left his lungs empty, "go!"

"No, don't look!" Tom faced the river, too, and swung his arm tightly around Bolt to keep him from turning. "It's bad. I want you to go to the police department and send me some help."

With a tortured yell, Bolt wrenched out of Tom's grip turned, and staggered a few steps.

"Emma!" he shouted.

"Bolton!" Tansy cried as his ravaged scream woke her. She jumped out of the rocking chair. "Bolton, wake up!"

Tansy rushed to his bedside and turned up the wick in the softly glowing lamp. Bolton was sitting up, clenching his fists to his eyes. Bare to where the sheet lay across his lap, there was a thin sheen of perspiration on his muscular chest. In her bed was not the tough bounty hunter whom people feared, but a man tortured by something unspeakable. Tansy sat down beside him and placed her hand on his upper arm which was as solid as a tree trunk. He flinched at her touch.

"Bolt?" she said, trying a new approach to pull him out of the blackness.

"Yeah?" he whispered, lowering his fists to his thighs.

"I think you had a nightmare," Tansy said, placing one hand on his shoulder as she gently put the other to his forehead. "Your fever has broken. You're on the road to recovery."

"I've traveled so many roads," he said with a sigh.

"You're in Deadwood now," she replied, easing his muscle-hard body back down in the bed. "In a room above the Crown Saloon. Remember?"

He squinted up at her as if concentrating hurt. "Tansy?"

"Yes," she murmured, a tremor passing through her at how intimately he'd said her name.

Pounding on the door jolted her.

"Jigger, are ya awright?" Gimpy asked. "Lupe 'n me heared ya both scream."

"Everything's fine," Tansy replied. "Thank you. Go back to bed."

With the soft edge of the sheet, she wiped cold sweat off Bolton's brow. When she made a move to stand, he grasped her hand.

"Don't leave," Bolton rasped.

What did he mean? Looking into his deep blue eyes, she glimpsed a soul full of loneliness, uncertainty, need, and desire. Mayhap he just meant for her not to go before he was well.

"I'm sorry I tried to leave town just because you had your boots on."

Bolton's sapphire eyes were dark and serious. "I'm sorry you've spent so many nights sleeping in that rocking chair because of me."

"I didn't mind, and you were right about my poor doctoring. But all the leather scraps are finally out now, and a poultice ridded you of the red streaks."

"I shouldn't have said—"

Tansy briefly touched a finger to his soft, sensual lips. "How does your foot feel?"

"A lot better," he replied, rotating his right ankle.

"You'll stay in bed this time until I say you can get up."

A thin chuckle brought on a rattling cough. Then this magnificent rogue stretched, his strong sinewy arms and long muscular legs spreading wide. He rolled onto his side, his naked body moving within an inch of her.

"Unless you're keeping me company, don't bet on me staying in this bed, angel."

Angel? Tansy's cheeks heated in a red hot blush. Her breasts tingled and her legs quivered at the thought of keeping him company...in bed.

"Bolton, I don't know how long you were in Deadwood before you were shot, but isn't someone somewhere worried about you?"

CHAPTER 11

"No," HE SAID, ROLLING TO HIS BACK. "THERE'S NO ONE."

Tansy wondered why he had no one. Why did she find herself caring? Who was this man, really? He was a gentleman who'd turned down Lupe when most men would have taken advantage of her. He'd been generous to Gimpy who was still talking about the ten dollars Bolton had given him.

Bolton's dry sense of humor was appealing. Her father's wit had been similar, and she realized she hadn't laughed since he'd been murdered. Remembering how she'd threatened to amputate Bolton's foot, she smiled at him. Her father had often used that amputation threat on ornery patients.

Ornery? Yes, Bolton was ornery, but she'd glimpsed a gentler side. He was a man who laughed instead of cursed, in order to keep his word. He must have a family who loved him very much. Surely there had been many women, many friends in his life.

"What about Marshal Tom Smith?"

"No." He laid his left arm over his eyes.

"No, because you can't remember?" she asked.

At this, his hand balled into a fist. Tansy wished she could take back the question.

"That fall in the saloon took a toll on my memory."

"I came to realize that might be the case."

Without warning, he pulled her down next to him! Facing him, her head settling on the feather pillow next to his, Tansy's heart rioted so wildly that she thought it might stop. Asleep in the rocker when his yell awakened her, she wore only a thin shift. She and Gimpy hadn't cut Bolton's pants off in a panic this time, but Gimpy had removed them so that he could convalesce comfortably. Thus, she was acutely aware that only her gauzy gown separated their skin.

"I don't confide much of anything because I can't afford to trust people," he said in a whisper. "They're all dead, Tansy."

"Your family?"

Bolton closed his eyes and told her how a family picnic had turned into three murders. His deep voice faltered as he described the deaths of his parents and a woman named Emma.

Tansy's throat was so constricted with emotion, she wasn't sure if she could speak. She gently placed her palm on his right cheek. Slowly his eyes opened, haunted with the sadness from these awakened memories. How much like a wandering orphan this man, who made the worst of the bad men quake, seemed at this moment.

"Bolton," she said in a soft voice and had to swallow before she was able to continue. "I believe God spared your life."

"I'd rather God had spared them than me," Bolton

said, staring up at the ceiling. "It's not fair they're dead and I'm not."

"I felt the same way when my father died," Tansy said as she caressed his chiseled jaw with her thumb. "Papa's death was a terrible waste of an excellent doctor who helped countless people. I was doing my best to follow in his footsteps until—" her voice trailed off.

"Until Rance cut off your path."

"Yes." When she started to move her hand, Bolton placed it on his chest. "It helps me to believe Papa didn't suffer long."

"It's been ten years since I lost my folks and the woman I was engaged to marry."

Fiancée. A spasm shot through Tansy like an arrow.

"I have no children. But as you said, it's for the best."

"I understand," she whispered with empathy. "Reliving the tragedy tonight has made the deaths seem like yesterday. Be patient. Time will heal both your heart and your memory."

"Tom's shots missed. After the funerals, Tom and I went back to search for clues to help track the killer down. All we found was that starving fawn. I took it took to Emma's parents."

"Yes, that was compassionate all the way around." Tansy was quiet a moment. When Bolton turned his head and looked at her, she said, "If you loved once, you'll love again Bolton. What do you miss most about Emma?"

"The way she played the piano."

"What was your favorite tune?"

"When Johnny Comes Marching Home Again."

"A fine Yankee tune. Popular in New York when you were engaged to Emma."

"Yeah, a lifetime ago. I was seventeen in sixty-three and you were only nine." He grinned then. "I'd have tossed you out of my bed back then, little girl."

Tansy giggled as if she were nine again. It felt really good to laugh. Bolton's low chuckle sprinkled goose-bumps over Tansy's warm skin. Bolton entwined his fingers with hers and then leaned over her. His long hair fell down both sides of his neck and his sapphire eyes locked on hers.

"Papa was so protective, I never had a beau," she said nervously.

"You *do* have an entertaining bedside manner. I want you."

"No, you don't." Tansy put a hand to his shoulder and tried to explain, "Clyde and Rance didn't want me and neither do you."

"I don't care about Crown or Rance. I know what I want and it's you."

Bolton pushed his body against hers and with soul deep shock Tansy felt his arousal. She had no time to turn away from his kiss. His lips were warm, his eyes closed. His kiss was a first and she closed her eyes to experience it. Feeling as weightless as a butterfly she wanted the kiss to go on and on.

Tansy yearned to feel safe, to be comforted, to be happy. To be loved. Her heart cried for more as Bolton's lips moved to her neck. Savoring these new sensations, he created in her, Tansy drew in her next breath with a staccato gasp.

"Settle down," Bolton said huskily near her ear.

In Bolton's strong arms she could forget her prob-lems and give in to the desire she was feeling. She sensed this man would love her, at least in the physical sense, better than any man she'd ever meet for the rest of her life. Wouldn't she regret it forever if she didn't seize this moment?

"Don't try to figure it all out, angel, just enjoy it," he whispered in her ear.

Bolton's insight into her thoughts had the impact of dynamite, exploding her doubts. When his mouth met hers again, she kissed him with abandon. He groaned and like a moth, desperate to fly into the flame that would engulf it, she wanted this man.

"Bolton." She must warn him. "For more than a year my life has been a kite. I want to touch the ground. But angry winds blew me to Deadwood, and they could become angry again. Remember when you asked me if I'd told you the whole—"

"Tansy, don't chatterbox me right now," Bolton urged. "If you kiss me, I'll weigh you down, so you don't fly away."

No man as thrilling, as amusing, or as sexy as Bolton Rivers would ever cross her path again, she thought. If she were destroyed by this man's hypnotic fire, so be it. She wound her arms around his neck and buried her fingers in his long, luxurious hair. She shut her eyes and pulled him down until his lips covered hers. When his tongue slid into her mouth she moaned with pleasure.

His hand molded to her ribs, and she fidgeted. But when he tenderly caressed her breast, she stilled to fully experience his exciting touch. Then his hand slipped down her side to her hip. He tugged up her gown, sliding his right leg between her thighs.

"Damn," he said, grumbling in pain.

"Please stop before you hurt yourself." Tansy opened her eyes and noticed the morning light outside.

"That would be a first."

"Taking care of that wound is what's most important right now," she said, gently pushing him away. "I have to get up."

"You own the place, stay in bed with me today."

Yes, stay for a week, her heart cried. Her mind said no, sleep on it...alone. Mayhap if Bolton stayed on for a while there would be another chance. No. Even if he didn't force her to go back to Rance, he was a marshal and a bounty hunter. He'd be gone soon. Agitated and confused she sat up.

"I have to open the saloon."

"You don't have morning customers." With a grin, Bolton tugged her back into his arms. "You'll stay in bed until I say you can get up."

Hearing Bolton echoes the words she'd once said to him, Tansy laughed. When he pressed his mouth to hers, she touched her tongue to his lips. He groaned and tightened his embrace around her.

"Bolt?" Gimpy called at the door.

"What?" Bolton barked.

"Well-sir," Gimpy began, "I was checkin' to see if you was awake and feelin' any better."

"I was feeling better until," Bolton grinned at Tansy, "now."

"Want me to bring ya up some breakfast?"

"Yeah, and please get Lightning from the livery for me."

"I thought his name was Silverheels," Gimpy said.

"It's Lightning." Bolton let go of Tansy. "Don't try to ride him. Just leave him at the hitching post."

"Sure thing, Bolt."

Gimpy's uneven walk receded, and Tansy jumped out of bed, fixing her hands on her hips.

"And just where do you think you're going? On a horse no less?"

"To track down the wanted posters in the godforsaken gulch," Bolton said, sitting up.

"Wanted posters?" she gasped and put her hands to his shoulders. "No, you can't!"

CHAPTER 12

"WHY NOT?" BOLTON ASKED, A SUPERIOR, MASCULINE GRIN spreading across his sensual lips as he prevented her from making him lie down. "I let you push me back in bed. When you're out of my bed, you'll find it's a different story."

"Please, Bolton." Tansy pulled her hands to her breast and clasped her fingers so tightly her knuckles turned white. "I've worked so hard on your foot. Give it a few days to heal."

"Maybe I'll go to the hospital to recover, so you can stop feeling responsible for me."

"No!" She never knew what this unpredictable rogue was going to say next. "The only hospital is a pest house for folks with smallpox or other deadly diseases."

"If I'm a bounty hunter, killers are a deadly disease all their own," he replied nonchalantly and keeping the sheet across his lap, swung his legs out of bed.

"*If* you are a bounty hunter? Haven't you remembered that you are one?"

"No."

"Well, I believe you are! And a bounty hunter wouldn't come to a godforsaken gulch like this for no reason. It suddenly occurs to me that amnesia is your game to keep me off guard until you're truly well enough to drag me back to Texarkana!"

As Tansy stood before him, Bolt couldn't believe his ears. He'd bared his soul, confided about his memory loss, and relived the murders of the people he loved. Ready to make love to him one minute she denounced him the next. He stared down at the floor and jerked his thumb toward the door.

"If that's what you really think, then leave," he said sternly.

"Leave this room? Or leave town?"

"This room. If I am who you think I am I don't want to bring you and your friends any trouble," he said. "I'll check into a hotel."

"You're my patient and I'll decide when you can be discharged from my care."

"You can decide all you want to and then I'll do as I damn well please," he said with a growl, raising his head and giving her the glare, he'd used to intimidate Crazy Earl and Larson. "I don't mean to hurt your feelings, but you need to go."

"You aren't the first man to hurt my feelings. If I hurt yours with my suspicions, I'm truly sorry. But by being too trusting in the past I've had worse than my feelings hurt."

"Dammit, Tansy!" He smacked his hands onto his thighs, and she took a step back. "Don't trust me. Just get out of here so I can get dressed, get my horse, and move on."

"I'll be happy to get a hotel room for you after I take your stitches out on Sunday and no sooner."

She whirled away, yanked open the door, and slammed it behind her. Bolt started to yell after her that he could take his own damn stitches out but looked back to the floor where he'd noticed something. From under the bed, he picked up a paper folded in thirds. Written on the outside, in a feminine hand, he read his name.

"Well, I'll be damned," Bolt breathed. "The deed to the Crown Saloon."

Tansy dressed in the smaller bedroom and went down to the saloon. At the bottom of the stairs, she noticed Gimpy through the window with Lightning in tow. He tethered the big, black stallion to the hitching post and came inside. With a nod to Tansy, Gimpy headed upstairs. She made a quick detour to the kitchen and then went outside to the horse.

"Hello, Lightning." Tansy petted his soft nose and pulled the apple from the kitchen out of her pocket. "Do you suppose that owner of yours is doing something stupid like trying to put on his boot?" The horse snorted. "Oh, you think so, too? Well, I think he tried, but since he hasn't made it down here, yet I'm betting he won't be riding you anywhere today."

Gimpy returned to the hitching post and untethered Lightning. The large animal pranced.

"He's accustomed to Bolton," Tansy said.

"Yeah, that's why Bolt told me to walk him," Gimpy turned the horse toward Main Street and finished over his shoulder, "back to the livery."

A reprieve on the wanted posters.

With that relief washing over her, Tansy opened the saloon. She glanced at the corner table where Bolton had sat and suddenly stopped in her tracks. Where was her deed to the saloon? She had last seen it...when? Right before climbing out the window and almost falling to her death. She had strategically placed the deed under the bed, so he'd find it and then forgotten about it.

Whether Bolton decided to turn her over to Rance or not, her saloon now belonged to...she gulped to...United States Marshal Bolton Rivers!

FOR THE NEXT FEW DAYS, Tansy avoided Bolton completely and tried to figure out what to do next.Gimpy raved about Bolton constantly and Lupe raced up to his room at night after the saloon closed. Had Bolton changed his mind about considering Lupe's age? Keeping Lupe out of Deadwood Dolly's clutches was one thing. But it was common around these parts for girls Lupe's age to be married. So, was it jealousy or protectiveness that made her want to keep Lupe out of Bolton's bed?

"Protectiveness," Tansy whispered to the four walls as she undressed after closing the saloon on Saturday night. She lay down on the small bed and sighed as their low voices drifted from down the hall. Her situation had gone from bad to desperate. A tear slid down her cheek. "What have I done?"

TANSY AWAKENED Sunday morning to the familiar chirping of birds. Her first waking thought was that she had to take Bolton's stitches out. He would no longer be her patient. If he had found that deed, he would certainly not be the one checking into a hotel. He'd have the saloon and she'd have her freedom. Freedom meant she had no claim to her job or the roof over her head.

Making matters worse, if that were even possible, the last time she had seen Bolton she'd accused him of lying about his memory. She didn't believe that for a minute, but her pride hadn't let her tell him so. True, she had apologized but he was still angry because he hadn't sought her out. Why should he? There was no reason to forgive her at this late date. He held all the cards.

And she would die before she played a damsel in distress card.

If Rance had sent Bolton after her other bounty hunters would find her here, too. She had to run again and soon. These past few days she'd been seeking a way out of Deadwood to no avail. Turmoil twisting inside her, Tansy went to the staircase. Each step down felt like sinking into quicksand.

"Mornin'!" Gimpy called merrily from behind the bar.

"You're in a good mood," she mumbled as he held up two coffee pots, one in each hand. "What are you doing with those?"

"Bolt said since most saloons don't serve coffee, we could capture some mornin' business. He gave me money to buy coffee beans, these here pots, and two dozen man-sized cups."

Bolton was exercising his authority as the new owner. She had no one to blame but herself. Tansy sat down at the bar with a heavy heart. Gimpy made the coffee and announced they needed a sign in the window advertising the coffee. He handed Tansy her pen, an ink well, and a piece of paper.

Tansy nodded and was almost finished with the sign when Lupe came down the stairs. Tansy patted the stool beside her. Lupe plopped down, set her elbow on the bar, and rested her chin on her palm.

"Want a cup of coffee? The new morning specialty?" Tansy asked.

Lupe sighed. "Sí."

"Mornin,' Lupe," Gimpy said, setting the cups on the bar. "Coffee'll fix whatever's ailin' ya." He pointed to the boardwalk from behind the bar. "There's Mr. Deetken from the Pioneer Drug Store. Too bad the sign Bolt said we need weren't in the winder fer him to see."

So, the sign was Bolton's idea, too. He was wasting no time in letting her know who was boss.

"Jigger, the only thing he's willing to teach me is how to read," Lupe said.

"Bolton?"

"Sí, my *novio.*"

So, that's what they had been doing at night, Tansy thought.

"Lupe, you'll find a boy your age."

Lupe nodded and shrugged at the same time. "Señor Rivers pines for somebody else."

"Yes," Tansy said. "But she's dead."

"Oh, no."

"Yes." Tansy said, "It breaks my heart, knowing how hard that's been on him."

"I didn't know you liked Señor Rivers. I thought you tried to leave because of him. I don't understand."

"Bolt won't explain nothin,' neither" Gimpy said.

"I don't want to burden either of you with an explanation."

"We don't deserve none?" Gimpy asked.

They did and it was time. Tansy hesitated not knowing where to start. She put the pen down.

"My name isn't Jigger."

Tansy told them everything. When she had finished, Lupe flung her arms around Tansy and hugged her tightly. Gimpy came around the bar and hugged Tansy, too.

"Clyde Crown was a nice ol' feller. But I'll get even with Rance if he shows up!" Gimpy said.

Over Gimpy's head, a movement at the top of the stairs caught Tansy's eye.

"You could have had a helluva head start if you'd left Deadwood after giving me the Crown Saloon," Bolton said nonchalantly, picking up right where she'd left off with her story.

"But you don't have the deed!" she said, hoping against all hope that was true.

"Yes, ma'm. I sure do. It's signed over to me lock, stock, and barrel."

"Then I have my freedom!" she said and inwardly cringed.

Bolton, decked out in black from head to toe, sauntered down the staircase. Lupe quickly vanished into the kitchen and Gimpy busied himself unlocking the doors of the saloon. Letting in the fresh morning breeze, he went outside, pulled a rag out of his pocket, and began polishing the window. Bolton swaggered to the bar. Tansy was mad at Bolton, mad at herself and loathing Lewis Whip Rance!

Bolton sat down on a stool next to hers and picked up the sign. "Coffee has two e's."

Trembling with anxiety, Tansy offered him the pen, but he ignored it.

"If the saloon's going to be open in the morning it needs customers. Maybe then it could show enough profit to pay its employees," he said.

Tansy so wished she'd thought of that. They always opened early, but none of the beer and whiskey drinkers patronized them. Bolton put down the sign and took the pen from her.

"Cat got your tongue, angel?"

Tansy had worked herself into such a state, her body jostled with tension from head to toes.

"You kinda look like a bubbling coffee pot about to boil over," he taunted.

Tansy was so furious and frantic over her predicament; she couldn't even think of a reply.

"Since you're free," Bolton began in a voice tinged with amusement, "why haven't you tied yourself to a kite and flown away?"

Tansy pictured shoving his broad shoulders hard enough to knock him to the floor.

"Well," she breathed out slowly, trying to unruffle herself, "I stayed to remove your stitches."

"Nah, you haven't even checked on me. The rumor is that you're still here because no one will take you out of this gulch since word spread that I threatened Larson."

"Yes, you're right!" Tansy threw her hands in the air and then spread her arms wide. "The whole town knows I'm not allowed to leave! As for checking on you, there's no need. I have daily, no hourly reports, from your rumor spreading friend, Gimpy, and your best amigo, Lupe!" She was losing her mind. "As for your stitches, I'm sure you could yank them out of your thick hide all by yourself."

"Yes, and I did," Bolton said as he made the second 'e' bigger and bolder than hers.

Tansy slid off her stool and clenched her fists at her sides. "Would you care to hire me?"

"What?" Bolton put the pen down and stared at her.

CHAPTER 13

"I need to earn wages to buy my own horse because even the wagon train won't take me!"

"What makes you think anybody's gonna sell you a horse?"

Tansy drew back both hands, palms out. Bolton grabbed her wrists and yanked her between his muscular legs, pinning her there. Moving her arms behind her, he held her wrists with one hand.

"Gimpy!" Bolton called out just as Gimpy pushed through the swinging doors. Glaring at Tansy he said, "Go get Lightning."

"Yes, sir!" Gimpy replied and headed back out to the plank walk.

"Lighting will do just fine," Tansy said and wrestled out of his grasp. "Thank you. I'll leave today."

"The hell you will," Bolton growled and stood. "Blazes!" he barked, making her jump. "How mad do I have to make you before you trust that I won't hurt you?"

"I trust you're mad enough to hurt me just like Lewis Rance," she said, raising her chin.

"Never." He clamped his hands on her shoulders and gently squeezed for emphasis. "How did he hurt you?" She didn't answer. "Dammit! Stop running from him or you'll be running forever."

"Stop scaring me!" she shot back.

Bolt folded the delicate woman into his embrace. Her ivory dress was soft under his hands as her full breasts pressed against his chest. The scooped neck of the form-fitting bodice of her frock allowed a hint of her cleavage to brush his open leather vest.

"Why don't you try believing me instead of fearing me?"

"I do believe you," she admitted, her head on his shoulder. "I never doubted your memory loss."

"Worth giving you the time to figure out I was telling the truth."

Giving her that time had been hard for Bolt. He had wanted her in his arms like this since the night she'd slammed his door. His reputation had kept her in town where she was safe, but she lived every day afraid, looking over her shoulder, ready to run. At that moment Bolt hated Lewis Rance as much as he hated the red-haired killer.

"I also believe Lewis Rance is a grudge holder. I will always live in fear of him."

"As for the Texas toad, take a stand."

"Like General Custer's last one?" she asked, looking up at him.

"No."

"But it would be *exactly* like Custer's." Her emerald eyes beseeched him to understand as she pushed out of his embrace. "I'm outnumbered, too, and there's no cavalry coming. I'll be on the run until the day I die."

"No, you won't."

Lupe ventured out of the kitchen, picked up the coffee sign, and placed it in the window. Then heading out of the swinging doors she skipped off on a mission. Tansy glided away from Bolt.

"Where are you going?" he asked.

Tansy turned to him with a perplexed expression as if he should know. "To get my bags, find a job and a room."

"Hey, there, Jigger Crown!" a woman hollered at the saloon doors.

An orange parasol was twirling above an orange hat nesting on brassy red hair. Below black eyebrows, dark eyes heavily lined in black. Pumpkin color rouge stained pale cheeks and thin lips were reddish orange. Snapping her parasol shut, she pushed through the swinging doors.

"I see I have some competition," she said, touching the tip of her parasol to the floor. She thrust out her overly endowed bosom and swayed into the saloon, shifting wide hips with each step. "Who's he?" she asked Tansy, her eyes on Bolt as she came to a stop in front of him.

"Bolton Rivers, this is Deadwood Dolly," Tansy said graciously, returning to Bolt's side.

"Ahhh, yes, the bounty hunter," was Dolly's greeting.

"And the badlands madam." Bolt nodded curtly.

"You've scared half my customers plumb out of town, Mr. Rivers," Dolly said, looking him up and down. "What? No apology for putting a dent in Dolly's Doves and Dance Hall?" Not waiting for an answer from Bolt, she asked Tansy, "Not much of a gentleman, is he?"

"Oh, yes! He certainly can be," Tansy said, jumping to his defense.

Dolly's strong perfume turned Bolt's stomach. Lupe was back so he swiveled on his stool. Lupe scooted behind the bar and handed him the *Black Hills Weekly Pioneer*. The newspaper was what they used for her reading lessons. Lupe grabbed up a coffee pot and Bolt nodded that he'd take a cup.

"Since when does the Crown Saloon serve coffee in the morning?" Dolly asked.

"Since today," Tansy replied.

"I sure don't need you stealin' my morning customers."

"You'll have to take up the coffee issue with Mr. Rivers. It's his saloon now."

"Ain't that interestin'? How'd you come to give up your saloon, Jigger?"

"I never planned to stay in Deadwood forever. I prefer warm weather."

"Are you leaving?" Dolly asked.

"Yes, as soon as I earn some traveling money."

"How can you be short on money if you just sold your saloon?" Dolly's shrill laughter cut the air. "Don't tell me you lost the place to him in a game of five card draw!"

"That's how it started," Tansy said.

Dolly hooted with amusement. "Don't worry, Jigger, my soiled doves only make two dollars a customer. But for a beauty like you, I can get three ounces of gold dust. That's near seven dollars a customer. And I'll only take forty percent of everything you make. Hell, Al Swearingen's probably gonna take fifty percent at the place he's opening in the Cricket Saloon."

Bolt slowly swung around on the stool and rested his

back against the bar. All three women focused their attention on him as he folded his arms across his chest.

"Only forty percent," Bolt said. "That's damn generous of you."

"You won't know how generous I am, gorgeous," Dolly purred, her eyes dipping to his crotch, "until you've paid me a visit."

"I've paid before," Bolt said casually, placing his hand on Tansy's shoulder and sliding his fingers under her long, silky curls. "But it's not as good as the real thing."

The madam raised her chin. "Proof you never patronized *my* establishment." She turned to Tansy. "I've got a door with your name on it, Jigger. If you don't like the color, it'll be painted any color you like."

"Why are the doors painted?" Lupe asked.

Dolly directed her answer to Tansy. "When a saloon or dance hall has a colored door upstairs, the men know they can pay the dove behind that door for her favors. If the woman's already spoken for then she's behind a plain door meanin' she ain't for sale."

"Jigger's not for sale," Bolt said firmly.

"I don't see why you have any say in this matter, Mr. Rivers," Dolly said with a smile and perused his crotch a second time.

"Because Jigger works for me," Bolt said and meaningfully tugged Tansy between his spread legs.

"Wouldn't you rather work for me, Jigger, honey? You'd make a lot more money and you can bring the half-breed with ya."

"Please don't call Lupe that," Tansy said. "My dream is to open a clinic and specialize in midwifery. Lupe's learning to be my assistant."

Dolly turned cold dark eyes on Tansy. "Without me

and my dance hall, you'll never earn enough money for traveling outa this gulch much less for a clinic, Jigger!"

"Oh," she drawled as only she could. "Bolton has given me an idea how to do it."

"I'll bet he has!" Dolly said with a hoot. "Hell, no hard feelin's on my part, folks." At that, she turned and swayed toward the doors, over her shoulder offering, "If any of you change your mind about visiting my place you know where to find me. My house is at the end of the alley, Rivers."

"Don't let the swinging doors hit you in the as—" Bolt said before Tansy's elbow hit his ribs.

Gimpy shoved against a swinging door at the same time Dolly did. Larger than Gimpy, Dolly pushed her way onto the boardwalk. Gimpy tottered, regained his balance, and entered the saloon.

"Lightning's here, Bolt," Gimpy said. "And I been tellin' ever'body 'bout our coffee. Some of 'em are plannin' on visitin' us this mornin'."

"Much obliged, Gimpy."

Gimpy said to Lupe, "Let's get eggs like Bolt said, in case coffee ain't enough for some folks."

Bolt turned Tansy to face him. "Will you work with me?"

"May I also keep this roof over my head?"

"Yes. You'll have a job, room and board, and money."

What Bolt really wanted was the same bedroom roof over her head as his. When Tansy slid her arms around his neck and hugged him, he was pleasantly surprised. He splayed his hands on her back and held her to him.

"Yes, I'll work with you," Tansy whispered in his ear.

"What idea did I give you?"

"Where are you going on Lightning?"

She eased out of his embrace, and he stood. Neither answered the other. Another standoff.

"Raise the price on the red-eye and beer," Bolt said and with that he stepped past her, smacking her fanny on his way. When she gasped in his wake, he chuckled and swaggered across the saloon.

"Dolly said you weren't a gentleman!"

"I *certainly can be* when properly motivated."

"What's that supposed to mean?"

"Figure it out," he replied over his shoulder on this way through the doors.

"It means if you're nice to him, he will be nice to you," Lupe said, coming up behind her.

Tansy glanced at Lupe. She saw both love and understanding in her young eyes. She smiled at Lupe and then rushed across the saloon to the swinging doors. Bolton stood a head taller than the prospectors and miners who were just beginning to flood the town.

As Bolton mounted the stallion, Tansy hurried across the plank walk and stopped beside him. The man and horse were both larger than average and black on black, a sight to behold. His black hair, tied back with a rawhide strip hung down the back of the black vest. His black shirt stretched tautly across his muscular chest. His Colt.45s lay strapped to rigid thighs in black pants.

He motioned her to his side. "What?"

"Well...in case you're still intent on tracking down wanted posters, we don't have a sheriff to post them," she said.

"Gimpy told me Isaac Brown was elected sheriff right after Hickok was shot."

"That's right. I forgot," she said honestly.

"As my memory returns yours is slipping like a bunch of wet puppies?" he teased.

"Come back inside and rest your foot," she said placing a hand to Bolton's left leg.

Bolton leaned down and touched her chin. "Tonight." He straightened in the saddle. "There are enemies like the hatchet killer and Rance to concentrate on. I'm headed to the jail."

"Our enemies won't be there."

"True, but I might get some information there."

"You have a saloon to run now. You don't have time to track down dangerous men, who would sooner shoot you in the back than look you in the eye."

"You'll get your saloon back if that happens," he said.

Jolted at hearing him admit he might get shot again she said, "I'm going with you."

"No."

The muscles in Bolton's leg flexed under her hand as his attention focused on two armed men shuffling away from the Number 10 Saloon. The heavy one jerked a thumb at Bolton and the skinny one grunted. The heavier man had a milky white left eye, the socket sunken into his skull, a jagged scar stretching across his cheek.

Bolton's face looked chiseled in ice, blue eyes glacial, mouth in a frigid line. Tansy shivered.

"Howdy, sir," the man with the scarred face said in a friendly manner, tipping his hat. "Nice mornin,' ain't it?"

Bolton nodded almost imperceptibly as the two kept going.

"Damnation, Sweet Pete," the thin man swore under his breath. "I ain't never seen you boot-lick nobody afore! Who was that?"

"I swear yer more daft than deaf, Skinny. That was Bolt Rivers."

The skeletal man threw a shifty-eyed, fearful glance

over his shoulder at Bolton as both men picked up their pace. Stumbling down the boardwalk, Skinny all but shouted his gratitude to Sweet Pete for warning him. Sweet Pete yelled back that Skinny could pay for him at Deadwood Dolly's. Reaching their horses, Skinny then shot off Sweet Pete's hat. Wide-eyed, their horses shied away trying to pull free from the hitching post as the men howled like animals.

Tansy looked up at Bolton. Harnessed brute force radiated all over him. Unleashed, that power would be lethal.

"Glad you aren't working at Dolly's?"

CHAPTER 14

"YES," TANSY SAID. "WHY CAN'T I GO TO THE JAIL WITH you?"

"I have a reputation to uphold so I won't be riding a little girl around town."

"But Lewis Rance is my enemy, not yours."

Bolton didn't reply to that as he nudged Lightning into a gallop and down Main Street. Dolly, who was still out and about, called to him. He ignored her.

Tansy watched the mysterious man until he was out of sight. After scratching for a way out of her sinking plight for days, in a matter of minutes, he had put her back on solid ground. When Dolly looked her way, Tansy smiled politely and went into the crowded saloon. Gimpy and Lupe were raking in money hand over fist. It looked like The Crown Saloon was going to give Dolly, the Grand Central Hotel, and the IXL Hotel a run for their morning money. Tansy tied on her apron and began working.

During a lull in business, she wandered out the front doors of the saloon. Standing on a box in front of the

Pioneer Drug Store was Preacher Smith. Among the wagons and beasts of burden, a crowd of townsfolk, prospectors, and miners were gathered. Passing through the crowd, with his hat in hand, was Swill Barrel Johnny, a Main Street beggar.

"Don't fret," Gimpy said as he joined her on the boardwalk. "Bolt'll be back."

"Of course, he'll be back," Tansy said, realizing Gimpy had sensed she'd come outside to look for him. What if he rode up with a wanted poster for her in his hand? "He owns the saloon now. Aren't you the least bit concerned about that, Gimpy?"

"Nah, I trust the both of ya."

"What won you over to the side of an *infamous and notorious* bounty hunter?"

"His word."

"About what?"

"That he won't never hurt ya."

Swill Barrel Johnny appeared, chasing a rolling coin, on all fours. Tansy reached into her apron pocket, grabbed the tips she'd made, and gave them to him. Johnny put the money in his pants pocket and Tansy could hear the clinking of coins, so his pocket was full. Tansy thought a moment and frowned. She untied her apron and gave it to Gimpy.

"Hold down the fort, Gimpy."

Skirting around Preacher Smith's crowd, she darted through customers coming and going from the store and shops. On lower Main Street she passed Boughton's Dress Shop and the McAusland Brothers' Gunsmiths store. Rounding on Sherman Street she passed the sawmill. A little further down, she glimpsed the undertaker dragging a corpse into his place.

Quickening her pace, she passed the houses of year

round residents. Next came a sea of canvas tents and lean-tos, the camping area for prospectors and miners. On a hill above the camp, she put hands to her ribs and gulped air. Then picking up her skirts, she ran.

BOLT CAME out of the small shack-like office, stopping to shake hands with Sheriff Brown. They both mounted their horses and Brown headed back to town. From a distance of about a hundred feet, Bolt paused and stared at Deadwood's jail.

The jail was just a cave on the side of a rocky hill. Guard duties were carried out by merchants, saloon owners, miners, cowboys, or anybody who could be coerced into doing the job. Four by six foot iron bars touched rock around the opening to the cave. Bolt frowned at the jail's foul stench. Flashes of other jails touched his memory. None were as bad as this pit.

Inside were three vermin of the human kind who had been trapped and caged by Sheriff Brown. Earlier, the sheriff had pointed out two of the prisoners who'd stabbed a miner to death in a knife fight over a claim dispute. Those men were still clinging to the iron bars. The third prisoner pushed between them as an elderly guard positioned near the opening of the cave jail took notice.

Sheriff Brown had told Bolt that this third prisoner had gone on a drunken rampage the previous night. During the melee, he had murdered two of Deadwood Dolly's favorite girls. No wonder the madam had been out bright and early looking to hire replacements. A chill crept up Bolt's spine as he got a good look at the killer. Crazy Earl.

"Guard!" Crazy Earl hollered. "I'm sick. I need help. Quick!"

The old guard hurried forward.

"No, Mr. Beasley!" Tansy screamed.

Darting out of a copse of birch trees beside the cave, she flung herself between the elderly guard and the prisoner. Bolt kicked Lightning's flanks as Crazy Earl grabbed Tansy's arm and jerked her against the bars.

"Let her go, Earl!" the aged guard said, fumbling with the heavy gun in his holster. Shaking violently, he dropped the weapon on the ground.

In a dust swirling stop, Bolt raised his right hand, training his Colt .45 on Crazy Earl. Gasping for air, Tansy clawed at the killer's arm clamped around her neck. When she saw Bolt, Tansy stopped struggling against the murderer and held up a delicate hand as if to warn Bolt to be careful.

"One chance is all you're gonna get," Bolt warned Crazy Earl, gun cocked. "And only one."

"Well, now." Crazy Earl grinned, displaying his rotten teeth, as he recognized Bolt. "We got ourselves a little reunion, ain't we? Only this time I'm holdin'," he tightened his arm around Tansy's throat, "the winning card."

"Deal her into my hands or I'll put a bullet in your head," Bolt said calmly.

"If I ain't gettin' outa this here jail, maybe I'll just snap her neck to wake snakes, Rivers," Earl said, spittle frothing around his mouth.

"Let him out, Beasley," Bolt said

Beasley unlocked the jail door. Reaching around the bars, Crazy Earl grabbed Tansy's arm as Bolt's gun kept the other two prisoners in until Beasley could lock the bars again.

Dragging Tansy backward toward the copse of birch

trees, Earl sneered, "You're damn stupid for a bounty hunter." He pulled a knife out of his boot. "You shoulda knowed I'd use her to get outa this gulch," he said and laughed.

When Earl raised the knife to Tansy's throat, Bolt fired. The bullet slammed the killer into the trees where he lay sprawled on his back, eyes open but unseeing. The two killers in the jail scurried into the darkness of the dank pit.

Beasley rushed over to Crazy Earl, gawked for a moment, then turned to Bolt. "That bullet hit him square between his eyes!" Picking up the knife, Beasley said, "Crazy Earl's as dead as dead gets!"

Tansy, her long blond curls and soft ivory skirt gently billowing in the wind, looked every bit like an angel who'd wandered into hell. She stood transfixed staring at the dead man.

"Angel!" Bolt barked. The prisoners cowering in the cave didn't need to know her by any other name. "Run to me!"

Instantly, Tansy ran straight to him. Holstering his gun, Bolt scooped her up with his left arm and plopped her across his lap.

"Report this to Sheriff Brown, Beasley," Bolt said. "He might want to check the knife-boys for more weapons."

"Yes, sir! Marshal Rivers!" Beasley replied. "Thank you, sir!"

Bolt then turned Lightning around and headed toward town.

"Put your right leg on the other side of the saddle, Tansy. You're pinching the hell out of my—"

"Cannon?"

"Yeah." Damn, she was sexy! With his legs spread wide and her wiggling across his lap, Bolt clenched his jaw. He took hold of her right leg and as he adjusted her into a more comfortable position, he imagined how good it would feel to have her legs around his waist when he bedded her. But had he not been at the jail. "I'm madder than hell at you! What were you doing at the jail?"

"I don't know," she mumbled.

"Stop that!" he growled and tightened his arm around her waist. "Tell me!"

"I was looking for wanted posters."

"Brown says they post them at the newspaper office where they'll be seen by more people. Why do you care about wanted posters?"

"To see if I'm on one."

"If you haven't broken the law, why would there be a wanted poster on you?"

"Because...the rest of my story is that Rance won't care how he gets me to Texarkana or who drags me there as long as he can imprison me again."

"I'll give you to Rance when hell freezes over."

That gave her pause. She stared at him with profound relief, her green eyes glistening with gratitude. "Thank you, Bolton."

"I guess I should have said that out loud sooner."

"That's all right," she said softly. "You being here is what made me realize there could be a poster out on me and that anybody, even a main street beggar, could turn me in."

Bolt figured Rance had enough money to buy trumped up charges, wanted posters, or both. They traveled in silence until they reached the crest of the hill above the canvas camp of prospectors and miners. Tansy pulled on Lightning's reins and Bolt calmed the horse before it reared.

"Do you mostly drag them in dead or are they usually alive?" Tansy asked out of the blue.

"Tom Smith told me anybody can bring in a dead man," Bolt replied, the answer coming to him like a long lost friend. "So, I take them in alive if at all possible."

"All the way back to where they're wanted?"

"Just to the nearest marshal or sheriff. He locks 'em up and when I get the bounty I move on."

"I believe we've proven you are a bounty hunter once and for all."

"Yeah," he replied. He tipped up her chin and looked at her neck. He saw a single drop of blood and thumbed it away. "Maybe my memory will soon tell me that I already caught the hatchet killer."

Tansy looked into Bolton's sapphire blue eyes and could make out the tortures still lingering there. She prayed for the pain to fade. "Some things are better off forgotten."

Bolton cocked a rakish brow. "Like going to the newspaper office to see if you're on a wanted poster?" When she nodded, he said, "Wanted posters sometimes offer clues to a killer's whereabouts."

"I'll be happy to check the newspaper office for you. Maybe you'd better let me down now, so you don't ruin your reputation by riding a silly girl back into town."

"I said little girl, not silly. I doubt I'll have any trouble with my reputation when the latest tale about Crazy Earl hits the saloons."

"True," Tansy agreed. She had admitted believing this man. Trusting he wouldn't take her back to Rance, she let herself enjoy being captive in Bolton's strong arms.

"Tansy, you saved that old guard's life, just as sure as you saved my life and my foot."

"Thank you, Bolton, for saving my life today. We're even."

"Don't ever make me do it again."

Tansy wrapped an arm around his neck and whispered in his ear, "Because you'd miss my chatterboxing if I died?"

Bolton scanned the horizon and then slashed his mouth across hers. She wrapped her other arm around him and hugged him. The brim of his hat brushed her head as he slid his tongue into her mouth. He groaned low in his throat and tightened his arm around her. Kissing Bolton was the only rejuvenizer she needed after her brush with death. He raised his head and patted her hip.

"Let's get back to the saloon. Saving you made me thirsty."

"I'll fix you a cup of tansy tea."

"I'll drink it if you'll spend the night with me."

With that, Bolton turned her around in the saddle and nudged Lightning's flanks. Tansy wanted to spend the night with him. Her heart pounded so hard, she wondered if he could feel it against his forearm. Passing the townspeople's houses, Tansy asked Bolton to stop at the newspaper office.

At the *Black Hills Weekly Pioneer*, Bolton let her slide out of his arms. She missed his embrace the moment her feet touched the ground. There was no one in the office and no wanted posters. Going back outside, she paused. Bolton was talking to two strangers and motioned for her to walk to the saloon.

Tansy fretted the whole way.

CHAPTER 15

"WHAT ARE THOSE STRANGERS DOING BACK HERE AGAIN?" Tansy snapped, two days later to Gimpy and Lupe as they stood behind the bar at closing time.

"I don't know, but it looks like the meetin's over," Gimpy said.

The two men shook hands with Bolton and left the empty saloon. Without a word, Bolton headed up the staircase, turning toward the bedroom where he'd been holed up since the strangers had found him at the newspaper office.

Rubbing her temples, Tansy worried aloud, "What could they possibly want?"

"Jist go ask Bolt," Gimpy said. "Lupe an' me'll lock up for the night."

Tansy took off her apron, made her way up the stairs and down the hall. At his door, Tansy raised her fist to knock but lost her nerve. She jumped when he spoke from inside the bedroom.

"The doors open, Tansy."

"How did—" she didn't finish. She was getting to

know him, and he was a bounty hunter after all.

The door opened and an angel lifted Bolt's spirits. Lamplight made the room cozy and as Tansy entered, it felt perfect. Intimate. The window was open to the cool evening. When Tansy froze just inside the door, Bolt knew he was about to get a lecture. Fine. He'd missed her chatterboxing.

"What have you done to my bed?" she asked.

He'd stacked the frame against the far wall and rearranged the two mattresses that had been one on top of the other. Both were on the floor now with one turned sideways at the end of the other.

"It's the only way I could make the bed large enough to keep my feet from hanging over the edge," he replied. Sitting in the middle of the mattress with his back to the wall, he'd dealt a hand of solitaire between his knees. He held an eight of spades in one hand and a bottle of whiskey in the other. "It *is* my saloon."

"Yes, it is," she replied.

"Let's play cards."

When he crooked his finger Tansy came to him, her fresh soap scent wafting his way. She couldn't afford perfume. He wondered if she'd like some. Stopping at the edge of the mattress, she pursed her lips.

"I don't want to play cards. I want to discuss the nefarious business you've been conducting with those men in the saloon the past two days."

Bolt played the eight of spades on a red nine then pat the side of the bed for her to sit down.

"Those men are United States Marshals. They're passing through the Dakota Territory on their way to California. In Hay Camp, about forty or fifty miles east of Deadwood, they heard I was here."

"Who told them?" she asked as she sat on the edge of the mattress.

"Marshals tend to deal with sheriffs, judges, and other marshals."

"So, any number of outlaws who left Deadwood after you arrived. They got into trouble somewhere else and talked about the marshal in Deadwood?"

"The bounty hunter in Deadwood," Bolt said. "But the men who were here know me as both. They want me to go back to being a marshal."

"So, they want you to return to New York?"

"No."

Tansy smiled slightly. "What else did they say?"

"One of them knew Tom Smith and reminded me why Tom stopped being the marshal in Abilene."

"Why?"

Bolt took a swig of whiskey, deciding whether or not to tell her.

"Tom, your best friend who saved your life from the hatchet killer. Tom, whose horse was Silverheels." Tansy swallowed before saying, "Please tell me what happened to Tom."

Bolt took another drink from the bottle and looked her in the eye. "Tom was trying to serve a warrant on two men wanted in connection with a murder. Tom had a deputy with him, but when gunfire broke out, the deputy left the scene. One of the suspects shot Tom, then took an ax and decap..."

Bolt stopped. Tansy's hands were clasped so tightly in her lap, her knuckles were white. He reached for her, but she leaned away from him. This was a lot to take in for him, too. With a sigh, he rested his back against the wall again.

"I'm so sorry about Tom," Tansy said. "Do they want you to help them track down Tom's killers?"

"No, those two were captured and sentenced to life in prison back in seventy-one."

"Good." Tansy nodded. "Why did the marshals come all the way into this gulch to find you?"

"They want me to go to California with them."

Bolt thought he glimpsed a stricken look fleetingly across Tansy's lovely face. He reached for her again, but she shook her head.

"Are you going?"

Bolt looked down. What he should do, needed to do, and wanted to do were three different things. He casually played an eight of clubs on another red nine. Silence. Then the next two cards he played were the aces of clubs and spades.

"Aces and eights!" Tansy gasped.

Bolt set aside the whiskey bottle and swept the cards out of the way. He grabbed Tansy and pulled her between his legs.

"What do you care where I go, Tansy?"

"I don't want you to get killed."

"California is beautiful." He frowned at the bottle of red-eye. "It's wine country. And it's as far away from New York City as a man can get."

"So that means yes, you're going."

"Means I'll have two marshals for friends in California if I settle there. You're not the only one with dreams, angel."

"That's a lot of information for a bounty hunter to give up since he can't afford to trust people. Why did you tell me?"

"Let's just say that grinding my teeth and cracking my knuckles wore thin."

She tilted her pretty head and smiled that sunny smile that warmed him far more than he cared to admit. Then, perhaps needing relief from this conversation, Tansy pulled something out of her pocket.

"Since you're barefoot, I won't have to tug your boots off to see if these will fit."

She dangled a pair of socks. Moving to the end of the mattress with gentle hands she placed his right foot in her lap. Desire heated Bolt's lower body. She turned his foot this way and that as she inspected his heel. Her touch fanned the embers smoldering in his loins.

"Did you knit those socks for me or someone else?"

"You did a fine job of taking out your stitches. Your heel looks good. Put the socks on that I knitted especially for *you*, and we'll take a midnight stroll. You can tell me about your dream."

"Thanks for the socks, but it's not midnight. Why are you being extra nice to me?"

"I'm nice to most people."

"Blazes!" he barked. "This has something to do with me saying you could properly motivate me." Bolt yanked his foot out of her lap. "If you're wondering if the marshals knew anything about you, they didn't. Forget about the damn wanted posters."

"If you'd take your own advice, you wouldn't risk your life hunting down wanted killers while tracking down that red-haired giant!"

Bolt was out of plays on that one. He grabbed a handful of cards and hurled them across the room.

"Bolton!" Tansy cried as several cards fluttered around her. "You're being too scary!"

"Aww...Tansy."

Feeling like a bully, Bolt got to his knees and caught hold of her slender shoulders. Kneeling on the mattress, he pulled her delicate body into his arms, pressing his thighs to hers.

Tansy whispered, "Some days you're funny and friendly, like Clyde. Other times you're dark and dangerous like Rance. When I see you lost and alone, I want to be extra nice to you."

Tears glistened in Tansy's emerald eyes as the softest of smiles touched her pink lips. Holding her close, he never wanted to let her go and shut his eyes as if to forestall that day.

"I'm going to buy you something to repay you for my socks," he breathed against her soft neck. "What do you want?"

"I want you to repay me by telling me where you're brooding up here has gotten you."

"I don't brood," he grumbled and leaned back. When she tilted her head and raised an arched brow he said, "What I should do is take the job in California and look to the future. What I need to do is find a killer from my past." But what he really wanted most was the beautiful woman perched between his legs in Deadwood. It was impossible to be in three places at once.

"Don't try to figure it out all at right now," Tansy said. "Just enjoy your time here."

Bolt remembered saying something similar to her and he was enjoying his time here. Tansy reached around his neck and tugged his hair, tied with a leather strip, to his chest. Her every touch was sensual.

"How lucky you are."

"How do you figure?" he asked hoarsely.

"You can pick up your life from where it's been and take it anywhere you want to go."

"So can you."

Tansy lifted her shoulder in a shrug as if that might

not apply to her. "If you could have any bounty in the Black Hills, what would it be? A gold mine, maybe?"

"No."

"Mr. Beasley's job at the jail?"

"Hell, no!" He chuckled.

"Surely not the Crown Saloon."

"This saloon's not big enough to hold in all the secrets. And I've had my fill of living in the dark."

"What secrets?"

"Like the ones involving you and Rance and Crown. Tell me what you meant when you said those men didn't want you."

"We're talking about you, not me."

"You opened the door to that subject, so we're going to talk about you now," Bolt said. She tried to scoot away from him, but he kept her between his legs. When she looked longingly at the door, he touched his fingers to her soft cheek and turned her head. "Was Rance your lover?"

"I haven't asked you about your lovers, Bolton."

"There have been women, but only one lover," Bolt answered. "Your turn."

"Rance intended to be my lover, but his actions proved otherwise. Clyde said the opposite about his intentions and the end results were the same. Understand?"

Bolt shook his head. "No, I don't."

He studied the exquisite young widow before him, sure that in bed she'd be the perfect combination of bashful girl and experienced woman. But the next man in her life should be one whom she loved passionately, not a rich bastard who'd had her father murdered and not an old timer who'd mail-ordered her. Tansy deserved a husband who worked regular hours and came home every night, not one who was on the road for months at a time. She'd said once that she wanted children. She shouldn't conceive them with a man who could be shot dead in the next gunfight.

"Tansy, you confuse the hell out of me." Frowning, he let go of her. "It's late so unless you're going to spend the night with me, get off my bed and out of my room."

Tansy stood and flung a handful of cards at him. "Play solitaire forever!"

CHAPTER 16

BOLT WAS SITTING IN THE BUSY SALOON WITH HIS BACK TO the wall. His temperature hadn't been normal since the night, several days ago, when he'd held Tansy on the bed. It was nearing twilight now as Lupe delivered a shot of whiskey to his table. He'd had enough of this standoff. Maybe he'd ask Tansy to go to supper with him.

"Where's Jigger?" he asked casually.

"I can't say, *jefe*," Lupe replied, having switched *novio* to *jefe*, which was Spanish for boss.

"Can't or won't say, Lupe?"

Lupe wouldn't meet his gaze. "What I saw is behind the strictest of fences."

"Behind the—" Bolt smothered a grin. "In the strictest of confidence?"

"*Sí!*" Lupe said, leaving to wait on customers.

Bolt opened the ledger he'd started on the saloon. He made some notations about the plates and utensils bought to go with the coffee cups. Even with that purchase, they were showing a profit. No matter, he'd paid their wages out of his pocket. A few minutes later Gimpy stopped by his table.

"Where's Jigger?" Bolt asked. He downed the shot of whiskey and gave the glass to Gimpy.

Gimpy's eyes shifted to the window as he replied, "Not real sure."

A tousle-haired, gangly young man was darting across the red clay street. Pounding across the plank walk, the kid pushed open the saloon's swinging doors.

"Hell-fire, the town crier!" Gimpy said.

The youth, Bolt judged to be in his late teens, burst into the saloon with a wild look in his brown eyes. He swept a lock of dark brown hair off his brow and spied Bolt.

"Mr. Rivers! You gotta do something quick!"

Staying in his seat, Bolt asked, "Do I know you?"

"No, sir! But I know who you are!" he replied.

As the young man started working his way around customers, chairs, and tables Bolt could see muscle beginning to develop on his lanky frame. The kid stumbled and Bolt thought if the boy ever grew into his big feet, he'd be strapping.

"Mr. Rivers, sir, I was here the day Wild Bill Hickok shot ya in the foot," he said and stuck out his hand. "My name is Wilbur Hector."

"Wilbur Hector...what?" Bolt asked, shaking his hand.

"Just Wilbur Hector. My folks died of the pox when I was little, and I can't remember my last name. Dumb, huh?"

"It's frustrating."

"You can call me Willy or Will."

"What's on your mind, Will?"

"You gotta help Jigger. On accounta she's the most

beautiful, finest, kindest lady! She's a huckleberry above a persimmon if ever there was one!"

"Is Jigger in trouble?"

"Yes, probably so, Mr. Rivers." He nodded. "I work for the newspaper and saw her rip down a couple of wanted posters a little bit ago."

"What do you know about this, Gimpy?" Bolt asked.

"Well-sir," Gimpy gulped. "Jist that Lupe saw a gun in her pocket."

"Blazes!" Bolt growled and stood.

Most of the customers eyed Bolt warily and some began scooting back their chairs. Lupe hurried toward them as Bolt tied his hair back with a rawhide strip.

"Bolt, I made Jigger promise she'd give the hatchet killer's poster to you if she ever came across it," Gimpy said. "Didn't I, Lupe?"

"Sí, jefe, he did!"

Will grinned at Lupe until Bolt barked his name.

"Yes, sir!" Will said, redirecting his attention back to Bolt. "Jigger took off lickety-split to capture a man whose poster she done tore down!"

"Good God Almighty!" Bolt snatched his Stetson off the peg on the wall behind him.

"She sa—" Will's voice broke as Bolt glared at him. "Said you gave her the idea of turning outlaws in for the bounty and she was gonna use the money to start a clinic. I followed her along Main Street, trying to talk her out of it all the way. When she ducked down the alley leading to Dolly's Doves and Dance Hall in the badlands, she told me to go about my business, because she was playing solitaire!" He frowned with concern. "That's when I gave up talking to her and ran back to get you, Mr. Rivers."

"Dammit to hell," Bolt gritted through clenched teeth,

realizing that as cool and controlled with killers and other outlaws as he was, this adventuress angel made him lose his temper the way no one else ever had. He didn't understand it, but it was a fact. "Where are the badlands?"

"North, on the west side of Main Street. I'll show ya!" Will said excitedly. "Hot diggety damn! I'm going to a whorehouse."

Bolt stalked across the saloon and shoved open the swinging doors. With Will at this side, Bolt headed north.

"Think Jigger's gonna be put out with me for telling ya?" Will asked. "I'd be powerful sad if she wasn't my friend no more."

"She's gonna be powerful sad when I get my hands on her."

Reaching the north end of Main Street, they turned left down an alley and walked behind a row of saloons. At the edge of the saloons, there was a narrow, well-worn path through pine and birch trees. Will pointed to the badlands.

"Dolly's Doves and Dance Hall," Will said dramatically as if on a stage.

There were four shacks, two on one side of the trail and two on the other, all small and weathered. At the end of the path was a large, whitewashed house.

"Dolly's is the two story, white house with the flower box and hitching post," Will said. "Them four shacks're for the doves too soiled to live in the same house as Dolly. Where do you think Jigger is?"

"Inside the house."

"How do ya know?"

"I recognize the horses at that hitching post."

"Oh," Will whispered seriously as if making note of everything said.

Door after door was cut into the house, side-by-side, five across the front of the place, and from what Bolt could tell it looked like there were more doors cut into both sides of the dwelling as well.

"What are all those doors for?"

"My boss, Mr. Merrick owner of the newspaper, which is the *Black Hills Weekly Pioneer*, let me help him write a newspaper story about these doors. Dolly and the previous sheriff didn't get along. He thought he'd shut her down by boarding up her front door. It's old news now so it ain't no news. But I found out that Dolly—"

"Dammit, Will, just give me the answer, not the whole history."

"Dolly honey-fuggled him!"

"She what?"

"Out-smarted him. She had another door built right next to her front door. When the sheriff nailed up that door, men built a new one and last count there was seventeen doors. That's a door for every year of my life!"

"This is a damn strange town," Bolt mumbled under his breath.

"Looks like Dolly had somebody unboard some of the doors here and there," Will said, pointing. "I guess Brown ain't been sheriff long enough to shut Dolly down. Or maybe he just doesn't care."

"Will, I'll take it from here and I don't want to see one word of this in the newspaper."

"I swear not a word. But I wanna help."

"I don't have time to argue."

Bolt headed down the path to Dolly's main house. Will followed then jumped ahead of him and in a grand gesture, tried to open the center door. It was locked. Bolt kicked it open.

Sweet Pete, just inside and yanking up his suspenders, went slack-jawed at seeing Bolt.

"I—I don't want no trouble, Mr. Rivers!"

"Neither do I."

TANSY HAD SNUCK in through a small door on the side of the house. Hunting the wanted man, she had quietly made her way up to the second floor, knocking first on a door painted purple and then a yellow one, but the doves she'd disturbed were alone. She knocked on a gray door and it opened.

"Well, well, Jigger Crown," said a woman clad in a scarlet robe. "Dolly said yer highfalutin' self would come crawling to the badlands sooner or later. We done heard you lost yer saloon in a gambling bet or somethin'."

Tansy just nodded unsure she could speak without her voice breaking. Not knowing where or how she'd lost her mind, with each step into this place, she'd gone from afraid to terrified. Only her dream of starting a clinic kept her from running. She hoped this dove continued to think she was looking for work and not question why she was here. But sooner or later, she'd have to speak.

"Word is your wickedly handsome bounty hunter fixed Crazy Earl's flint in short order," the woman said.

Accurate, so Tansy nodded again. Stiffening her spine, she tried to peer around the puffy sleeve of the voluptuous woman's robe. The open robe revealed satin drawers and a shockingly low cut lace corset.

"I'd like to personally thank him," the prostitute said,

shoving at her hair. Tansy shrugged. "Is Rivers as good in bed as he is with his gun?"

Tansy cleared her throat and said, "In bed, he packs a cannon."

"Ooowhee!" the dove squealed. "I need him! Is he here with you?"

"He's taking a bath." Tansy had overheard him say he planned to do so.

"Be still my heart!" the woman exclaimed. "Bring him with you next time!"

At that moment, the door was jerked open and there stood the wanted outlaw clad in filthy, long underwear.

"I'm...I'm turning you into Sheriff Brown for the bounty," Tansy said fingering the small derringer in her pocket.

"Huh?" he said, not knowing what to make of her.

With a shaking hand, Tansy pulled the wanted poster out of her pocket and held it up. Then she stuffed the poster back into her pocket and yanked out the derringer. Arms trembling and legs quivering, she put both hands to the gun to steady it.

"What in tarnation happened to my favorite door? The only one that locked!" Dolly suddenly screeched from downstairs. "What's going on up there?"

Tansy swallowed hard and answered, "I'm turning in Cole Younger to the sheriff."

"Who?" Dolly shrieked.

"I'm not dying like them girls Crazy Earl knifed!" the dove entertaining the outlaw wailed and ran.

A few women, with heavily made up faces, quickly appeared in their doorways hearing the noise and one let the fleeing dove into her room. The doors shut just as fast and stayed firmly closed.

Alone with the outlaw, Tansy's abject fear became so

all-consuming she felt lightheaded. The tiny gun in her hand must weigh fifty pounds, she thought. She opened her mouth to order the outlaw to come along peaceably. But that result seemed so unlikely no words came out.

"He's not Cole Younger," a familiar voice said.

Bolton came around a corner and into the hall, a study in black and white. His black Stetson sat low on his head, black hair, shot through with the silver streak, hung down the back of his black vest. Under the vest, a white shirt, his thumbs casually hooked in the pockets of snug black pants. Below his low slung gun belt was the bulge of his cannon and further down polished black boots.

Tansy had never experienced such overwhelming relief.

"She—she—thinks   I'm—I'm—"   the   outlaw stammered.

"I heard everything she said."

"Cole Younger is masquerading as Skinny," Tansy whispered to Bolton as if it were a secret.

Bolt realized Tansy was near to being literally paralyzed with fright. Shaking caused her long blond curls to bounce just above the white bow at her tiny waist. In a pale pink dress with a white collar at the high neck, she was the picture of innocent goodness in this house of ill repute. And just as she'd protected his reputation by walking him down the street after he'd sent Larson packing, Bolt would get her out of this with her dignity intact.

"Jigger, did I forget to tell you the U.S. Marshals I talked to suspect Cole Younger's somewhere in Minnesota with the James boys?"

Tansy fixed her green-eyed gaze on him, lowering the gun to her side.

"Besides, Jigger," Will piped up, joining them. "The James-Younger gang robs trains which Deadwood don't have and hold up big banks which Deadwood's Mechanics' and Miners' bank, ain't."

"Well now, Will, Jigger, and I wrangled with a man who could have passed for Jesse James not long ago right in the middle of Main Street."

"Ya did, Jigger?" Will asked.

Eyes on Bolt, Jigger nodded.

"So can I go?" Skinny asked. "Mr. Rivers, sir?"

"No, you're Roy Skinner and there's a five hundred dollar bounty on your head for murder."

Skinny's expression confirmed that was true as Dolly came into view on the second floor.

"Are you gonna turn him in, Mr. Rivers?" Will asked excitedly.

"I don't risk my life for less than a five thousand dollar bounty like on Jesse and Cole. And Jigger feels the same way."

"Whew!" Will exclaimed, grinning ear-to-ear.

"Skinny's in my house and I'll turn him in!" Dolly said, a small cigar between thin lips colored orange.

"Jigger found him and she's turning him in. Right?" Bolt asked, turning to Tansy.

"Right," Tansy answered softly.

The look Bolt gave Skinny over Tansy's head moved the outlaw forward without Bolt saying a word. Desperation showed on the criminal's face when his eyes lowered to the derringer in Tansy's hand.

"A man using a derringer, risks the other man coming up off the floor," Bolt said. Skinny raised his head and looked down the barrel of a Colt. 45. "You won't get up." Bolt pulled handcuffs out of his vest pocket and Will reached toward them.

"I'll cuff him for ya," Will offered.

"Behind his back and make sure they're tight," Bolt ordered, handing the cuffs to him.

Bolt gently took the small weapon out of Tansy's hand and wasn't sure she'd even noticed. When Will had the cuffs on Skinny, Bolt put a hand on Tansy's shoulder and squeezed.

"Let's go, Mr. Skinner," Tansy said.

"Will," Bolt said, not wanting Skinny any closer to Tansy. "Make sure he doesn't run."

Will grabbed Skinny's arm shuffling him out of the bedroom and down the stairs. Tansy followed him, with Bolt at her back. Dolly began a slow clap and, doors opening, all her doves clapped, too. Dolly and several of the women followed him quoting prices; fifty cents to touch, a dollar to do. The woman in the scarlet robe ran her hand down Bolt's back and over his rear, offering herself for free.

Bolt felt not a trace of desire as he sauntered through the bordello.

"You offered him bargains, girls. Now, leave him be! Just because he's in the badlands don't mean we gotta act like we got bad manners," Dolly said in the foyer where she caught up with him.

CHAPTER 17

"GOOD RIDDANCE, WILBUR HECTOR!" DOLLY SHOUTED shrilly. "Good riddance, Jigger Crown!" she hissed as Tansy followed Will out of the house. Dolly then shooed the doves back upstairs. "Bolt here's the key to my dance hall," she said, pulling a key out of a low cut bodice barely covering her abundantly endowed bosom. "You'll never have to kick open my door again."

"There's no bounty big enough to make me take that key," Bolt replied.

Leaving Dolly in his wake Bolt noticed Gimpy at the end of the path, worry lining his face.

"Nobody turns me down!" Dolly screeched after him. "Did you hear me, Rivers? You sorry son-of-a-mule!"

Bolt had caught up with Tansy when he registered amusement on the faces of Gimpy and Will.

"I've been called a helluva lot worse." Bolt laughed and swung his arm around Tansy.

Tansy was white as a sheet and slumped against him. He quickly swept her up in his arms and kissed her full on the mouth. Hoots and hollers erupted from Dolly's doves. They'd never know Tansy had passed out. Gimpy said Dolly had stormed into the house. A gawking Will reported half naked women hanging out of all sorts of doors and windows.

"Will!" Bolt barked. "Pay attention! You're getting half the bounty."

"Yes, sir!" Will's eyes grew round. "I am?"

"Gimpy, Skinny won't be needing his horse. Take him to Red Clark at the livery and tell Clark I'll be responsible for the horse's keep," Bolt ordered, carrying Tansy down the alley.

Dusk dimmed any sparks of curiosity from the passersby on Main Street. Approaching the Crown Saloon its rustic charm was warmed by a sky tinted red and gold by the setting sun.

"What's wrong with Jigger?" Lupe asked coming to the swinging doors.

"Fainted," Bolt said.

"Sheriff Brown is here about what happened at the jail," Lupe said as he emerged from the saloon.

Bolt paused long enough for Brown to say he'd found two more knives on the prisoners and to thank him for dispatching Crazy Earl. Bolt told Will to turn Skinny over to the sheriff as Lupe opened a swinging door for him.

"Ya shoulda seen Mr. Rivers in the badlands!" Will said to Sheriff Brown and Gimpy as Lupe looked at Will with interest.

WHEN TANSY OPENED HER EYES, the bedroom was softly lit by a single oil lamp. She lay on the bed trying to get her bearings. Bolton was stretched out beside her, his black hair fanned out on the pillow, eyes closed. She wondered if he knew his straight nose was one of his best features. So were his lips. Intensifying the snarl on his chiseled face when confronted with criminals, his cocky grin could make her blush to her toes. His vest and gun belt hung over the back of a chair, his boots next to the bed, a couple of buttons open on his shirt. She rolled to her side and placed her hand on his arm.

"Bolton." His eyes opened just a sliver and then closed. "What you did for me today was far more than just saving my life again. Thank you."

"Don't try to sweet talk me," he said, gathering her to him. "You're in big damn trouble, little girl."

Clasped to Bolton's warm, muscular chest she breathed in his sexy, masculine scent. Though he said she was in trouble she couldn't have felt safer. She snuggled closer to him.

"When I found those posters, I remembered Mr. Skinner, who I thought was Cole Younger, talking about Dolly's and decided to look for him there." Tansy reached into her pocket, but where was it? Startled, she asked, "Where's my dress?"

"I have it and I might just keep all four of your dresses, so you can't leave this room."

"I'm in my camisole and drawers!" Tansy really wanted to be mad, but her body decided instead to tingle in mysterious places. "Did you undress me?"

His sapphire eyes opened again, making her shiver. "Yes."

"Where's my gun?"

"I have your peashooter and I'm keeping it. You," he kissed the tip of her nose, "are staying the hell away from jails, brothels, and outlaws."

"Hmm..." Tansy smiled as his protectiveness warmed her heart. Bolton was all male, confident and commanding, with muscles and power. "What if I don't do as you say?"

"I'll handcuff you to a chair and set you in the corner."

"You wouldn't dare!" she said, gooseflesh instantly popping out all over her.

"Are you flirting with me?"

"Mayhap."

"That bad girl would be naked in the chair until she convinced me she'd behave."

"Oh." It took Tansy a moment to picture that and recover. "You have the wanted posters that were in my pocket, don't you?" she asked shyly, changing the subject.

"Uh huh," Bolt said, rolling onto his back and stacking his hands under his head.

"Is the second poster of *him*?"

"Yeah, Hatchet Harless Parker. Worse than the worst," Bolt growled, staring at the ceiling before looking back at her. "You should have brought his poster to me immediately."

"I know," Tansy replied, placing her hand over her heart. "You told me not to make you save my life again and that's not what I intended, but it's what happened."

"Having to save you means I could have lost you."

In her glittering green eyes, Bolt saw an angel willing to risk her life, just to get the money for a clinic to help others. His heart said this compassionate beauty was a once-in-a-lifetime woman. Her shy flirtation had triggered a raging desire in him the likes of which he'd never known. The usual saloon noises drifted upstairs as he took her in his arms and pressed his lips to hers. When his mouth opened, hers did, too. This time her tongue touched his first.

"*Jefe* and Jigger!" Lupe suddenly called from the hallway. I've brought you a late supper and Gimpy's got a table with him. Open the door, por favor."

"Blazes," Bolt growled, giving Tansy's hip a familiar pat as he rolled out of bed.

He opened the door and Gimpy set down a small table. Bolt moved it near the rocking chair and Lupe placed a tray laden with stew, biscuits, cherry pie, whiskey, tea, and glasses on the table. Her eyes widened at seeing Tansy in her underclothes. Gimpy was already gone. Lupe said nothing and left.

With a soft blush on her cheeks, Tansy shrugged. She'd spent many nights in this room with him after all. He smiled at her, glad she was getting out of his bed and not the rocking chair this time. She took a seat in the rocker now and Bolt pulled up the chair which held his gun belt.

"I need a steak, but this'll do for tonight," Bolt said. He poured whiskey into his glass and Tansy poured tea into hers. Bolt took a sip of her tea, frowned, and added a shot of whiskey to it. "Tansy tea and whiskey. It's not bad," he teased, trying to keep a straight face.

She sipped, choked and her expression was so cute he poured her a half shot more. Both hungry, they finished supper before Tansy spoke.

"Tell me about that big bounty on Harless Parker's wanted poster."

"That poster's not the most current one. The bounty's grown."

"Because he keeps killing?" she asked.

Bolt clenched his jaw, scooted back his chair, and grabbing the whiskey bottle, moved to the window. Staring outside, it was a long moment before he turned to her and blew out a sigh.

"In eighteen sixty-six, when Parker first crossed my

path there was no bounty on him. Tom Smith and I hadn't heard of him and nobody else had, either." Bolt paused and took a drink. "New York City's entire police department looked for him. We had no identity on him. No sightings. No more hatchet murders. No leads." Bolt tapped his anger down with another swig of whiskey. "Tom and I met with Governor Fenton and when we left his office there was a bounty on a nameless, red-haired giant."

Shaking her head as if in wonder, Tansy asked, "How did you find out Parker's name?"

"By tracking him. The only way to do that across state lines was to become a United States Marshal. So, I left the police department and became a marshal, like Tom. A year later same time of year; late summer, early fall Parker killed again. When Tom and I got down to New Orleans where he'd murdered a family of five and raped the woman, he was long gone. But he left behind a police record."

"The authorities let him go?" Tansy asked in horror.

"No. They got his name out of him before he killed a deputy and broke through a wall of their jail," Bolt took another drink of whiskey. "Since then, he's left a trail of bodies all over the country." He looked back down on Main Street wishing Parker would lumber into view. "To collect the reward in full, he has to be brought in alive."

"Why alive?"

"So, Parker knows who put up twenty-five thousand dollars to catch his murdering hide."

"You?"

"Yeah," Bolt growled.

"But what if someone brings him in and demands the reward?"

Bolt turned away from the window and caught her

swigging the last of her whiskey-laced tea. He leaned against the wall, crossed his arms, and silently watched her until she grabbed his glass and choked on a swallow of straight whiskey.

"Tansy, let's stop talking about it."

"No." She coughed and gave herself a shake, making her breasts jiggle. "I wasn't prepared for the gruesomeness of the riverbank murders or what happened to Tom." She took another big gulp and said, "Tonight, I'm —hiccup—prepared. How will you pay the reward?"

"I've got money."

"When did you remember that?"

Caring, understanding, and innocence were so nakedly written on her face that he knew he could confide in her. He lit another oil lamp in the room before answering.

"I remembered after the manager from the Miners' and Mechanics' Bank came by the saloon a couple days ago and asked me when I was going to pick up the five hundred dollars sent from Sonoma."

"Where's Sonoma?"

"California."

"Do you have a home in Sonoma?"

"I'm not sure about that. Since Deadwood doesn't have a telegraph office, I sent a letter to the California bank to make some inquiries."

"It's a place to start." She nodded. "Do you think you're...that you might have a—"

"Wife?" Bolt finished for her. "I've never been married. I remember that for sure."

"Once you find Parker and turn him in, you can forget bounty hunting. Right?"

"Right." He wondered how soon Tansy would forget

him when he was gone. "But I'll see Parker in his grave before I retire, or I'll die trying."

"But Bolton?" she murmured and hiccupped. "For ten years, Parker's been impossible to find even though a lot of smart gunfighters and ruthless gunmen surely must have tried so they could collect that money. What makes you think you will ever find him?"

"When he vanishes for a year at a time, some say he hibernates like a grizzly bear. Others say he's the devil and descends into hell. Whatever the case, this time of year, every year, he surfaces and kills," Bolt replied. When Tansy visibly trembled, he whispered, "Come here, angel."

Though tipsy, she didn't hesitate. Tansy rocked forward trying to get out of the rocking chair. She launched herself out of the chair on her third try. She was so adorable, Bolt grinned. Weaving past the lamp, her thin camisole and drawers showed him every feminine curve from her full breasts to her shapely hips, to the sexy vee between her pretty legs.

"Mayhap someone's turned him in or mayhap he's already dead," she said and hiccupped.

"The Sonoma bank told the bank here that the reward hasn't been claimed," Bolt replied. He opened his arms, spread his feet and she walked into his embrace. He held her close before saying, "He's out there."

"Out where?"

"In the Black Hills."

CHAPTER 18

It was the dead of night as Tansy floated down French Creek in a canoe. She sensed someone with her. Bolton, she hoped. She reached out, surprised at the Indian who appeared and asked her to take Bolton to the Valley of the Moon. She promised she would. But...where was it?

"Are you Bolton's guardian angel?" Tansy whispered as she gripped the sides of the canoe. She wanted away from the scary darkness. "Please take me to Bolton," she asked as the vision faded.

"Tansy, I'm right here," Bolton said. "And you're the only guardian angel I see."

Tansy opened her eyes and looked around. She wasn't in a canoe. She was gripping the sides of the wooden bar downstairs in the empty saloon. And there was Bolton, his steadying hand gently holding her as she lay loosely swaddled in a blanket from the chest down.

"How did I get here?" she asked, looking up at the handsome man in the flickering lamplight.

"You fainted twice in one day," Bolton said, towering

over her. "To be on the safe side, I sent Lupe for a doctor. When Doc Youngblood finally got here, he said he was too tired to make it upstairs. So, I brought you down here."

Struggling to sit up, Bolton helped her. She remembered she was wearing only her camisole and drawers under the blanket. Her cheeks grew hot with a blush.

"The doctor checked you over, took your pulse, and said you'd be fine when your tansy tea and whiskey rejuvenizer wore off." Bolton chuckled. "Before the doctor arrived you had an admiring visitor." Tansy smiled at hearing of Wilbur Hector's concern and devotion to her. "Lupe and Gimpy turned in an hour ago. It's almost midnight now and I was about to take you back upstairs."

"No!" Tansy said abruptly and placed her hands on his chest. "You have to leave Deadwood right away and go to the Valley of the Moon."

"The Valley of the Moon?" Bolton shook his head. "That must have been some dream."

Tansy wrapped her arms around Bolton's neck and pulled herself to his muscular body. When his hands splayed on her back, she knew she'd hate herself for sending this gorgeous man away.

"It wasn't a dream. It was a vision from a Lakota Indian. Hatchet Harless Parker is in the Dakota Territory."

"I already told you Parker's here in the Black Hills."

Yes, she recalled that now. "How do you know?"

Bolton eased away from her and braced himself against the counter along the back wall. The ornate mirror, above the counter stacked with bottles, glasses, cups, coffee pots and plates reflected his powerfully built body and luxurious black hair.

"I've been remembering."

"Remembering what?"

"After Tom was murdered in Abilene, I wondered if he'd been killed with a hatchet instead of an ax. I went to Kansas and confirmed that a farmer was the one who killed him with an ax. As I was about to move on who should step off a train?"

"Hatchet Harless Parker?"

"Wild Bill Hickok," Bolton said, rubbing his forehead as if reliving their meeting. "Bill and I went to the Alamo Saloon where he later set up shop to take Tom's place as Abilene's new marshal. While we played five card draw, I told Bill about Parker. He said if ever there was a place to hibernate like a grizzly bear and hide among devils on the run it had to be this isolated gulch in the Hills. I was in Cheyenne when I heard Hickok was forced out of Abilene as a vagrant." Bolton shook his head, obviously troubled by that. "People in Cheyenne said Hickok had headed to Deadwood."

"Mayhap Mr. Hickok hoped to redeem his reputation by capturing Hatchet Harless Parker."

"We'll never know. I decided to come here on nothing more than a hunch. When I heard Bill was playing poker in the Number Ten Saloon, I decided to say hello. You know the rest." Bolton looked her straight in the eye. "I think my hunch about Parker being here has paid off."

"I think Mr. Hickok would have hated that he hurt your foot."

"Forget about my foot," Bolton said. "Think about Gimpy's foot."

"Oh, dear Lord, yes!" Tansy said, clasping her hands over her heart. "It was Parker who took off Gimpy's foot last summer! With a hatchet!" She paused a moment and said, "The wanted poster fits your description of Parker. But it doesn't look exactly like the man I saw last summer."

"How has he changed?"

"His hair is thinner and gray rather than red. But most different of all was the deep pockmarks scaring his face around a scraggly beard."

"Even smallpox couldn't kill him," Bolton muttered.

"Wouldn't he have moved on by now since that was a year ago?"

"Not if he's been recovering from smallpox in the pest house or holed up in a cave somewhere."

"He could be holed up right next door!"

"He's not next door. Calm down." Bolton held up both his hands. "The day I went to the jail, I described Parker to Sheriff Brown. He said he'd ask around."

"I hope he doesn't find out anything."

"Will knows Deadwood as well as anybody and maybe better than most. I asked him about Parker and explained Parker wouldn't use his real name. He was back within the hour. He went through old newspapers and found out there's a giant of a man who has a claim on a placer mine. I imagine you're aware that means he's panning for gold on creek in the Black Hills. Maybe he's got a mine inside a cave he's working, too. Will is going to see if he can find out where."

"What you need to find is the Valley of the Moon, not a monster," Tansy said.

"I'll find Parker then we can discuss the Valley of the Moon."

Tansy scooted to the edge of the bar and was about to jump down so that she could grab Bolton and shake some sense into him. But he stepped forward, flattened his hands on her thighs, and held her still. She tingled and lay her hands on top of his, curling her fingers under his palms. Not knowing what his reaction might be, she wouldn't admit how much she wished she could help him find that valley.

"I watched my mother and infant brother die in childbirth and that's why I want to be a midwife." Other than Papa, she'd never confided that to anyone. Until now. Until Bolton. "You know I saw Papa die, too. I don't want you to die because of Parker."

"Tansy, I'm sorry you lost everybody. I understand how that feels," Bolton said, squeezed her hands, and changed the subject. "I went to Boughton's today and bought you something to thank you for my new socks." He pulled one hand from hers, reached under the bar, and handed her a small package.

"What is it?" Tansy asked, but he only shrugged. Boughton's was the fancy dress shop on lower Main Street. She tilted her head and unwrapped the gift. "Perfume!" Tansy smiled, removed the stopper, and sniffed. "Honeysuckle." Dabbing the sweet scent behind her ears, she whispered, "I've never ever had perfume. I love it. Thank you so much, Bolton."

"You're welcome. Now, let's go back upstairs so you can get a good night's sleep."

"Not yet," she said. He shrugged and tucked a finger into the blanket in the crease between her breasts. Tansy craved this man's touch and couldn't stand the idea of him leaving Deadwood. But she said persistently, "Say you'll go to the Valley of the Moon."

"Not yet," he said and cocked a brow. "I'm just getting to know my beautiful barkeep."

Beautiful? Tansy was speechless. This man, who dreams were made of, thought she was beautiful.

Suddenly picturing Dolly's doves, she felt terribly self-conscious about her undergarments.

"I don't need satin and lace," Tansy said with a toss of her head.

"I have no objection to satin and lace. But it's the woman wearing them who matters. In bed, I want that woman to be naked and love me because she wants to and not because she'll be paid," Bolton said and took his finger out of the blanket. His eyes raised and locked on hers. "Want me, Tansy."

Want him? More than anything she wanted him. The challenge of his words and the bold glint in his hooded blue eyes unleashed raging desires that instantly ran rampant within her. She didn't fully understand these wild new yearnings, only that they were all tangled up with Bolton.

"Come to think of it I had a swallow of your tansy tea at supper," Bolton said, a sexy grin lifting a corner of his mouth. "So, you're spending the night with me."

"But...I just woke up," she said, as nervous thrills swept through her. "You can teach me five card draw." Warmth tingled Tansy's most intimate part. "Let's play cards."

Bolton sauntered around the end of the bar, walked to the window, and pulled down the shade. With catlike grace, he prowled toward her like a hungry lion in search of a mate. He lifted himself up on the bar and straddled it.

"Let's play," he said.

His voice was deep velvet. Captivated, Tansy focused on his sensuous lips. He smiled and she knew at this moment she was the luckiest woman alive. With every ounce of her being, she wanted this man's body, heart, and soul. She raised her eyes to his ready to play whatever game he wanted to teach her.

"Gimpy keeps the cards at the other end of the bar," she whispered and set her perfume aside.

Gently, Bolton slipped the camisole strap off her left shoulder and then her right. Tansy could hardly breathe. He pushed the blanket down and her camisole lowered, baring the swell of her breasts. Raking his fingers over the top of her right breast and then her left, he nudged the blanket to her waist. Spasms of heat flared between Tansy's legs as Bolton licked his lips and studied his work.

"I worried about you while you slept. But below the belt, I wanted to strip you naked."

"Strip me now, Bolton."

"Last chance to go upstairs like a good girl."

"I'm gonna be a bad girl."

His eyes narrowed. "Only with me."

"Only with you." She pulled the blanket from around her body and shoved it behind her.

Reaching down his leg, Bolton pulled a Bowie knife out of a scabbard and sliced her worn camisole down the front! She wished the lamp wasn't doing such a good job of spilling light over them. Bolton set his knife on the bar and almost reverently, inch by inch opened her camisole. She closed her eyes and silently prayed for his approval.

Bolt stared. Never in his wildest fantasies had he imagined such perfect breasts. They were the color of pale moonlight, with nipples the shade of California's finest red wines. He took their soft weight in his palms and brushing his thumbs over the tips, watched them bead.

"Unlike any woman, anywhere, you have a passion I feel even across the crowded saloon."

When she trembled, Bolt pulled her closer, lifted her long hair to one side, and kissed her neck. Placing a gentle hand on her naked back, he saw. And he knew.

"No!" Tansy cried out.

CHAPTER 19

"TANSY!" BOLT BARKED AS SHE SHOVED HIM AWAY.

Tears gathered in her emerald eyes as she quickly covered herself with what was left of her camisole. "You...you..."

"I what?" he asked.

"Find me distasteful!" she replied.

"The hell I do."

"I knew you'd think I'm so unappealing you wouldn't make love to me."

"Who was impotent, Rance or Crown?" Bolt asked intuitively.

"How did you know?"

"It's the only thing that finally makes sense of things you said about them. Any man with eyes would want you. Which one was impotent?"

"Both."

"Who blamed you?"

Tansy pulled her legs up to her chest. "Rance."

Bolt clenched his jaw. "I've wondered why Rance didn't force himself on you. It was because he couldn't."

He ached to pull her into his arms, but he'd work the poison out of this wound first. "You didn't answer me when I asked you what happened when you refused to marry him or how he hurt you. Tell me now."

A tear trailed down her cheek. "He had a fit. He said my refusals had turned him from a stallion into a gelding. He said only if I married him and willingly went to bed with him would he be cured."

"When he had this *fit* did, he have the bullwhip in his hand?"

"I don't know."

"Tansy, did he put that mark on your back?"

"Yes!"

That was exactly what Bolt had figured upon seeing the mark when he'd pulled her hair aside and kissed her neck. Murderous rage slammed through him.

"That sonofabitch!" he yelled.

When Tansy scooted back, Bolt protectively folded his muscular body around her delicate one. A moment later, a sleepy Gimpy, clad in a nightshirt, trotted out of his room near the kitchen. Bolt shook his head, Gimpy pivoted, and went back to his room.

"That's when you accepted his proposal. Rance lifted his guard, and you ran for the Hills. Literally."

"Yes." Tansy choked back a sob. She smelled of honeysuckle and felt just as sweet in his arms.

"What did Crown say about the whip mark?"

"All Clyde asked of me was to play the piano. He never saw me undressed and we never shared a bed. He slept downstairs. After Gimpy was hired, Clyde bought an extra cot and shared his room with Gimpy down here. I helped Gimpy dress Clyde for his funeral and that's when I glimpsed his..."

"Peashooter."

Bolt meant no disrespect to the dead. But he couldn't imagine being married to Tansy and not seeing, touching, and kissing every inch of her naked body. Pressing her breasts to his chest, he eased the camisole down her slender back. Though faded, the whip mark stretched from her left shoulder blade to the right side of her ribs. Damning proof of Lewis Rance's cruelty.

"It won't be long before the mark's completely gone, angel."

"It would have been worse if not for my dress."

"Rance never saw you naked, either?"

"No! Never!" she replied, sitting back and looking him in the eye. "No man has! Ever!"

"Damn glad to hear it," Bolt said with a smile. "And you didn't cause Rance's impotency."

"But he said I did."

"He's a liar. What man would want to marry a woman who'd changed him from a stallion to a gelding?" Bolt cocked a brow. "Trust me, when Rance was flat on his back in bed and looking at you every day while you took care of him and his wife, he damn well knew he was impotent. He was hoping you could cure him."

"Are you saying when you were sick in bed, you—"

"Wanted you? Hell, yes!" He took her hands in his. "When you came into the room, I had to think about the weather to keep from making a tent of the sheet. I could have pulled you into bed and made love to you all day and all night."

"Rance honey-fuggled me?"

"Yes." Bolt gently squeezed her delicate hands for emphasis. "Was it your father or Rance who said the horse kicked Rance in the stomach?"

"Rance. Why?"

"I think that horse kicked Rance between the legs.

My guess is he didn't tell your father he was impotent because he didn't want your father steering you away from marriage."

"Come to think of it, Rance couldn't walk for a while."

"When he could walk, he had a limp rope in his pants." Bolt felt Tansy's tension ebb when she giggled just a little at his description of Rance's anatomy.

"I wonder if Papa found out about Rance's problem and paid for it with his life?"

The marshal in Bolt wondered how Mrs. Rance died. "Whatever happened or didn't happen, none of it is your fault."

"And Clyde?"

"Age may have been his problem. He probably felt he'd cheated you all the way around and tried to make that right by leaving you this saloon."

"Does that whip mark bother you?"

"Do my bullet wounds and knife scar bother you?"

"Are you going to love me tonight, Bolton?"

"Tansy, I do lo—" Bolt cut himself off, surprised by what he'd almost said. He couldn't afford to fall in love. He had a killer to catch. Reining in his thoughts, he said, "Until tonight, I figured you'd been to bed with a couple of men. I didn't like it, but I thought I was dealing with an experienced widow, not an innocent virgin."

Tansy lowered her fingers and began unfastening the buttons on his shirt. "Think of me as a *willing adventuress*." With one finger she traced the thin line of hair down the middle of his stomach.

"Willing is one thing," he said, savoring the feel of her touch and craving it lower. "But an innocent assumes once a man takes her virginity, he will be hers forever."

"I've told you that you owe me nothing," she said, tugging his shirt out of his pants.

"Nothing is exactly what you might get from a bounty hunter."

"I know better. I will have everything."

"What would you have?"

"Tonight," she drawled, pulling herself close, her breath warming his neck. "If Crazy Earl had sliced my throat or Skinny had shot me, I'd have gone to my grave without ever making love to you. I want you to hold me and kiss me and love me all night long."

"You serve up your truth as strong as the whiskey," Bolt said, knowing he couldn't resist this sensual siren much longer. He ran his hands down his thighs and splayed his fingers.

Tucking her fingers into the waist of his pants, she undid the top button. Doing so pushed her creamy breasts together and let the wine-red tips peek through the locks of her long blond curls. Bolt's stomach muscles tightened as a sweet heat thrummed into his loins. His heart pounded with yearning, slamming blood through his veins, and hardening him.

"Let's go up to the bedroom, angel."

"Let's stay right here."

Bolton was agreeable now, but Tansy feared on the way upstairs, he'd talk himself out of taking her virginity. Keeping her eyes on his lap she slowly proceeded.

Bolton's manhood rose out of his pants one button at a time until all the buttons were undone. His black hair which fascinated her so on his upper body swirled around his indented navel and traveled lower. Nesting in lush, male fur was his dark pink arousal; long, hard, and thick.

"You've seen me before, Tansy," Bolton said with

amusement and masculine pride touching his deep voice.

"Very fleetingly and never like this. Did I do that to you?"

"Definitely."

Bolton peeled off his shirt. Tearing her eyes from his lower body, Tansy watched the muscles in his chest and arms ripple as he tossed the shirt. He smiled and tucked his fingers into her underwear.

"Stand up and I'll pull 'em down."

"Just cut them off," she said, too bashful to stand and be stripped. With his Bowie knife, he carefully did so. When he pulled her drawers out from under her, Tansy squeezed her legs together. "Am I being too bad of a girl?"

CHAPTER 20

"ARE YOU HANDCUFFED TO A CHAIR IN THE CORNER?"
Bolton looked between her legs and groaned. "C'mere,"
he said huskily.

Bolton brought her to him, his eyes closed, and his
mouth slashed across hers. She wrapped her arms
around his neck and his tongue slid into her mouth in a
kiss as thrilling as the man himself. Exactly when had
she forgotten that Bolton was a lot of man to handle for
more than a few minutes?

He slipped his hands under her arms and raised her
to her knees. She started to cover her breasts, but he
whispered no. Tansy slowly ran her hands across his
broad shoulders and through his long, loose hair. He
gently rubbed the pads of his thumbs over her nipples
and watched the tips bead. He held her closer, and his
lips closed over the left nipple! His mouth was warm and
wet, causing Tansy to moan his name. Leaving a path of
fire in his wake, he kissed his way to her right breast,
closing his lips around the tip and brushing her nipple
with his tongue.

"Tansy, from head to toe, you are incredibly beautiful."

Tansy's most private place sizzled like a fever burning her up inside.

Bolton lay back and brought his long legs up on the bar, trapping Tansy's hips between his thighs as he pulled her on top of him. Her hair fell forward, and she tossed it over her shoulder, catching their reflections in the mirror behind the bar. Her breasts were crushed to his muscular chest and her hips rested on his unfastened pants. Tansy trembled with eager giddiness.

Bolton stroked the back of her head and pressed his mouth to hers. She wound her arms under his neck as he slowly slid his hands down her back. When Bolton's hands kneaded her bare bottom a whimper of excitement vibrated her lips against his.

Lying atop him, Tansy could feel the muscles rippling in his chest, arms, and legs as he pushed his pants down his hips. Then she was suddenly aware of what was hard as his knife handle and as scorching as a heated iron pressing into her stomach.

"You do have a battle gun," she whispered in awe.

"And it's gonna hurt when it shoots through you."

"I don't care."

"Touch me," he said quietly.

Tansy moved her hand between their bodies and gently gloved his rock hard male flesh.

"Mmm..." Bolton's voice was intimate, deep, and masculine. "I've been waiting for that."

He gripped her waist as his knees came up between hers and she gasped as he spread her legs wide. His fingers touching that which no one had ever touched, she realized the warm tingling had made her damp. He parted her tenderly, his hardness replacing his fingers.

As he pushed into her, she could barely contain her desire for him.

"Little girl, I feel that barrier—"

"I want all of you." She raised up.

"Don't sit down."

"Ouch!" As she'd tried to sit, raging fire speared her. She tried to wiggle off Bolton but before she could separate her body from his, he tightened his grip and thrust into her. "That hurts!" she cried and collapsed atop his muscular chest. Her tears wet his shoulder as her legs clamped against his thighs.

Bolton's gentle hands pressed the small of her back and her body adjusted itself around his erection. She clung tightly to him and as he spread her legs wider her body accommodated his to the hilt. He pulled almost out, before tenderly sliding in again. This time Tansy felt no pain, only pleasure.

Yes, this was what she had desired. Bolton Rivers was her *wanted* man.

Bolton then carefully pulled out, rolled her over, and stretched out on top of her. She wound her arms around his neck as he settled between her legs. She parted her lips for his kiss and his tongue slipped into her mouth as he slid into her body. With each rocking motion of his hips, Bolton turned her sweet surrender to him into her most amazing adventure.

Their mating dance quickly built a storm in Tansy's lower body. Suddenly it thundered and struck like lighting raining pleasure through her entire being. He arched his hips and plunged all the way into her as his sexy, low groan escaped against her mouth.

Tansy felt hard, throbbing inside of her, his heart pounding against her breasts. When he kissed her again it was softer. She opened her eyes and looked into his. She smiled at him thrilled beyond belief.

"Bolton," she purred, with him still inside her. "You've given me a night to remember."

When the pulsing stopped, Bolton said, "If the pleasure you gave me is any indication, I probably just gave you my first child."

Shocked at that flattering realization, Tansy combed his hair back with her fingers and smiled. Would Bolton's baby have black hair? How wonderful to have this man as the father of her child. His sapphire eyes narrowed, and she was sure a baby would have his blue eyes.

"I lost control with you, Tansy," he separated from her and sat up. "I shouldn't have."

"I'm happy you did. Unless I have your baby, I'll have no one's because I..." No. She wouldn't admit her all-consuming love for him since he'd said virgins thought their first lover was forever. She sat up beside him on the bar.

"Because?" he asked.

"Because no other man could possibly measure up to you."

"I'll take that as a promise and a compliment."

Bolton slid off the bar, tugged up his pants, and grabbed the blanket for her. She wrapped the blanket around her as he fastened a couple of the buttons on his pants. Then he braced his hands on both sides of her hips.

"Before you and Will split the bounty on Skinny—"

"No!" Tansy said. "I could have gotten you and Will both killed! I don't deserve anything!"

"Not open for discussion," Bolton said. "Tell me

where you intended to run both times you tried to escape me."

"I don't know."

"You're already naked and I *will* handcuff you and set you in a corner."

She laughed and whispered shyly, "Let's go upstairs."

"As soon as you answer me, I'll carry you upstairs."

"The Black Hills are beautiful but too cold." She lowered her gaze from his blue glare to his broad chest, splaying her fingers on his naked shoulders. "But because of Rance, I can't go south."

"Give me a one word answer, chatterbox."

"Canada."

"Talk about cold!" he barked. "I cannot imagine a little girl like you wandering the frozen wilds of Canada."

"Where would you go?"

"California. It's the last frontier. A place for new beginnings."

He was reminding her that giving him her virginity didn't mean he was hers. They were eventually headed in opposite directions. As he put on his boots, she pictured him walking away and was thankful she hadn't embarrassed herself by offering to help him find the Valley of the Moon. Reminded again of her promise to the Lakota ghost to get Bolton out of the Black Hills, she put a voice to that thought.

"California would be a perfect new beginning, Bolton."

His broad smile broke her heart. But she laughed when he snatched her off the bar. Cradling her in his arms, he carried her up the stairs.

. . .

BOLT WAS at his table in the saloon at suppertime the next day, fighting a grin as happiness tried its damnedest to put a smile on his face. He couldn't allow that. It would send the wrong message to the wrong people. Marshals and bounty hunters had enemies everywhere, especially in an untamed, reckless gulch like Deadwood. He glanced up from the account ledger as Will and Gimpy headed toward him.

"Mr. Rivers?" Will said respectfully.

"Bolt," he said. Will grinned and Gimpy rolled his eyes. Bolt liked these characters and motioned for them to sit down.

"I ain't found out where that placer mine is, yet. But I'm working on it," Will said.

"I have no doubt," Bolt replied.

"I'm also working on a story about General Crook chasing Crazy Horse and the Sioux, who helped massacre Custer and his Seventh Cavalry, in the direction of Deadwood."

CHAPTER 21

"The Crow, fierce enemies of the Sioux, are helping General Crook track them," Will said.

"Our government shouldn't have lied to and cheated the Indians," Bolt said.

"Jigger gives sermons on bein' fair to the Indians better'n Preacher Smith," Gimpy added.

Bolt chuckled. "She dragged me out of here this morning and down to the Pioneer Drug Store to hear Smith preach his Sunday street sermon." Bolt sobered. "But the Indians *are* out for blood."

Will then handed Bolt a copy of a rough draft of the newspaper story he was writing about it.

"Replace ain't with aren't, Will," Bolt said absent-mindedly and kept reading.

"That's right," Will said seriously.

"Glad you didn't write nothin' 'bout Bolt and Tansy at Dolly's." It was a bad slip on Gimpy's part.

"Who's Tansy?" Will asked. When Gimpy's shoulders slumped, Will guessed. "Sir, I'll take that information to my grave," he vowed, looking Bolt in the eye.

"People travel in and out of Deadwood with the newspaper tucked under their arm, Will. That's why I didn't want any mention of Jigger or any description of her in the newspaper. Without even asking me why you swore you wouldn't write a story and you kept your word."

"Yes, sir! I did!" Will nodded his head for emphasis. "You can always count on me!"

"I counted on you the other day at Dolly's, and you handled yourself well." Bolt feared the smile on Will's face might split his head wide open.

As conversation switched back to General Crook and the Sioux, Bolt's mind wandered. The Indians and the United States Army might be at war, but he hadn't felt so at peace in ten long years.

Gazing at the back of the saloon, his memory served him up with a picture of Tansy and him atop the long bar. He visualized slicing off her underclothes and revealing the most gorgeous body he'd ever seen. Her breasts, more succulent than sweet red wine, made his mouth water. His palms itched to knead her shapely body and his fingers ached to caress the petal soft skin between her thighs.

An inexperienced innocent who'd cried in his arms in one breath, with the next she became his tantalizing lover. With his hands at her waist, he'd held her atop him as he pierced her squeezing tight interior. Bolt quickly forced his mind away from their lovemaking to keep his body from betraying him.

His thoughts turned to their talk about a new beginning. Carrying her upstairs, he realized she hadn't said she wanted to go with him to California. In their room, Bolt decided he would absolutely not follow in Rance's footsteps; a former patient who pressured her with demands. Lying in bed, with the moonlight streaming across their bodies, he'd asked her if she regretted giving him the gift she could give to only one man, one time. She'd said no but sounded vulnerable as she snuggled closer to him. Instead of making love to her again, with a will of iron, he'd simply held her all night.

Bolt had awakened to Tansy's sweet kiss on his cheek. She murmured that it was Sunday and time to go hear Preacher Smith. Bolt had struck a deal. He'd go with her if she'd go with him to the Grand Central Hotel's restaurant for a steak supper. She had politely declined. He'd then threatened to handcuff her and drag her to Boughton's Dress Shop, so she would be the best dressed woman there. Since Sunday was the busiest day of the week in the gulch, that shop and most of the stores on Main Street were open for business.

"Don't she look purdy!" Gimpy whistled.

Tansy was standing at the top of the stairs. Blue satin covered her from the neck down as intimately as Bolt's hands had covered her body the previous night. White lace trimmed the frock's collar and the cuffs of three-quarter length sleeves. A blue satin shawl trimmed with white fringe draped her shoulders.

Tansy's long blond locks were pulled high on her head. Lupe stood next to her adjusting a couple of the ringlet-like curls dancing at her shoulders.

Prospectors, gamblers, miners, cowboys, merchants, hell every last man in the room openly gawked at her with lust on their faces. Truth be known, Bolt couldn't blame them for staring. She was indeed a spectacular vision of beauty to behold.

"Jigger!" Bolt bellowed, cementing in their minds to whom they would answer if they got out of line with her. "Come here!"

Smiling, shaking their heads, and greatly envious of Bolt's good fortune, customers slowly returned to their cards, conversations, beer, and whiskey.

Regally, Tansy descended the stairs, with Lupe behind her. Will shot to his feet so quickly he nearly knocked over his chair. Bolt stood and Gimpy followed suit.

Honeysuckle wafted his way and Bolt smiled recalling how Tansy had touched the stopper between her breasts while clad only in the satin and lace underneath the dress. This sexy siren was femininity and fantasy beyond compare.

"Evenin,' Jigger," Will said, ducking his head and then glancing at Lupe.

"Evening," Tansy answered. "Will, have you been properly introduced to Lupe?"

"Recently, I've seen Lupe getting a newspaper from out front of our office. Hello, Lupe," Will said.

"Nice to meet you, Will," Lupe said with a shy smile.

"Same here, Lupe." Will nodded politely. "Jigger, you look like you're feeling better than the last time I saw you."

"I am. Thank you, Will."

"I got a story to finish about General Crook, Crazy Horse, Sitting Bull, and the Sioux," Will said. "So, I'll be seein' you folks."

"I hope so," Lupe said softly before Will turned and left. "I helped with Jigger's hair! Doesn't it look lovely, *jefe*?"

"It sure does, ladies," Bolt replied.

With a last glance at the swinging doors, Lupe returned to tending customers.

"Bolt, I ran into Sheriff Brown earlier," Gimpy said. "He asked to tell ya the Board of Health is gonna pay

Skinny's bounty tomorrow, so ya don't hafta wait for it to be brung by pony express."

"Is that usual?" Tansy asked Bolt.

"No, but Deadwood is far from usual."

"Town officials're hopin' to get on yer good side, Bolt, so you don't leave." With that, Gimpy trotted to his place behind the bar.

"Angel, you are a heavenly vision," Bolt said.

"My dress matches someone's sapphire blue eyes," Tansy said shyly. When he cocked his brow, she smiled and smoothed her skirt. "I've never had such a lovely gown and...and underclothes."

"Come on, let's go to the restaurant for supper," he said with a grin and winked at her.

As she slipped her dainty hand into his, Bolt's hand felt large and crushing. He swung open one of the doors and followed her out of the saloon.

"Do you have any idea how handsome you are, Marshal Rivers?" she asked. "Quite the dashing man in your new black suit and tie."

Earlier, when she'd been clad only in her satin and lace undergarments and he in his black pants and boots, she'd brushed his hair and tied it back with a rawhide strip. He could get used to that.

"Will you sleep with me again tonight?" he asked.

"Mayhap I will and mayhap I won't," she flirted.

Bolt smiled down at her, moving her hand to the crook of his arm and pulling her close. At the Grand Central Hotel, Tansy glided as royally as the queen Bolt felt she was into the restaurant. The men inside fixed the same lustful gazes on her that had shown on the faces of the men in the Crown Saloon.

After seating Tansy in a corner of the restaurant, Bolt put his back to the wall. Always keeping a wary eye out, he didn't peruse the menu. Bolt ordered two specials: buffalo steaks, potato pancakes, green beans, and sourdough rolls. But they were out of wine and Bolt sighed with disappointment.

The waiter left and Tansy said, "I miss the Mexican food in Texarkana."

"Shh," Bolt said softly at the mention of her former home. When Tansy's eyes grew wide at her error, Bolt reached across the table and patted her hand.

"I'll make a Mexican supper for us and if you like the brown betty dessert that comes with the special, I'll ask the waiter for the recipe," Tansy said, bestowing on him one of her sunniest smiles.

Bolt wondered if a man could get any luckier than he felt at this moment.

Tansy grew a little quiet then. Dinner was served and after dessert, she asked for the recipe. They left the restaurant and walked down the boardwalk. The night had cooled, and Bolt was glad he had urged Tansy to buy the shawl. On both sides of Main Street, soft lights twinkled in saloons and stores.

"That was my first restaurant meal since Papa died."

"Were you thinking of your father at dinner?"

"Yes." Tansy tightened her shawl. "Papa had a portrait taken of us a while back. But I couldn't find it the night I walked away from Rance. I have nothing to remind me now." She looked up at him. "It hurts so much to lose someone you love with all your heart."

Bolt hadn't expected to love again. But now he felt a love he had never known before. He'd had no idea such powerful love existed; boundless, unrestrained, irrevocable. As they drifted down the plank walk Bolt hoped by the time he found Parker, Tansy would trust him enough to leave Deadwood with him. He'd whisk her out of the cold Dakota Territory she disliked so much and settle her in warm and sunny Sonoma, California.

Breaking into his thoughts, Will suddenly skidded around a corner, making a beeline south toward the office of the *Black Hills Weekly Pioneer*.

"Will!" Bolt shouted, "What's going on?"

Will whipped his head around. "Bolt! Jigger!" He raced toward them. "Preacher Smith is dead!"

CHAPTER 22

"A RANCHER JUST FOUND PREACHER SMITH'S BODY AT THE Rest. You know that trailside breathin' spot five miles south of town?" Will said.

Bolt saw sadness and shock touch Tansy's face as she nodded. She'd just said how hard it was to lose people and here was another death.

"What happened to Smith?" Bolt asked.

"You was right about the Indians wantin' blood. They killed him!"

"Have they been caught?"

"I—I don't know, sir."

"Tell me what you do know," Bolt said and placed a steadying hand on Will's shoulder.

"The preacher's sermon notes were still stuffed in his pocket," Will said and seemed to collect himself. "Smith's hands were folded 'cross his chest and he was holding his Bible. I reckon since he was a holy man in the Indians' eyes they didn't mutilate or scalp him."

Instinctively, Bolt moved his hand from Will's shoulder to his Colt .45.

"Here comes Preacher Smith's body now!" Will said, smacking a hand over his heart.

Clattering up the red clay street was a wagon loaded with hay and the corpse of Preacher Smith. Half a dozen men circled the wagon as it rolled past.

"The struggle is over for him," Tansy whispered. "Each day a person lives through the violence in Deadwood is a miracle."

Bolt felt the same way. The Black Hills were picturesque, but a deadly place to live.

"I gotta get more facts about what happened," Will said and took off after the wagon.

"There's nothing we can do for Preacher Smith," Bolt said, taking Tansy's hand. She stared over her shoulder at the wagon carrying the dead preacher until Bolt gave her a tug down the boardwalk. "I have a surprise for you that might take your mind off this."

They stopped in front of the McDaniels/Langrishe Theater. The bill posted outside touted: 'First Class Male and Female Comedy Company.'

"I got tickets for us earlier," Bolt said, and Tansy nodded.

Inside, they laughed, and Bolt felt some of Tansy's tension ebb. By the time they left the theater, her spirits and his were brighter.

Halfway home, a gathering of men had formed in front of Robinson and Ross Grocery. Voices were raised in angry shouts. Will was in the middle of the fracas but spotted them and came running.

"Mr. Merrick told me to find Mayor Farnum quick!" Will said. "I been lookin' everywhere, but I can't find him."

"Why do you need the mayor?" Bolt asked.

"Sheriff Isaac Brown has been shot!"

Bolt clenched his jaw. "Is he dead?"

"Yes!" Will was wild-eyed. "Shot right through the heart."

"Try looking for the mayor at the theater," Bolt said.

Will thanked him and ran down Main Street crying out his horrible news.

"My God," Bolt gritted out. "Can't these people rest on Sunday?"

"They don't," Tansy replied, resignation in her soft drawl.

Tansy had been right when she told him Deadwood was soaked in blood, whiskey, and corruption. As they continued toward the Crown Saloon, all hell broke loose as word of the sheriff's murder spread. Frantic merchants poured out of their shops. Drunken men staggered from saloons and dance halls. Some of those who'd liked Isaac Brown scuffled with the sheriff's detractors. People were speculating on who'd done the sheriff in while others said it didn't matter. Deadwood was lawless with or without a sheriff.

At the Crown Saloon, the bar had cleared out due to the murders of Preacher Smith and Sheriff Brown. Lupe was frantically pacing.

"Mi Dios, you're finally back!" Lupe crossed herself. "The preacher is dead! The sheriff is dead!" Lupe flapped her arms. "I feared you were both dead!"

"Lupe, why would we be dead?" Tansy asked, putting her arms around her.

"Jigger, it's only a matter of time before it's our turn to be killed!" Lupe wailed.

"Lupe! Calm down!" Bolt ordered. "Where's Gimpy?"

"Trying to help Will find the mayor," Lupe whimpered, clinging to Tansy. "Gimpy's going to die!"

"No, he isn't," Bolt said. "I'll find him.

"I'll go with you," Tansy said, letting go of Lupe.

"No. Lock up after I'm gone," Bolt replied. "Then go upstairs to bed."

"With all that chaos, you're sure to be hurt or worse," Tansy said. "You can't go!"

"Who's gonna stop me?"

"Me," Tansy said and when Bolt chuckled, added, "Lupe and me."

"*Sí, jefe!*" Lupe nodded.

Bolt walked out of the saloon alone.

TANSY AND LUPE closed and locked the front doors to the saloon but stayed downstairs. After a few minutes of watching the melee out in the street, Tansy distracted Lupe by asking her to go upstairs and light the bedroom lamps. Tansy went over to the piano and sat on the bench that was back now.

Making love to Bolton was the best thing that had ever happened to her. During the night Tansy's determination to flee Deadwood ceased and her desire to stay with Bolton flourished. As he'd held her in his arms, she had decided to stay in the Black Hills as long as Bolton remained, so she could send him to safety in the Valley of the Moon.

Tansy couldn't pinpoint the exact moment she fell in love with Bolton, but she loved him so much she had admitted wanting to have his baby. However, he had made no promises. He had even warned her that nothing was exactly what she might get from a bounty hunter, making it clear she didn't fit into his new frontier in California.

Tansy plunked at the piano keys. "Love me." Plunk, plunk. "Love me."

Then a realization hit her so hard her fingers froze on the piano keys. Even if by some miracle Bolton offered to take her with him to California, she couldn't go. Staying with her placed Bolton in Lewis Rance's deadly path! Though Bolton would assure her that he could handle Rance, she had felt the bite of Rance's bullwhip and had witnessed his hireling kill Papa in cold blood.

Bolton had to leave Deadwood alone at all costs and the cost would be to her heart. More than ever, Tansy resolved to send Bolton away from her to the safety of the Valley of the Moon.

Decisions made; Tansy plunked away. "Broken heart." Plunk, plunk. "Broken heart."

But for now, if only 'Johnny' would come marching home again, she would hurrah. It seemed like an eternity before Lupe's squeal brought Tansy to her feet.

"Jigger, here they come!" Lupe exclaimed, pointing at the window from the bottom of the staircase.

Tansy jumped up from the piano and hurried to unlock the doors. Bolton and Gimpy blew into the saloon on a midnight breeze. Tansy silently hurrahed as Lupe crossed herself.

Dashing in his black suit and dangerous with the Colt .45s slung low on his hips Bolton took Tansy's glare of concern in his stride. In fact, under the brim of his Stetson was a reckless gleam in Bolton's blue eyes. He was in his element. But Gimpy, so small in comparison to Bolton, nervously tugged on his drooping, gray mustache as he eyed the dark street.

"Lock up, Gimpy," Bolt ordered.

"Where have you two been?" Tansy asked, trying not to let her voice shake.

"We was seein' the elephant!" Gimpy said, meaning everything.

Gimpy quickly locked the doors and Lupe wagged a scolding finger at him.

Bolton swaggered across the saloon and around in back of the bar. He placed a hand on the bar, in the exact place where they'd made love, and met Tansy's gaze. He cocked a slashing brow, his long fingers stroking the worn wood. Heat crawled up Tansy's neck and her cheeks flamed. A tingle between her legs brought with it a picture of Bolton's magnificent naked body. The effect this man had on her was outrageous! She joined Gimpy and Lupe at the bar where Bolton was setting out four whiskey glasses.

"Did you catch up with Will?" Lupe asked Gimpy who nodded.

"We found Will who was with the mayor, who was with the bank manager, who's part of the Board of Health!" Gimpy said all in one breath. His eyes twinkling now, Gimpy smacked a package full of money down on the bar. "Will didn't wanna take his two hundred and fifty, but Bolt made him. Said he earned it. And here's yers, Jigger."

"Oh, no! Give that money to Bolton."

"What about saving up for that clinic?" Bolton asked, grabbing a bottle of red-eye, and pouring some into the glasses.

"*Sí*! I'm going to be your assistant, Jigger!"

"Let's toast to the clinic," Bolton said.

Bolton and Gimpy raised their shots. He'd poured Tansy half a shot and Lupe a swallow. Tansy looked into three smiling faces and clinked her glass to theirs. Bolton treated all but Lupe to a second round. Good naturedly, Lupe hugged them and went upstairs to bed. After a yawning Gimpy headed for his room, Bolton smiled at her.

"What's that look in your eye, Tansy?"

"Last one upstairs is a silly girl!" she said and whirled toward the staircase.

Bolton quickly extinguished the lamps. When he started after her, Tansy shrieked and grabbed the staircase handrail. Hurrying as fast as she could, she heard Bolton's footsteps behind her and giggled.

"No fair taking the steps two at a time!" Tansy said as he passed her.

Bolton's deep laughter was laced with the knowledge of his masculine strength, and he reached the second floor well ahead of her. She raced down the hallway only to find him blocking the bedroom door.

His blue eyes narrowed and only the faintest of smiles formed on his sensual lips. Bracing his forearms against the door frame, his legs spread wide, he cocked a brow. Tansy grasped him low on his hips, just above his gun belt. His eyes smoldered as his jaw muscle clenched.

"What do you want, silly girl?"

"You," she breathed.

Instantly, Bolton swept Tansy inside the cozy bedroom and kicked the door shut. Leaning against the door, he tugged her to him and slashed his mouth across hers. Standing on tiptoes between his booted feet and winding her arms around his neck, she poured herself into the kiss. He lifted her off the ground and with a groan, put her feet back on the floor before breaking off the kiss.

"Last night, you started out on top. Tonight," Bolton's grin was wicked, "it's my turn."

Bolton stripped off his suit coat and dropped it over a chair. His rakish grin fanned the spark in Tansy's most secret place into flames. He unbuttoned his white shirt, pulled it out of his snug pants, and tossed it along with his gun belt over the chair. Leaning against the wall, he yanked off his boots and Tansy's heart melted as she saw he wore the socks she'd knitted for him. When the half-naked man sauntered toward her, his magnetism was more delicious than dinner and more thrilling than the theater.

"Stop!" Tansy held up her hands, having just thought of a very important question at this most inopportune moment. He didn't stop and she shivered with sweet anticipation. "What will Sheriff Brown's death do to your plans to find Parker?"

"Well, Gimpy says it puts a gimp in them," Bolton replied. "Forget about that."

Bolton wrapped her in his arms. His warm flesh rippled over hard muscle, his sapphire gaze burning with desire. All man, he smelled of soap and leather.

"Yes, forget about Parker," Tansy whispered. "I want you to leave the Hills."

"So, you've told me." Sliding his hands down her back, he unbuttoned her dress and slowly peeled it away from her shoulders. "If I leave, what happens to my saloon and my beautiful barkeep?"

"I'll buy the saloon back," she replied, knowing that was unrealistic.

"I thought your dream was to go to a warmer climate and open your clinic."

"That's true," she said, not reminding him that she couldn't go south because of Rance. "But you must go to the Valley—"

"Of the Moon," he grumbled, placing his hands to his tapered hips. "How do you expect me to go someplace when we don't know where it is?"

"We must find out because the Indian's vision fore-told a meeting with Parker will result in death."

"Yeah, Parker's." Bolton's voice softened and he said, "In the meantime, love me, Tansy."

Love. Her heart skipped a beat. But he just meant make love to him, of course. If it wouldn't put him in danger or make him feel trapped, she would tell Bolton she loved him so completely with body, heart, and soul she would follow him to the end of the world. And never look back.

"I will love you on one condition, Bolton."

"Name it."

"If I locate the Valley of the Moon before you find Parker, you must go there and forget about him." She stuck out a trembling hand. "Deal?"

Bolton grabbed her hand and pulled her to him. "Maybe."

With that Bolton eased her dress down, letting it float to the floor where it looked like a pool of deep blue water. Off came her petticoat before he swung her up in his arms and carried her across the room. At the edge of the bed, he stood her down and stripped off her lace and satin underwear.

Nude before him, Tansy unbuttoned his snug black pants and pushed them down. Backing onto the mattress she stretched out on the bed. Bolton stepped out of his pants and naked, lay down on top of her, spreading her legs with his and touching his hard manhood to her moist softness.

"I'm going to work on locating that valley, Bolton Rivers."

"Just work on loving me, Tansy Wiley."

CHAPTER 23

Tansy stared at the calendar behind the counter in Robinson and Ross Grocers. September twentieth. Tansy smiled. It was exactly one month since giving herself to Bolton. She wondered how much longer she had with him.

"Somebody's going to have a good supper tonight, isn't he?" Mr. Robinson asked as he put her purchases into a paperboard box.

"I hope he likes it," Tansy replied, feeling a slight blush as she dug into her dress pocket to pay.

"No." Mr. Robinson shook his head. "Please tell Mr. Rivers his supper's on me."

Thanking him Tansy left the store, her mind on the man who occupied all her waking thoughts.

Remembering his strong, muscular arms which had held her to a rock-hard body the previous night, Tansy smiled her way past Dr. Fuller's dentistry office. Passing the drug store where Preacher Smith had given street sermons, she said a prayer of thanks for letting her be the one to come to Bolton's aid the afternoon he was shot. Nearing the Number 10 Saloon, she hugged the box to her heart, wishing her arms were around a certain sexy man.

Yes, the past thirty days had been heaven on earth. And the nights...Some nights they rode the mattresses to the farthest corners of the room. There were nights they made love only once but many nights they didn't sleep until dawn.

Tansy was in love with a marshal turned bounty hunter. Though she wouldn't care if it were front page news, she'd not told a soul. Just as Bolton had kept her badlands escapade out of the newspaper, she vowed to keep Bolton out of Rance's path. To that end, she had asked Will to help her by discreetly asking around about the Valley of the Moon.

"Careful, Jigger."

Tansy was startled as Will grabbed her arm. Not realizing it, she had almost walked off the edge of the boardwalk.

"Thank you, Will," she said, redirecting her stroll.

Will took the box of groceries and chuckled. "A penny for your thoughts and I reckon they start with a 'B.'"

"A 'B,' huh?"

"As in Bolt, the bounty hunter?"

"Oh, him." She laughed and nodded. "Any news?"

"No news about your valley or the mine Bolt's looking for. I'm sorry."

Tansy was both disappointed and relieved. They walked in silence until they reached the saloon. Tansy pushed open the swinging door, but Will hung back, handing the box over to her. He stared down at the plank walk and kicked aimlessly at pebbles.

"What is it, Will?"

"Uh...well, uh..." He glanced through the open door to where Lupe was waiting on a couple of customers. Then looking back at Tansy, he blew out a sigh. "Never mind."

"Will, please tell me," she said and let the door close.

He squared his shoulders and filled his chest with air. "Does Lupe have a suitor?"

"You mean a novio?" Tansy asked. "Novio means sweetheart in Spanish."

"Does she have one?"

"No, but I think she'd like to have one. Do you know of someone?" Tansy asked, knowing well what Will's question meant.

Ducking his head he mumbled, "Uh, yeah."

"Tell him to come by at six for supper with us. We're having brown betty for dessert."

Will smacked a hand over his heart and grinned. He nodded and hopped off the boardwalk. As he loped across the street Tansy figured it took every ounce of his restraint not to shout his good news. She turned and thanked a regular customer as he swung open the door for her. Their coffee and breakfast patrons, along with their beer and whiskey drinkers, were turning quite the profit for the Crown Saloon.

"Good morning!" she called to everybody, smiling at one gorgeous man in particular.

He was reading the newspaper, probably the story he had helped Will with on the Northfield, Minnesota bank the James-Younger gang had attempted to rob on September seventh. Bolton predicted the failed raid on the bank would end what was left of the gang and Will had concluded his article with that quote. Bolton sat at his favorite table his back to the wall, his Stetson hanging on its peg behind him.

It had been hard to leave Bolton's side that morning

as he lay sprawled across the mattresses. With a sheet riding low across his naked back, his arms folded around his pillow, he'd been the picture of a dozing sated lion. But when he was on the prowl, Tansy was his lioness with pleasure.

Over the top of his paper, Bolton grinned knowing the blush on Tansy's face meant she was thinking about their lovemaking. She had planned to rush into the kitchen and hide what was in the box. But his smile put air under her feet, slowing her to a snail's pace.

His winter-streaked, midnight mane fell loose down his back. Under his long hair, his broad shoulders strained against his blue shirt, sleeves rolled to his elbows, exposing his forearms. His hands were big and strong, square palms and long blunt fingers. Oh, how she enjoyed what those hands did to her. He put his paper down and crooked a finger at her. Fireflies danced in her stomach. Yes, he was the most wickedly handsome, dangerously irresistible man on earth.

"Where did you go without telling me?" Bolton scolded, folding his arms over his leather vest.

"If it's any of your business, I went shopping. I needed some things for a special supper this evening," she replied with mock haughtiness.

"Satin and lace? Since when do they put that in a grocer's box?"

"Not a dress, silly boy!"

Bolton furrowed his brows as a hush fell over the saloon. Glancing over her shoulder, Tansy saw twenty some customers covertly watching to see what Bolton would do about being called a silly boy. Gimpy poured whiskey over the top of a glass and Lupe gaped open-mouthed from a nearby table.

Bolton's chair scraped the floor as he stood and took

the box from her, smacking it onto the table.

"What did you call me, *little girl?*"

But before she could answer, he yanked her to him and kissed her. With a chuckle, he sat down and pulled her onto his lap. Tansy could almost hear a collective sigh of relief in the saloon.

"I have groceries in that box. Mr. Robinson said to tell you supper's on him."

"You've cooked for me many times. What's so special about today?"

"You know, don't you?"

"Yeah." A cocky grin lifted one corner of his mouth. "A month never flew by so fast."

"We're going to celebrate with our special supper and then—"

"Let me treat you to supper somewhere."

"But the Deadwood restaurants offer American food." She clapped a hand over her big mouth.

"Let the cat out of the bag? You're going to cook Mexican food like you talked about."

"My father and I loved it."

Bolton smiled. "Tell me what I can look forward to."

"Burritos which are tortillas wrapped around beef tips and cheese. Rice and frijoles as side dishes. Frijoles are beans."

"I'm going to help Jigger cook," Lupe said, having overheard and walking to the table.

"That reminds me, Lupe, you have a gentleman coming to call on you this evening and he'll be dining with us."

"Will?" Lupe's dark eyes lit up.

"Yes," Tansy answered with a smile.

Will was a head taller and probably sixty pounds heavier than Lupe who had just turned fifteen.

"Oh, I'm so glad I'm wearing my flowered birthday dress you gave me today, Jigger! Tonight, I'll wear the shawl you gave me, *jefe*!"

Lupe hugged both Jigger and Bolton at once, giving Tansy a kiss on the cheek. Tansy's eyes teared at Lupe's long overdue joy. Lupe left their table and Tansy returned to the subject of supper.

"Dessert will be an American favorite." She touched her mouth to Bolton's and whispered against his lips, "Brown Betty."

"You're my favorite American dessert."

"Then you may have me at the Grand Central Hotel. They boast the best lodging department, with the finest furniture in all of Western Dakota Territory. Let's spend our one month anniversary—"

"Hush," Bolton suddenly said, shifting Tansy onto a chair beside him.

Immediately, the swinging doors burst open smacking against the walls, as a solidly built man blocked the morning sun. His face was leathery, weathered by harsh winds and weather. Frowning, he wore a wide-brimmed slouch hat low over his creased brow and a red neckerchief around his throat. An Army shirt showed under his fringed jacket and revolvers were strapped tight against his buckskin-clad legs. On his feet were moccasins which reached halfway up his calves.

Bringing the dust of the street into the saloon, the stranger crossed the room and bellied up to the bar. Oblivious to everyone's stares, the stranger pulled five grimy bottles out of his shirt, two with a brown liquid, two with a clear liquid, and a fifth with a red mixture. He lined them up on the bar and turned to the gawking customers.

"Come on, boys! Have a drink on Calamity Jane!"

CHAPTER 24

"THE ONE AND ONLY MARTHA JANE CANNARY," BOLTON said to a startled Tansy.

"I heard Calamity Jane was a close friend of Mr. Hickok's, but I've never met her. Have your paths crossed?"

"Oh yeah." Bolton nodded. "It was a while back in Fort Laramie, Wyoming."

"Well-sir, uh...ma'am—?" stammered a flustered Gimpy. "Miss Calamity, we serve our own whiskey and beer, and we don't serve it to no women."

"Barkeeps in better saloons'n this have served me." Calamity Jane raised a bottle and looked around. "Can't say I've danced with comelier whores'n that one in the corner."

Bolton winked at Tansy meaning just to ignore Jane's comment.

"I'll go introduce myself," Tansy said, raising her chin a notch.

"Just wait, I'll do it," Bolton replied.

"Now shut yer trap and set up some shot glasses,"

Jane said to Gimpy. "I'll pour."

At the bar, Gimpy tugged on his drooping mustache. "If you wanna pour the men a shot it hasta be from the red-eye the Crown Saloon serves."

Calamity Jane swiped off her hat, exposing dark braids that hadn't seen soap for quite a spell. She slapped the hat onto the bar, shoved up her sleeves, and snarled, "Why you leaky-mouthed, paper-backed varmint! Jist try to make me swallow yer local skull varnish and I'll give you an Injun haircut!" With that, she gripped a long bladed knife resting in a scabbard strapped to her waist. "Or maybe the Injuns done scalped-cha!"

With a hand going to his bald head, Gimpy hurried around the end of the bar and said, "I'll show ya to the door, Miss Jane."

"I'll show yer peg-legged carcass this here knife, afore ya can throw me out!"

"No, you will not!" Tansy dashed across the saloon to Gimpy and said to the woman armed with at least two guns and a knife, "There's no reason to hurt anyone."

"So, the cat fur can meow." Jane squalled like an angry cat. "I can tame yer whiskers with a swipe o' my knife and then one o' these miners'll put ya to bed with his pick 'n shovel."

"¡Mi Dios, you smell worse than podrido huevos!" Lupe said, hurrying to Tansy and Gimpy.

"Beg pardon?" Jane asked, fixing her glare on Lupe.

"You smell like rotten eggs," Lupe answered.

"Fer that, I'ma gonna catawamptiously chaw all three of ya up and spit ya out like bits o' teeth on my tongue!" Jane warned.

"Leave my friends alone!" Will shouted, pushing through the doors of the saloon.

"Get on outa here you green-as-unsunned-pumpkin

kid lookin' to lose his manhood afore he's even dipped it!"

Will's face reddened. Calamity Jane had hit home. Will stood his ground as customers gauged their reaction to Bolton. Since he'd not even stood up no one fled. It was quite the show after all. Knife in one hand, Calamity Jane pulled a gun with her other one.

"Jane!" Bolton barked.

"Damn my poor ol' eyes!" Jane squinted and then a grin split her weather worn face. "Is that you, Bolt Rivers, you bodaciously good lookin' hunk o' man, bounty hunter, you?"

"Come over here and I'll buy you a drink."

Jane put away the knife and gun, grabbed her hat, smacked it on her head, and tromped toward Bolton. He holstered his Colt .45 and crooked two fingers at Tansy.

"You could catch a weasel asleep quicker'n you can surprise Calamity Jane, butcha did just that!" Jane said, fixating on Bolton.

Tansy gave Lupe a nudge toward Will. Will looked at Bolton who nodded at the door. Will handed Lupe a small bouquet of wildflowers. Lupe blushed and disappeared outside with him.

"I ain't seen you in a coon's age, Bolt." Jane pulled out a chair and gave it a half turn, throwing a leg over it and sitting down across from Bolton.

"I guess you heard Hickok's dead," Bolton said as Tansy reached him. He put his hand on the back of her chair and she sat beside him.

"Cold as a wagon wheel," Jane replied. She then bit off a chunk from a plug of tobacco. "Wish I could get my hands on the tinhorn gambler who put that bullet in the back of my Bill's purdy head." She eyed Tansy then and, around the tobacco, said, "I ain't never seen you take up with a lady, Mister Catch Me If You Can. But near up, that's what this here gal looks to be."

"That she is." Bolton nodded at Jane. "That's as close as you'll get to an apology from Jane," he said, patting Tansy's shoulder. "Martha Jane Cannary meet Jigger Crown. She owns the place."

"No, I don't," Tansy gasped. "You own it."

"Purdy, but dumb, huh?" Jane asked Bolton rhetorically and said to Tansy, "You can call me Jane if'n you have a *mind* to."

"Pleased to meet you, Jane," Tansy said, wondering if Bolton never considered himself the true owner or if he was giving the saloon back to her because he planned to leave soon.

Jane turned to Bolton. "Was Hickok right about Hatchet Harless Parker being in the Hills?"

"Haven't found him, yet. But he's here."

"Parker 'vaporates into thin air," Jane said, shaking her head. "I done been an Army scout, stagecoach driver, bull freighter, mule skinner, and dance hall bawd. Ain't never been no bounty hunter. If'n I was one I'da tried to collect that big reward on Parker."

"I'll get him."

"Ya always do."

"Taking too damn long," Bolton growled.

"Just makes Parker all the deader when ya find him." Jane then hollered to Gimpy, "Hey, barkeep! Bring me and Bolt my bottles."

Gimpy waited for Bolt to nod. Lupe returned to the saloon with her wildflowers and humming a tune, she picked up the groceries and headed for the kitchen.

"I guess ya done checked with the local law?" Jane asked as Gimpy brought the bottles.

"Yes," Bolton replied. "There was a man named Isaac

Brown who was elected sheriff after Hickok was shot. A month ago, Brown was shot." Bolton rubbed his forehead. "Then a barkeep, named Young, shot a vagrant at the Number Ten Saloon next door where Bill died. Young said he thought the vagrant was Laughing Sam, who was in Young's words, a desperado who was after him. Young turned himself into the Board of Health and a de facto sheriff was hired to gather a jury for Young's trial."

"Damnation! If I'da knowed the barkeeps 'round here shoot their customers, I wouldn'ta pulled ol' peg's wooden leg." Jane laughed, grabbed up one of her bottles, raised it to Gimpy, and then took a swig. "Who's the new sheriff?"

"Seth Bullock," Bolton said and poured himself a shot of red-eye. "After Young was found not guilty, it was suggested that an election for a lawfully authorized marshal should be held."

Sitting beside Bolton, Tansy knew exactly who had made that suggestion. I haven't seen this side of Bolton Tansy thought, talking business with an old friend...of sorts.

"A man named Con Stapleton won the election," Bolton said. "So, Deadwood's got a marshal and a sheriff for all the good it'll do in this town."

"Hell, they oughta elected you, Bolt. Yer big enough to beat law and order into men with yer fists, just like that Irish pardner of yers, Tom Smith, done in Abilene."

"Not for the paltry hundred and fifty dollars a month Bullock and Stapleton get paid."

"True 'nough. You get a helluva lot more'n that fer bringin' in one wanted man instead corrallin' a whole town fulla buffalo chips."

Bolton smiled over at Tansy, and she figured he was

thinking of the *paltry* five hundred dollar bounty she and Will had split.

"If Parker's here as I suspect, he's due to surface," Bolton said. "We know he likes whiskey, so he'll come to Deadwood. I'm not going to be out looking for him when he shows up."

"Jane," Tansy cut in, "have you ever come across a place called the Valley of the Moon?"

"No, I ain't, Jigger."

"It was nice visiting with you, Jane," Tansy said and stood. She couldn't take any more talk about Parker. "Now if you'll both excuse me I have a meal to cook."

In the kitchen, as she started preparations, all Tansy could think about were the ingredients for Bolton's death. First and foremost, there was Harless Parker, an insane hatchet murderer. Next, were the Black Hills themselves, a virtual maze of dense forest. Last, Bullock and Stapleton were as yet unknowns, far from the trusted best friend Bolton once had in Marshal Tom Smith.

"I'D LIKE to jaw a while longer," Calamity Jane said around her chaw of tobacco as Bolt glanced toward the kitchen. "But I figure ya wanna get back to yer lady and I gotta take care o' the bull team that brung me here."

Bolt stood up as Jane stuffed her bottles of gin and whiskey, along with the red mixture she said was catsup, inside her shirt. Then he led her across the saloon and through the swinging doors to the boardwalk.

"Nice seeing you again, Jane," Bolt said, breathing in fresh air.

"The pleasure was all mine, handsome." Jane added gravely, "Be careful if'n you catch up with Parker. We done lost one purdy man when Bill died. Let's not lose one who's even purdier."

"Thanks. I'll be careful."

Bolt watched as the hard looking, hard drinking enigma trudged down Main Street. Then his thoughts turned to the beautiful adventuress who'd found him the day Hickok lost his life. In his mind's eye, Bolt saw an angelic face with a body to match. How quickly her sunny smiles, tinkling laugh, and sense of humor had banished his years of brooding.

The past few weeks this emerald-eyed goddess had spoiled him day and night in a way that no mortal man deserved to be loved, in or out of bed. What he had taught an innocent atop the bar, she'd taken to their bedroom. With eagerness, she learned and with enthusiasm, she perfected. When he made love to Tansy, she responded with nothing short of wild and wanton abandonment.

Damn, he was one happy man.

Will rode into view on the horse that had been liberated from Skinny. Bolt had given Will this chestnut coated horse after he'd been fed, groomed, and fitted with new horseshoes at Red Clark's Livery. Will had smacked a hand over his heart and said he couldn't take the horse. But Tansy and Gimpy helped convinced him otherwise. Will shook Bolt's hand and with a choke in his voice, thanked him for his first horse. Will had used some of his bounty money to buy a new saddle and maybe the brown cowboy hat he sported today. Probably not a Stetson, but similar.

Bolt stifled a chuckle now as Will waved off something Jane was hollering at him. Then he sensed honeysuckle. And there she was, flour dusting her cute nose and peach cheeks. When he kissed her pink lips, he tasted sugar.

"Just the lady, with the sunny smile, I needed to see."

"I learned something from Calamity Jane," Tansy said.

"Hell, I hope not," Bolt replied, wondering what it could be and why Will was here well ahead of supper-time. "Hey, pardner," he said to Will as he reached them.

"Howdy," Will said, then dismounted his horse and tethered him to a post. Will patted the big reddish brown horse's nose and the animal nuzzled his new owner. "I decided on a name for my horse."

"What is it?" Tansy asked.

"I named him Wild Bill." Will hopped up on the plank walk and peering down at new boots that looked a lot like Bolt's, he said, "On accounta running into you, Bolt, the day Mr. Hickok got shot."

"Will and Bill." Tansy nudged Bolt and smiled up at him. "I like it."

"Me, too," Bolt agreed.

"I learned when you were talking to Calamity Jane that you stopped trying to find out where Parker's mine is because you're waiting for him to come to you," Tansy said, satisfying Bolt's wondering about what she'd learned from Jane.

"Yeah." Bolt gently brushed the flour off Tansy's nose and cheeks then swung an arm around her slender shoulders.

"A showdown's acomin'," Will said.

"You have *news*?" Bolt asked.

Will nodded. "I just found a box of old stories written before there was a newspaper. There's been hatchet murders this time of year for a long spell." He glanced at Tansy and back to Bolt. "One story specifically mentioned a giant seen near a hatchet murder on a

French Creek placer mine. I guess old news can be new news."

"Oh, Will!" Tansy said, not wanting to hear about leads on Parker.

"I'm sorry Jigger," Will said.

Bolt thanked Will, who said he was looking forward to supper. Will then swung himself up in the saddle, patted Bill's neck, and headed off toward the newspaper office.

"Please don't face Parker alone," Tansy said as Bolt took her hand and started for the swinging doors. "Let Sheriff Bullock or Marshal Stapleton help you."

"I don't need any help killing that bastard."

"Is killing a man fair?"

"In this case, yes. If he isn't stopped, he will keep murdering and raping innocent people."

Galloping hooves pounded their way. Will and Bill were heading straight toward them.

"Go inside, angel." Bolt said.

"I'm staying," she replied firmly.

"Hatchet murder!" Will shouted, dismounted, and hopped onto the boardwalk.

"Where did it take place?" Bolt calmly asked.

"The Rest, the same trailside breathin' spot five miles out where Preacher Smith was killed."

Bolt's eyes narrowed. "How do you know it was a hatchet murder?"

"I ran into a member of The Board of Health," Will nodded in the direction of the newspaper office, "who told me two prospectors' bodies was just brought to 'em! A hatchet was still stuck in one poor feller's skull!"

Bolt took a deep breath. This was as close as he'd been to Parker since that day on the riverbank.

"I heard," Gimpy said, pushing through the swinging doors.

"Me, too," Lupe whimpered.

"Get Lightning from the livery for me, Gimpy," Bolt said in a calm, but firm voice. "I'll meet you back here in an hour."

"Bolton, let Parker come to us for this showdown," Tansy pleaded and grabbed his arm.

"He has," Bolt replied, stepping back.

"Where are you going?" she asked, with fear in her voice.

"First to the Board of Health office and then to McAusland Brothers' Gunsmiths store."

Tansy lost her grip on Bolton and Will fell into step beside him. When the men were out of sight, she went into the saloon and for the next hour mechanically made tortillas. Lupe worked alongside her in empathic silence.

When tears threatened, Tansy slipped out the back door, wiped her eyes, and scattered feed to the chickens. Then she collected the last of the jerked meat she'd laid out to dry in the sun. She'd never made beef jerky before, but Bolton said he liked it, so she had made several batches of it as a surprise.

When she went back inside, she froze. Filling the doorway between the saloon and kitchen stood the bounty hunter. He had on the leather chaps he'd not worn since he'd arrived in Deadwood. His Stetson was pulled down low and he'd tied his hair back, a sure sign he meant business. Over his black shirt and vest, he wore a knee length, black leather coat, split up the sides so he could ride.

And he was armed. To the hilt.

Slung over one shoulder was a Winchester rifle and a belt filled with cartridges. Riding low on his hips were the pearl handled Colt .45s and on his thigh, strapped in the sheath, was his Bowie knife.

"I don't know when I'll be back," he said in a tone of voice Tansy had never heard.

"You mean you don't know *if* you'll be back," she replied.

Lupe nodded and fled the kitchen bawling.

"I will come back," Bolton said.

"Forget Parker! Forget the Valley of the Moon. Beautiful dreams await you in Sonoma, California."

"I'm not taking off to California when Parker's dropping mutilated bodies at my feet in the Black Hills. If I don't catch him now, it might be years before I get this close again."

The kitchen was hot, and the spicy dishes were blending into one sickening odor. Tansy wiped sweat off her brow. In a few short hours, she'd gone from walking on air to fighting for breath.

"Bolton, forget revenge. Let someone else get Parker."

"It's not revenge and deep down I want to be the one to stop him."

Bolton's dark blue eyes asked her to understand. And she did. She nodded and held out the beef jerky she'd just gathered. He took it.

"I pray you get Parker, so he can never kill again. When it's over, you can celebrate with this." She dug into the grocer's box and retrieved a bottle of red wine she had bought from the Grand Central Hotel's restaurant. He didn't take it.

"I promise I'll be back as soon as I can, and we'll celebrate together."

"Just promise me you'll go to California after you stop Parker," she said.

"I was planning to, Tansy. I promise."

"Good." Tansy clasped the bottle to her heart and knew this was her one and only chance to steer Bolton out of Lewis Whip Rance's path. "I don't want you to come back to the saloon."

All she wanted was to fall at his feet and beg him to stay. She itched to slap his face and push him out the door. Her world was spiraling out of control and there was no stopping the anguish washing over her like a hurricane hitting the Gulf of Texas.

"What do you mean?" he asked.

"If I'm expecting you to come back from this showdown with Parker and you don't, I'll know you're dead. If I know you're going to California after you face Parker, then when you don't come back, I will believe you lived to make your dreams come true."

She suddenly understood why he had never invited her to go with him. Deadwood Dolly took her for a potential whore and Calamity Jane had called her a whore. Bolton was a United States Marshal. He had money. Deep down, he knew a woman on the run would never fit into his new beginning in the California wine country.

Mister Catch Me If You Can.

Tansy had not been able to catch Bolton Rivers. She envied the California lady who'd lose her very soul in his smoldering eyes, kiss his hungry mouth, and be loved by his magnificent body.

"Bolton," she rasped. "Your foot is healed, and your memory has returned. I've done all I care to do for you." She wished God would strike her dead for the lie. "Find a lady who wants to share your dreams and don't come back."

CHAPTER 25

"He had to go, Jigger," Gimpy said matter-of-factly. "After years of tryin' to find that killer, you'd be wrong to 'spect Bolt not to get him."

Instead of serving a special Mexican supper, Tansy, Gimpy and Lupe were serving up whiskey and beer. Suppertime had come and gone without any of them eating a bite of food. As they stood behind the bar, Gimpy's eyes watered, and he looked away.

"I hate that Parker took off your foot, Gimpy," Tansy said with heartfelt sympathy. "He'll pay for that when Bolton catches up with him."

"Don't matter 'bout my foot," Gimpy said. "What matters is Bolt. You yanked the rug out from under Bolt by tellin' him not to come back."

Like a forest fire, word had spread that the bounty hunter had gone after a hatchet murderer. He'd ridden his big black stallion down Main Street, leaving a whirl-wind of dust, fear, and hope in his wake. Talk drifting in and out of the saloon was that the townspeople appreci-ated Bolton Rivers and were concerned about him. Only those on the wrong side of the law hoped he didn't return.

Those closest to Bolton were forever changed by him. Gimpy no longer broke up saloon fights, Lupe was learning to read, and Will was a man with a horse. All, including Tansy, had money in their pockets nowadays thanks to Bolton.

After speaking his mind, Gimpy had avoided Tansy. Lupe refused to even look at Tansy, much less speak to her. There was no sign of Will who'd been so excited to come to supper. Tansy's chest felt hollow. She could hardly make it from one second to the next. Finally, she caught up with Gimpy again.

"I told Bolton not to come back to keep him out of Lewis Rance's path," she said.

"It just might keep him from livin'."

Gimpy gave her a curt nod and drifted to the far end of the bar to take care of a group of regular customers. The hurricane swirled inside Tansy and with each movement came indescribable pain. Every breath fueled terrifying panic. The beating of her heart echoed soul wrenching sorrow.

Tansy glimpsed herself in the mirror behind the bar. She looked haggard. The hours since Bolton left had crawled. On any other night, he'd teach her a new card game, tease her, and ask her to play the piano for him. She would count the minutes until she could race Bolton up to their bedroom. He always won and she was always a silly girl. What was he doing right now? Was he hungry? Was he afraid? Had he found Parker? Had Bolton killed or been killed?

"Jigger," Gimpy said, breaking into her thoughts. "Time to close up."

"Yes, all right, Gimpy," she said.

Lupe was at the window where she'd been every ten minutes since Bolton had ridden off on Lightning. It was late now and shoulders sagging, Lupe dragged herself across the nearly empty saloon to Gimpy. Sobs wracked Lupe's body as Gimpy hugged her.

Tansy stood apart. Oh, how she wished a gorgeous man with a streak of silver in his black hair, would ride up on a shiny black stallion. They'd come to a dust swirling stop, that man would shove open the swinging doors, and swagger into the saloon like only he could do.

A shadow fell across the plank walk outside.

"Bounty hunter!" a voice blared. "Sellin' Injuns!"

"What's that about?" Tansy asked nerves frayed as she turned to Gimpy.

"It's Arkansas Hank," Gimpy replied. "He hunts the Sioux and Cheyenne. I ain't seen him since Bolt...fer a spell."

Arkansas Hank stopped at the big window outside and stared in at them. His face was fat and looked like someone had pushed the heavy brows toward the meaty chin, barely leaving room for beady eyes and a bulbous nose. A dirty hat sat on a square head. The man's grin said he was hiding some evil secret. Coming through the swinging doors, he displayed two heads, mounted on sticks.

"Evenin' folks. Arkansas Hank, bounty hunter, here," he announced, entering the saloon. "Twenty-five dollars buys an Injun head."

Two cowboys on their way out of the saloon shoved past Arkansas Hank. One covered his mouth and the other yelled for the sheriff.

"You'd think cowboys would appreciate seein' Injun heads," he said, laughing.

"Blazes!" Tansy spat the word she'd learned from Bolton. "Those are children's heads!"

"Well, now—" Arkansas Hank shrugged. "That's why they ain't fifty dollars apiece."

"Get out!" Tansy ordered and pointed to the swinging doors.

"Forty dollars fer both heads," the odious man howled, instead of leaving and shook the heads in the air. "I done heard that two's better'n one!"

"A real bounty hunter brings in criminals like you who murder innocent people," Tansy said through clenched teeth.

"Criminal?" Arkansas Hank scowled. "I'm riddin' the Black Hills of Injuns. So called real bounty hunters, like Rivers who I know done left town, kill white folks."

"Bolton Rivers deserves a medal for the work he's done," Tansy shot back.

"Rivers deserves fer me to put his head on one o' my sticks."

"As if the pathetic likes of you could wrangle him and live to tell about it!"

"So, ya *hankerin'* fer one head er two?" he asked.

"I said get out!" Tansy screamed, grabbed up a heavy shot glass, and hurled it.

Arkansas Hank squatted and the glass missed him, shattering on the wall.

"Missed all three of us," he guffawed and waved the heads at her.

The swinging doors burst open, and Will yanked Arkansas Hank onto the boardwalk, smashing his fist into the ugly bulldog-like face, dropping him into the street.

Tansy rushed outside, followed by Lupe and Gimpy, as a crowd quickly gathered to see what was happening.

Frowning, Will loomed over an unconscious Arkansas Hank. Tansy and Lupe removed their aprons, handing them to two merchants who gently wrapped the children's heads in the soft cloth. The men carried the heads away as the two cowboys dragged the headhunter out of sight.

"Thank you," Tansy called to the men and then turned to Will. "Are you all right?"

"Yeah," he replied, rubbing his fist.

Gimpy clapped Will on the shoulder. "Thanks for riddin' the saloon of that varmint."

"*Sí, muchas gracias*, Will," Lupe said, smiling at him.

"Happy to oblige," Will said with a shrug. "With Bolt gone, I just came to tell you General Crook's troops are expected in Deadwood late tomorrow."

Tansy nodded. "Bolton told me that Crazy Horse and his people were running in our direction. He said General Crook was trying to catch them or divert them before they got here."

"I guess Arkansas Hank caught a couple of little ones," Will growled. "I don't have no details yet but looks like both General Crook and his men and Crazy Horse and his tribe are tired and starving. Crook's troops are killin' their horses for meat."

"And there's Bolton smack in the middle of the pursuing Army and fleeing Indians," Tansy said.

"At least he knowed that goin' in," Gimpy pointed out. "If anybody can slip between the Army and the Injuns, kill a killer, and get back out alive, it's Bolt Rivers."

"I'm going after him," Tansy said.

"No!" Gimpy yelped as if she'd kicked him. "It would be the death of ya!"

"I'm going and sticking with you all the way there this time, Jigger," Will said.

IT WAS midnight when Bolt reined in Lightning deep in the dark forest of the Black Hills. He'd easily picked up Parker's trail at The Rest. By the hoof prints, Bolt could tell Parker was as usual riding a bull since a horse couldn't support the man's enormous bulk. Some miles back Parker had ridden the bull into Whitewood Creek, an old trick meant to throw someone off your trail. Bolt had found Parker's trail again, several miles downstream, on the other side of the ice cold water. For hours through birch, aspen, black maple, pine, and other evergreen trees Bolt had steadily gained on him.

Parker was nearby. He could feel it. Bolt couldn't risk sleeping. But he and Lightning should rest, so Bolt dismounted and led the horse to the creek for a drink.

Bolt remembered seeing his reflection in Whitewood Creek earlier in the daylight. He'd looked like he felt; strangely apathetic at being so close to Parker.

When Lightning was watered, Bolt let him graze, but left him saddled, just in case. Bolt then eased down under a black maple tree. He hadn't eaten since breakfast and though he had plenty of the beef jerky, Tansy had given him, he had no appetite. He sighed, wishing he'd been able to enjoy that special Mexican supper with her. They should be in bed at the Grand Central Hotel right about now.

Placing his rifle across his lap, he kept his finger near the trigger, his thoughts filled not with facing Harless Parker, but of loving Tansy Wiley. Shivering in the cold autumn air, Bolt was glad she was safe and warm at the Crown Saloon. Had she put her dismantled bed back together? Would some other man enjoy her sunny smile, eager kisses, and perfect body as much as he had? Hell, yes. A siren's song, tantalizing Tansy was everything a man could want.

She's a huckleberry above a persimmon.

Tansy, Will, Gimpy, and Lupe were the closest thing he'd had to a family since losing his to Parker's hatchet. Will was as loyal as the day was long and shaping up to be a fine friend. Gimpy always had a grin, a shot of whiskey, and his deck of cards ready when Bolt entered the saloon. Lupe could read better every day and was holding her head high. I miss them, he thought.

How he had loved letting Tansy spoil him. She'd fawned over his health, brushed his hair, and pressed his shirts. She fed him hearty meals, poured him coffee or tea instead of whiskey, and raced him up to bed at a reasonable hour every night.

If only his emerald-eyed beautiful barkeep were here he'd make everything right. Bolt imagined her slender arms wrapping around his neck and folding him to her soft breasts. He'd plow his fingers up through her silky curls, tilt her pretty head back, and kiss her sweet lips. Honeysuckle would waft around him as she whispered in his ear, asking him to make love to her. He'd peel off her clothing and shrug out of his, lay her on the soft grass and love her. A familiar heat coiled in his lower body.

But that would never happen again because she didn't want him back. He had asked her to work on loving him. But she said only that she would work on finding that mystery valley.

"Tansy, what did I do wrong?"

Although she'd begged him not to go after Parker, she'd also made him promise to go to California. Tansy was too kind to wish him dead, she just wanted him gone.

I've done all I care to do for you.

Bolt no longer gave a damn about prevailing in the fight against a murdering madman without the sunshine of an adventuress angel. He closed his burning eyes and hung his head in despair.

An eagle screamed and Bolt realized it was dawn. Hell, he'd fallen asleep and lost several hours. Getting to his feet in this cold, dank forest was a far cry from waking up in a warm bed with Tansy snuggled cozily at his side.

"Never again, Tansy. I'm gone."

CHAPTER 26

"IT'S TAKEN US FOREVER TO GET HERE AND NOW WE'RE UP the creek without a paddle," Will said as they stood beside Whitewood Creek watching the horses drink. "We rode all night and ain't...haven't seen hide nor hair of Bolt."

In the light of dawn, Tansy's mind drifted back a few hours. After she'd said she was going to follow Bolton, she wondered how since she didn't have a horse. Lupe had nudged Gimpy. Motioning for her to follow, they led her to Red Clark's Livery where they woke up the stable hand.

Tansy's mouth had fallen open as she stared at the palomino mare with a blond mane. Tansy's eyes filled with tears as the stable hand placed a brand new saddle on the single most beautiful horse she had ever seen. As if in a dream, she walked over to the mare and rubbed her soft nose. Hugging the horse around the neck, Tansy wished she could hug the man who had, according to Gimpy, spared no expense in finding and getting the horse to Deadwood by September twentieth.

At Lupe's urging, Tansy reached inside one of the saddlebags. She pulled out a card, the queen of hearts. On the back, written in Bolton's bold hand, was the horse's name, *Angel*.

"I wish Marshal Stapleton or Sheriff Bullock could have come with us," Will said, breaking into Tansy's thoughts.

Seth Bullock had found a note, dated on the day Isaac Brown had died, and brought it to the Crown Saloon as Tansy and Will were leaving. A prisoner had mentioned a giant and Brown had gotten the location of the giant's mine from him. Tansy and Will hoped they were heading toward that mine.

"I wish they could have too, Will." Tansy wiped a tear off her cheek. "But they couldn't leave town with Crazy Horse and General Crook heading in the direction of Deadwood."

"Did you hear that?" Will asked, glancing right, and left.

"Shh," Tansy said, also alarmed by the sudden swishing of tree branches and the crunching of leaves and twigs.

"Think it could be that one-eyed bear that killed Lupe's folks? She said it appeared at the edge of the forest and was on them before they knew it."

"There really aren't many bears in the Black Hills."

"Only takes one big mean one to kill us," Will said, turning in a circle as he scanned the woods. "The Army and the Indians could have that bear all riled up and running straight for us!"

Tansy cringed knowing that was all too true. She listened but didn't hear anything else from the woods. If Bolton were with her, she wouldn't feel as though these towering trees were swallowing her...or that a killer bear might be about to do so. But it was Will at her side, and she was fairly certain they were hopelessly lost within the vastness of the thick forest.

As exhausted as she was afraid, she wanted to take a nap. When Bolton said 'let's take a nap' he wanted to do something entirely different than sleep. There would be a hooded expression in his deep blue eyes and a sensuous curve to his lips that always made Tansy weak with desire.

"Angel and Bill aren't reacting, so maybe it's a sign they don't sense a bear close by. Let's press on." Holding Angel's reins, Tansy patted the mare's nose. "Bolton has a six hour head start and ten years' experience on us."

Will nodded and then they both stopped in their tracks. Dead ahead stood an Indian.

"Eaten by a bear or scalped by Indians," Will began, "either way, we're goners."

The Indian was a woman and the fear Tansy felt was mirrored in the woman's eyes. Her long braids needed redoing and her buckskin dress was torn, but there was pride in her stance. A little boy came out from behind her and tugged on the woman's hand. As though it went terribly against her grain, the woman held out her other hand.

"They're starving," Tansy whispered.

Suddenly, three males on horseback galloped out of the forest, splashing across the creek.

"The woman and boy lured us in," Will said.

"No, I think they're as surprised as we are."

The Indians were now only a few feet away, the fiercest of the men reminding Tansy of Bolton. Perhaps a little older, with long straight black hair, power radiated from him. Yet, when he looked at the woman and child Tansy sensed in him, as she'd seen in Bolton, a protective side. Tansy wasn't as afraid of him as she'd been of Crazy Earl and Skinny.

The men sat erect, but their buckskin clothing hung loosely on their too-lean frames. They must be some of Crazy Horse's tribe, Tansy thought.

"Mayhap if we can make friends with these Lakota people, they'll let us live," she said.

"Lakota?" repeated the eldest of the three men, who looked to be in his mid-sixties.

"Do—do you speak English?" Tansy asked.

The men spoke in guttural tones to each other in a language that sounded harsh to Tansy.

"They can't speak English, they're Sioux," Will suggested.

"Sioux...ssssnake," the fierce one hissed.

"They're Cheyenne." Will swallowed hard. "Or Crow!"

The two younger men grew agitated at the name Crow. Tansy knew the Crow were their mortal enemies, along with most white men.

"No." Tansy gulped. "I believe he's telling us their enemies say Sioux means snake."

"Lakota!" the oldest one, who seemed to be in charge, tapped his chest. "Friend."

"Yes, Lakota means friends or allies!" Tansy agreed enthusiastically.

"How do you know what Lakota means, Jigger?"

Addressing the oldest man, Tansy said, "My late husband's first wife was part Lakota. Clyde Crown said she was his best *friend*." The Indian's faces grew puzzled. "Stop chatterboxing them," she mumbled and slowed down. "His wife walked across the Rainbow Bridge a few winters ago."

"She did what?" Will asked.

"It means she died," Tansy replied. "Her name was Lark Who Sings." Extending her arms, she flapped her hands and sang the first verse of Little Brown Jug. The two younger men and the woman looked stunned. The little boy grinned. The eldest man nodded, and Tansy said, "Lark Who Sings Crown."

"Lark," said the man in charge, touching what appeared to be an eagle's feather in his hair. He seemed to understand some of what she'd said. "Tanksi."

"Tanksi?" Will repeated. "What's that, Jigger?"

"Tanksi is sister." Desperately, Tansy pulled at the Lakota words she could remember. "And brother is...I can't remember the word for brother."

"Try," Will pleaded.

"Tatanka!" Tansy said and pointed to the man in charge.

The fierce one frowned and his woman laid a hand to his knee. Both of the warriors flanked the oldest one more closely and yelled at Tansy.

"Blazes!" Will yelped. "I think you said the wrong thing."

"Yes, I did." Raising her hands into the air, Tansy waved them as if to erase what she'd said. "I just called him a buffalo."

"Well, why don't we just scalp ourselves and get it over with?"

"Tiblo!" Tansy said. "You are Lakota, and Lark was part Lakota, so you are like a brother—tiblo?"

"Tiblo!" the eldest man said, hitting his fist against his heart.

Tansy looked into the Indians' tired faces. "I know General Crook is an enemy who is chasing you, but I am a friend of the Lakota," she said, placing a hand over her heart. "My name is Tansy." When she reached into her saddlebag, the braves drew their arrows from quivers. "Eat...yuta."

Tansy retrieved tortillas and the little boy ran to her. Offering the food to the boy and his mother, Tansy then dug out some beef jerky and divided it among the Indians. Only the one in charge hesitated in accepting the food from her.

"Wapiya," he grunted, tapping his chest.

"Wapiya?" Tansy thought. "Healer? I am a wapiya, too."

The wapiya nodded knowingly. "See," he said quietly.

"You've seen me before?"

He pointed to his head and then to the sky.

"You saw me in a...a vision! I saw you, too!" Tansy said, gooseflesh covering her whole body. "Please, please tell me...where is the Valley of the Moon?"

SHORTLY BEFORE DUSK, Bolt dropped Lightning's reins and reached into his saddlebag, pulling his Model '73 Winchester Repeating Rifle out of the open-mouthed scabbard. Stealthily, he eased to the edge of the trees and crouched behind a boulder.

Not far from the ominous dark hole to the mine entrance, Bolt spotted a huge bull tethered to a tree. Strapped to the animal were pans, picks, and shovels. As Bolt had presumed, Parker was digging for gold inside the cave and panning in French Creek right alongside it.

Bolt figured Parker had ventured from the mine to begin his annual killing spree. He'd killed at The Rest, then feeling tracked, Parker had scurried back into his hole. Bolt wondered if this mine was where Parker hibernated for a year at a time. Made sense as mines in caves, opposed to placer mines, afforded the miner some protection against the bitterly frigid Dakota Territory winters.

An eerie quiet surrounded Bolt like the calm before a storm. A cold breeze rustled through his long, black coat like a thieving pickpocket.

In the next instant, a streak of lightning ripped out of the clouds, just like the tempest that had hit during Bolt's birth. Grimly he thought it only right the same should happen on a day of death.

As thunder clapped, Bolt noticed large, muddy foot-prints leading from the bull to the mine's entrance. He'd have to draw the butchering son-of-a-bitch out of the cave. That bull. Bulls could live to be twenty-five years old or more. Parker had ridden a big black bull forever and the tethered bull looked to be an old one. It was probably the only thing Parker cared about, besides killing.

With his eyes on the mine, Bolt moved closer to the bull. This animal was going to *wake snakes* in a minute and Bolt was ready.

Holding his rifle in his right hand, Bolt retrieved the derringer from his coat pocket, aiming Tansy's peashooter at the bull's thick skinned flank. A decade forever lost in tracking Parker flashed before Bolt's eyes. Remembering how his father, mother, and Emma were so ruthlessly slaughtered by Parker, Bolt pulled the trigger.

The bullet grazed the bull's dense hide, sending it mooing and bucking, eyes bulged, and nostrils flared. It swung its head and jerked its body so violently it dragged the tree it was tethered to out of the ground, roots and all. Pans, picks, and shovels clattering, the bull lumbered toward the mine entrance.

"Come out," Bolt gritted between his teeth.

A hunkered down mass of man soon emerged. He grabbed the bull's reins and jerked them hard, using the animal as a shield. A few yards was all that separated Bolt from Parker.

"Rivers!" boomed a voice to fit the size of the beast. "If yer out there, you can have all my gold if you'll leave me be!"

Bolt took a calming breath. Unleashing one's temper, he'd explained to Tansy, was one thing. Losing his temper was not an option.

"I knowed you been after me fer years. What I don't know is why yer the only man among all of them other bounty hunters, fortune seekers, and gunslingers who's still doggin' my trail when all the rest of 'em done give up."

Bolt took a second deep breath of rain scented air. Lightning flashed as Harless Parker chanced a look over the bull's back. Just as Tansy had described, there were patches of scraggly gray hair on the man's head and a dirty beard grew here and there on Parker's pockmarked face.

"What do you want?" Parker bellowed.

"Justice for my family."

"Yer gonna join 'em in hell today, Rivers."

"Why do you kill, you bastard?" Bolt shouted.

"I hate men and kids and I need women."

"Women hate you, don't they?"

"Shut yer lyin' mouth, Rivers!"

"And men stand in your way."

"I like seein' 'em all beg and bleed!"

Bolt raised his repeating rifle. He'd bought it in 1873 when Winchester first offered it. Like most marshals, he preferred this .44 caliber repeating rifle because it didn't need to be reloaded between shots. It was the largest caliber made and he'd bought plenty of ammunition from the McAusland brothers.

Changing tactics, Parker hollered, "The wanted poster says I gotta be brung in alive."

"Then drop your weapons," Bolt ordered, knowing he was never without his hatchets.

Parker slowly unbuckled a belt that dropped with a clang of hatchets.

"I'm unarmed, *Marshal* Rivers!" Parker blared and came out from behind the bull.

Parker was as tall as Bolt remembered and heavier now. His enormous shoulders sloped away from his neck at a deformed angle, his upper arms the size of a man's thigh, his belly hanging out.

Bolt stepped into view. Their eyes had met only once before. This time Bolt stared down the barrel of his rifle pointed straight at Parker's head. It was a sight he'd waited a long time to see.

Thunder broke directly overhead, and the skittish bull ran. A streak of lightning touched down so close to Parker it looked like the finger of an angel pointing to a devil.

"You ain't gonna make it outa this storm alive, Rivers!" Parker hollered.

"I *am* the storm," Bolt growled.

Instantly, a flash of silver flew in Bolt's direction. He dodged it and pulled the trigger twice just before a second hatchet hissed past his left ear.

"Aaahhh!" Parker shrieked, staggering backward into the mine.

The reverberating rifle blasts stopped the world, or so it seemed to Bolt. Silence from the devil, from the heavens, from the hatchets, and from the rifle. Silence.

The silence from Bolt's heart...reigned supreme.

Parker had landed a few feet inside the mine. Bolt walked to the entrance. Blood covered the piece of human debris' face. The back of his head dripped down a far wall. Both eyes were gone. Hatchet Harless Parker would never see another man, woman, or child beg and bleed again.

To the right of Parker's body was a large shaft maybe thirty feet deep. From the odor of decayed flesh, it was hard to say how many bodies Parker had dumped down there. Bolt heard water running and rats scurrying in the hellish pit.

As good a grave as any.

CHAPTER 27

FROM THE CREST OF THE HILL, TANSY SAW HIM.

In the looming twilight, just inside a cave, Bolton stood over a giant. Something in his stance said he was exhausted over the death instead of vindicated.

"Bolton!" she cried out.

In a blur of swirling black hat, black hair, and black coat, Bolton swung around. He never flinched as he faced her, Will, and five Lakota Indians. Tansy nudged Angel into the gully as Bolton whistled to Lightning, bringing him out of the woods. The Lakota men, on their horses, followed. The woman rode behind the fierce one and the boy sat behind the other warrior.

Nearing Bolton, his steely blue eyes chilled Tansy far worse than the cold breeze off French Creek. A muscle flexed in his chiseled jaw suggesting latent fury and whisker stubble added depth to danger.

Overwhelmingly, a sensual aura of strength and masculinity, from a righteous battle fought and won, surrounded this mysterious man. Like never before Tansy saw Bolt Rivers, the fearsome bounty hunter, and respected United States Marshal. Drawn to every irresistible, magnificent inch of him, Tansy reined in Angel a few feet from Bolton and Lightning.

"Bolton," she breathed. She slid out of her saddle and took a step toward him.

"Your cheek's dirty, your hair's knotted, and your dress is torn. What the hell are you doing here, Jigger?"

Jigger? Tansy was riveted to the spot. She swiped at both cheeks and tried to smooth her hair, glancing down at the hole she'd put in her skirt when she'd caught it in the stirrup.

"Bolt!" Will smacked a hand over his heart. He all but jumped off Bill covered the ground between him and Bolton and hugged his hero.

"Howdy, pardner," Bolton said easily and clapped him on the back. "Who are your friends?"

"They're Lakota Indians!" Will exclaimed. "Jigger can talk to them some. She told them about Parker killing people. When we reached the gully, we heard thunder and saw lightning. We got here just in time to see you shoot down Hatchet Harless Parker!"

"How'd you find me?" Bolton asked Will.

Will filled him in as to Sheriff Bullock bringing the note, he'd found of Sheriff Brown's.

Tansy's mind was racing. This was not the reception she had envisioned from Bolton.

"Their wapiya, which means healer," Tansy began, indicating him, "is a Lakota medicine man. Clyde Crown's first wife was part Lakota. She was the wapiya's tanksi, his sister, or at the very least the wapiya feels a kinship to her. He saw me in a vision, and they brought us here."

"Good thing because we were lost," Will acknowledged. "But they knew where this mine was."

Bolton didn't ask about the vision but nodded to the Indians. The fierce one looked at Tansy and pointed to the bull.

"Tatanka," the warrior informed her.

"Yes," Tansy agreed softy, knowing he was making sure she knew what tatanka meant.

The medicine man made eye contact with Bolton and then looked at the bull. Bolton indicated the animal was theirs. Both warriors dismounted and went into the mine. The wapiya dismounted then as did the woman and boy. There were guttural remarks between the warriors as they emerged from the cave, staring with respect at Bolton.

"Wophika!" the fierce one shouted to the other Indians, pointing to his eyes.

"What's that mean, Jigger?" Will asked.

"Lark Who Sings was a wophika songstress." Tansy scratched her head. "Expert!"

"You shot both his eyes out at that distance, Bolt?" Will asked Bolton in amazement.

Bolton lifted one shoulder in a slight shrug, walked over to Lightning, and slipped his rifle into a scabbard. Tansy didn't doubt it. She'd seen Bolton in action at the jail. The medicine man nodded at Bolton indicating the death of the murderer was justice. Then the wapiya, mother, and child joined the two Lakota warriors who were removing the pans, picks, and shovels from the bull.

"We're here because we were so worried about you," Tansy said, answering Bolton's earlier question.

"Parker's dead. You can stop worrying," Bolton said.

"I'll water our horses," Will said, gathered up reins, and left.

"I see you got your mare," Bolton grumbled.

"Yes." Tansy's eyes teared. "Angel is sweet and beautiful. I love her. Thank you so much."

"Yeah."

"Bolton, what's wrong?"

His brow furrowed and that muscle flexed in his jaw. From the moment she'd told him goodbye in the kitchen she'd longed to have him pressed to her heart. Stepping forward, she wrapped her arms around Bolton's rigid body, hardly believing he was alive and well. When he made no move to return her hug, Tansy tilted her chin up and smiled. Any second now he'd grin and kiss her. He didn't.

"Gimpy and Lupe miss you. We were afraid we'd never see you again, Bolton."

"Why would you expect to see me again? You told me not to come back."

There it was. Bolton pushed out of her arms and strode to where the Lakota had surrounded the bull. Bolton took Parker's saddlebag off the bull and flung it over his shoulder. Then he returned to the cave where he picked up a hatchet belt. Bolton dropped the clanking belt into what must be a mine shaft. The time the belt took to hit bottom said the hole was deep.

Witnessing an intangible bond strengthen between Bolton and Will, much like the bond she knew had existed between Bolton and Tom Smith, Tansy watched mesmerized. Just as he'd done when they had captured Skinny, Will took a stand beside Bolton. Without a word to Will, Bolton put his booted foot to Parker's body. Will followed Bolton's lead and together they shoved Parker's corpse into oblivion.

When Bolton and Will came toward her, Tansy said, "You're finally free, Bolton?"

"That I am, Jigger," he replied coolly.

"What do you think is in Parker's saddlebag, Bolt? Will asked.

"Parker told me if I would leave him be I could have his gold." Bolton pulled out a large, heavy looking pouch, opened it, and then pulled the strings tight again. "I'll be doing just that now, so I figure this gold is mine to do with what I want." He offered the pouch to Tansy. "Give this to Gimpy."

"I told Gimpy you'd make Parker pay for his foot. But Gimpy said his foot didn't matter. You mattered. You give him the gold," Tansy said.

"Here, Will," Bolton said. "Tell Gimpy, Parker paid."

"Gimpy will want to hear it from you, Bolt. Besides, we don't know how to get back to Deadwood without you," Will said.

Bolton clenched his jaw and shoved the pouch into the pocket of his long black coat. "I'll take you back as far as The Rest and then we'll part company."

Before a stunned Tansy could respond, the medicine man and the boy approached.

The wapiya pointed to Bolton, touched his own head, and gestured to the sky. "See wica."

"Wica means man," Tansy said. "He told us on the way here that he saw," she paused, wondering how Bolton would react, "you in his vision, too."

As lightning flashed in the far distance, the healer took the feather from his hair and stuck it into the leather strip tied around Bolton's hair, letting the feather trail down Bolton's back. He had given Bolton the only thing he had to give in thanks for the life-saving bull.

"Tiblo, pilayama." The gratitude in the wapiya's voice and eyes spoke volumes.

"Tiblo means brother and I think pilayama is thank you," Tansy translated in a shaky voice.

"Pilayama," Bolton said, for the feather.

"I will never forget you," Tansy said and in spite of her worry over Bolton's anger with her, took the healer's hand. "Thank you for bringing Will and me through the Black Hills—the Paha Sapa. For the vision, you helped me see this morning, pilayama." She lightly squeezed his hand. "Goodbye, Wapiya."

After a moment, he said, "Goodbye, Wapiya."

The little boy stepped forward then, stopping in front of Bolton who towered over him. The child looked over his shoulder and the fierce one motioned to him. Bolton knelt down on one knee.

"Pilayama," the little boy said softly.

Bolton held out his right hand. Trustingly, the boy placed both of his small hands in Bolton's. Covering the little hands with his hands, Bolton gave them a gentle shake. The boy slowly smiled. Tears burned Tansy's eyes and throat. Will sniffled and then coughed beside her.

Bolton stood and the wapiya and child returned to the other Indians who raised their hands in farewell. Bolton nodded at them and then whistled bringing Lightning trotting to him. Bolton placed the pouch filled with gold into Lightning's saddlebag and mounted the huge black stallion.

"Let's ride!" Bolton barked.

Tansy stood numb from head to toe at being so alienated from Bolton. Will's eyes met Tansy's and he shrugged self-consciously. When Will mounted his horse, Tansy did so with Angel, and they fell in behind Bolton who was already heading out of the gully. Tansy took a final glance at the Indians. The wapiya pointed to the full moon reminding her to take Bolton to the Valley of the Moon.

The horses crested the hill and under the light of the

bright moon, they traveled two or three miles before Will became the first to speak.

"Bolt, did you notice how fast the storm stopped after Parker was dead?"

"I've seen thunder and lightning hit the Hills with no rain," Bolt replied.

"Still, I don't remember ever reportin' on a storm quite like that one," Will said.

Bolton didn't comment. The horses' gallop slowed as darkness descended. Tansy studied him riding ahead of her, silhouetted by the moonlight. She noticed the streak in his hair and thought of the bolt of lightning he'd been named for. Was this the eye of the tornado? If the full fury of this cyclone hit them, where would they all be when the rage of this storm blew over?

"At least we won't have to spend the night sleeping in the rain," Tansy said, trying to get Bolton's attention by picking up the conversation Will had started.

"Being at that saloon was the longest I've gone without sleeping in the rain for years," he replied stoically.

"Having you at the saloon has changed all our lives for the better," Tansy said.

"She's right about that, Bolt," Will agreed.

"We'll part even," Bolton growled.

Those three words caused the tension around Tansy's heart to tighten and twist her like a dish rag. Will then told Bolton about the encounter with Arkansas Hank, but Bolton said nothing.

"Jigger was plum petrified that Parker was gonna kill you, Bolt," Will said next. "She pushed us through the Hills relentlessly. Even so, I don't know how we caught up with you."

"I fell asleep."

It might just keep him from livin.'

At that, Bolton reined in and pointing to a copse of trees announced they would make camp alongside the nearby creek. Tansy hoped he'd come to her and let her slide into his arms. Instead, he dismounted and unsaddled Lightning. Tansy dismounted her horse and Will unsaddled Bill as Bolton went to Angel. He patted the pretty palomino, took off her saddle, and walked away.

As Bolton led all three horses to the creek, he asked Will to gather wood for a campfire. Tansy helped Will and when the horses were watered and grazing, Bolton used the wood to kindle a fire. Yes, Tansy thought, Bolton had no trouble starting raging, passionate fires.

"I was sure the bear that killed Lupe's folks had found us when we were lost," Will said to Bolton, concern sounding in his voice as he placed another pile of wood near the crackling fire. "But this campfire should keep any bears away. Don't you think so?"

"Yeah," Bolton replied, moving off to tether the horses near the campfire. "I caught sight of a large black bear just before sundown my first day out of Deadwood."

Following him, Will asked, "Did it have one eye gone?"

"Couldn't tell. It had a raccoon in its mouth and disappeared into the forest."

Then as he'd surely done all those years he'd slept under the stars, Bolton spread out his bedroll. Tansy imagined him grinning at her and crooking his finger for her to come to sleep beside him. He took off his long black coat and tossed it on the ground beside him. He sat down on his bedroll, propping himself against a fallen tree and stretching his long legs. Will spread out Bill's saddle blanket and sat down across the fire from Bolton. Tansy found Angel's saddle blanket and retrieved the jerky and tortillas from her saddlebag. She lay her blanket halfway between the men. Unwrapping a cloth, she handed Will some of the food, but Bolt didn't look in her direction. She had no appetite, so placed the remaining tortillas and jerky on her blanket.

"I'll take the first watch," Bolton told them. "You two get some shut-eye."

Tansy wanted to get her shut-eye in the protective curve of Bolton's muscular body. Ignoring her, he folded his arms across his chest and crossed his ankles.

"Jigger, are you going to tell Bolt where the Valley of the Moon is?" Will asked.

Tansy glanced at Bolton, but he didn't turn to her or encourage her to explain. Tansy could barely shake her head at Will.

"Bolt, you shoulda seen the way Jigger made friends with the Lakota Indians," Will said.

Bolton nodded at Will. As he continued to shut her out Tansy remembered Bolton had not planned to see them back to Deadwood until Will said they didn't know their way home.

"Bolton," Tansy asked. "Where were you planning to go next?"

"Fort Laramie," he mumbled.

Tansy felt as if she were dying little by little.

"What's in Fort Laramie?" Will asked.

"A telegraph office. I'm going to wire Rance from there and tell him I've got her," Bolton replied, looking directly at Tansy.

CHAPTER 28

"WHEN HE SHOWS UP, AND I KNOW HE WILL, I'LL TAKE HIM into custody and prove he was an accessory to your father's murder," Bolton said.

"Oh, no!" Tansy gasped, dumbfounded. "Bolton, proving he killed my father is not your responsibility. Why would you bring Rance and his henchmen down on you?"

"I won't be around to protect you. So, I'll get him off your back once and for all."

"What about California?" Tansy asked, trying to process everything as quickly as possible.

Bolton didn't reply.

"I'm working on a story for the newspaper about California gold mining. Lupe told me California means hot oven," Will said, perhaps trying to ease the tension.

"California is *sunny* and warm," Bolton said.

"Deadwood is too cold and gets too much snow. I'm tired of it. I'd go with you, Bolt, and find a newspaper job," Will said.

"What about Lupe?" Bolton asked with a tease in his voice.

"If she'd go, I'd take her with me. You taught her to read. She could help me with my stories. Would you be a marshal in California?"

A faraway expression crossed Bolton's face as he stared into the dancing flames.

"When I was your age, Will, I heard about a place called Sonoma and the Bear Flag Revolt. Back in forty-six, the area was proclaimed an independent republic. Maybe because I was born that same year, I felt an affinity for Sonoma. I knew California was the last frontier." Not even glancing at Tansy, Bolton looked at Will, who was hanging on his every word. "Once I left New York, I started buying land in Sonoma. Someday, it'll be famous for its wine and vineyards."

"So, you'll grow grapes and make wine for a living," Will said.

"Red wine, I'll bet," Tansy said. "When did you remember that?"

"After you told me what I said when I was delirious," Bolton replied in a flat tone.

"You mean owning a big house and seeing acres of land?" Tansy clearly recalled that's when she began thinking of him as a beautiful dreamer.

"Time to get some rest," Bolton said, putting an end to the conversation.

"Yeah," Will said, lying down and facing away from them. "Goodnight."

Tansy studied Bolton as he stared into the fire. Such fury was so evident in his tight profile she looked down his broad chest to the strong hands folded over his flat stomach. Having his muscular legs crossed formed a sexy bulge at his crotch. Would he ever thrust the cannon he had in those snug pants inside her again? She looked into the fire, too, where it seemed her *silly girl* dreams of a life with Bolton were going up in smoke.

No! Her mind screamed. Explain yourself to him.

"Bolton!" she said more insistently than she'd intended. He frowned in surprise, and she said, "I have something to say."

"You've said it."

"No, I haven't." Staring across the fire, she said, "I've been coddling you like a baby because you've been through hell. But I've been through hell, too! If I have the strength to talk, you can at least hear me out."

"I'm listening."

"I made the worst mistake of my life by telling you not to come back to Deadwood. I'd hoped to accomplish two things. First, I wanted to pretend you were alive so I could go on living in case Parker killed you," Tansy reminded him, gripping her hands in her lap. "But when you rode Lightning down Main Street, I realized I didn't want to live if it meant living without you."

Bolton stared straight ahead. Not a single argument occurred to Tansy as to why he should care whether she lived or died.

"Secondly, I saw it as my one and only chance to steer you out of Rance's path."

Bolton's jaw clenched as if he were stopping himself from commenting on that.

"I assure you I did not ride relentlessly, watch for that killer bear, face down three Lakota warriors, and risk meeting up with Parker instead of you, because of my lack of caring about you."

Bolton didn't move a muscle. Tansy felt her throat constricting with emotion and swallowed to keep her voice from breaking. Turning her wishbone into a back-bone, she continued.

"The image that drove me night and day without stopping was finding you. Alive. Never did it occur to me that Will and I might miss you by a few minutes. But now I know we almost did which means you would have been gone from me. Always and forever. Until the end of time."

Bolton's blue eyes misted, and he blinked a couple of times. Suddenly getting up he threw some wood on the fire. Had the shadows of mistrust lessened on his hand-some face?

"May I sit closer to you, so—so that we don't wake up Will?" Tansy asked after he sat back down. Bolton didn't reply, so Tansy scooted around the fire to the edge of his bedroll.

"I don't want to part company with you at The Rest." She reached out and took his hand. He didn't pull it away and that gave her courage. "If you're determined to deal with Rance, with or without me, please let it be with me." Her eyes filled with tears, and she finished raggedly, "Please forgive me. I want a second chance, Mister Catch Me if You Can."

"Aww, Tansy," Bolton said softly, pulling her into his strong arms. "I want a second chance, too."

"You do?" Tansy asked, incredulously.

"Where else am I gonna find another huckleberry above a persimmon?"

"Oh, Bolton." Boldly, she straddled his lap, placed her hands to his face, and gazed into his sapphire eyes. She closed her eyes and touched her lips to his. Winding her arms around his neck she hugged him tightly. "Thank you," she cried against his lips.

Bolton plowed the fingers of his right hand through

her hair and splayed his left hand across her back. "Thank you, for talking some sense into me," he said in a raspy voice.

Tears of joy coursed down Tansy's face. He pressed her to him and when their mouths met again, Tansy tasted her salty tears on his lips. Bolton pulled back and gently brushed her tears away. He clamped his hands on her waist and arched his hips under her. Feeling his rock-hard arousal pressed to her secret place, Tansy tingled.

"Think he'd notice if we made love on my bedroll?" Bolton asked, tilting his head toward Will.

"Who cares?" Tansy whispered with a smile. "Let's move your bedroll."

"No," he chuckled and then groaned as if in pain. "But the second we get back to Deadwood, we're heading to the Grand Central Hotel. In the meantime, tell me about the Valley of the Moon."

"I will." Tansy started to scoot off his lap, but his hands tightened on her waist, so she stayed put. "The Lakota wapiya turned a spot on the ground into a valley by fashioning hills out of mounds of dirt." Tansy moved her hands as the healer had done. "He drew a big house and sprinkled blades of grass around it. Then he pinched dirt between his finger and thumb making rows and rows of what must have been grapevines. When I asked him where the valley was, he pointed west." She ventured, "Sonoma?"

Bolton ran a hand across his forehead. "We can certainly find out if Sonoma is known as the Valley of the Moon."

"Yes," Tansy said. "That's where your beautiful dreams are waiting for you."

"Our dreams, Tansy."

Tansy hugged him and whispered, "I can't explain how I saw him in a dream or how he saw us in a vision, but I believe in miracles. Don't you?"

"I'm holding one," he said softly. "I've slept. You haven't and it's time you did."

Bolt kissed her before easing her over beside him. Tansy rolled Angel's saddle blanket into a pillow. Yawning, she curled up at his side and was already out as he covered her with his long coat. She sighed in her sleep and Bolt smiled. When he'd seen her this evening his first thought was to spank her bottom for riding into danger. But that was the adventuress in her. Quickly, his anger gave way to the desire to kiss the smudges on her beautiful face.

But then he'd remembered she had wanted him gone. So, he'd hidden his happiness at seeing her by barking about her pretty hair which appeared clawed by every tree branch in the hills. Now, as he carefully plucked a leaf out of a tangle, he decided to replace the dress she'd ruined in her desperate flight to find him. If only she could love him as he loved her. But she had never once mentioned love. He could not make her love him and he had vowed not to pressure her to be with him as Rance had done.

Bolt had never known he could love a woman the way he loved Tansy. He loved her totally, passionately with every breath in his body. She had given her bed to a stranger and welcomed a bounty hunter into her family. She'd teased the silly boy as her friend and taken the man as her lover. She'd made him laugh and tonight, as he'd sat beside the campfire, she had made him cry.

Dreams of California meant nothing without Tansy because along with the vineyards he wanted children. But his children had to be with Tansy.

Then Bolt's thoughts took a sudden heart stabbing turn. She had told him she couldn't go south because of Rance. Was that just an excuse not to go southwest with him to California? Hell, Sonoma was further away from Texarkana than Deadwood. Besides, he'd said he would deal with Rance. But instead of trusting him to do so, she'd planned to wander Canada alone.

As of tonight, Tansy knew he intended to confront Rance, with or without her. So, had she quickly asked not to part company with him to ensure he kept his word to finally free her of Rance? She'd then be free of himself, too. Two things accomplished after all.

"Damn you," he muttered, loving her so much.

THE NEXT MORNING, Tansy awoke to the sound of voices. Bolton and Will had already saddled all three horses. She got up, feeling she'd missed something. Had she only dreamed Bolton wanted a second chance? No, the fact she was gathering up his bedroll now was proof she'd slept beside him all night. Or had she? She didn't remember him hugging her during the night.

Bolton's back was to her as he spoke sternly to Will, "At The Rest, you take Jigger and get her to Deadwood safe and sound."

"What happens if we meet up with Indians like the ones who killed Preacher Smith there? Or with the people who shot Sheriff Brown?" Will asked.

"No, Bolton!" Tansy said breaking into their conversation as she stomped up behind Bolton who was holding the reins to Lightning and Angel. "You said last night we were going to Deadwood."

"Blazes!" Bolton whirled on her, black hair and coat

flying, booted feet spread wide and hands clenching into fists at his sides.

"And to the Grand Central Hotel!"

"That's enough, Jigger!"

Jigger again? Though his stance alone was intimidating enough, it was the icy cold fury in his steely blue eyes which seared Tansy's mouth shut from pushing him any further at the moment. He took his bedroll from her and swung himself on Lightning. Tansy glanced at Will who shrugged.

"Mount up!" Bolton barked.

Bolton's anger speared her soul and stuffed her into the saddle on the pretty palomino. Bolton led the way and the fast clip at which they traveled made it unquestionably clear to Tansy that Bolton could hardly wait to be rid of her.

"THANK GOD, YER BACK!" Gimpy exclaimed, pacing the boardwalk in the moonlight as they rode up.

Lupe flew out of the swinging doors, looked toward the heavens, and crossed herself. Gimpy helped Tansy dismount as Will jumped off his horse and caught Lupe up in his arms. In the middle of the boardwalk, Will gave Lupe what was probably their very first kiss.

"I been aprayin' and aworrin' since they left to go get ya, Bolt," Gimpy said, his frail body visibly shaking. "I'm powerful glad yer all back!"

"We've got so much to tell you!" Will said excitedly to Lupe and Gimpy.

Bolton, still in the saddle, tossed the pouch of gold to Gimpy who had to take a side step to balance the weight of it.

"Parker paid, Gimpy." And with that, Bolton tugged

Lightning away from the hitching post.

"Where are you going, *jefe?*" Lupe asked, running into the street. She grabbed Bolton's long coat and looked up at him. "What's wrong?"

Bolton leaned down and whispered something that sounded like "novio" and inclined his head toward Will.

"Adios," Bolton said, sitting tall in the saddle again. His broad shoulders squared as he turned Lightning and headed down Main Street.

"Bolt!" Will yelled, joining Lupe in the street.

"Nooo!" Lupe screamed after Bolton and whirled on Tansy. "What have you done?"

"I asked him for a second chance," Tansy said, her throat aching as she placed her hands over her heart. "I love Bolton."

"I don't believe you!" Lupe said vehemently. "And neither does he or he would not be leaving!"

"That's because I haven't told him."

Lupe threw her hands into the air. "Mi Dios, why not, Jigger?"

"It wouldn't be fair to him. He doesn't love me, Lupe!" Bolton would take her virginity. But Emma he would marry. "He still loves Emma."

"You fight to save him from death and hand him over to a ghost!" Lupe's expression was a mixture of outrage and pity. "You deserve to lose him!" Lupe turned to Will then and cried in his arms.

Was she giving Bolton up to a ghost, Tansy wondered? Couldn't she love him until he loved her back? What if that day never came? But what if it did? Pressing her fingers to her temples, she had to stop her world from spiraling into a cyclone.

"Bolton!" Tansy screamed at the top of her lungs. "Don't go!"

CHAPTER 29

"You can't go in there," Will said to Tansy. "Bolt and Gimpy aren't decent."

Tansy was sitting astride Angel in front of the Deadwood bathhouse the next evening. The bathhouse boasted several large bathtubs of fresh water from Whitewood Creek. The weather had cooled, thus Bolton and Gimpy were the sole patrons.

Only Gimpy's shout to Bolton had stopped him the night before. Bolton had glanced over his shoulder to see Gimpy fall as he rushed after him. Tansy had instinctively held back. Will reported Bolton had gotten two rooms at the IXL Hotel. She hadn't seen either of them since.

"So, when will they be done?" Tansy asked.

"When they're done, I guess," Will replied, standing beside the closed door.

The bathhouse keeper, sitting atop a barrel on the other side of the wooden door unnerved Tansy when his long tongue darted out of his mouth like that of a snake.

"Studyin' on it I got an idee the town crier's posted

here to make sure you cain't get to 'em," the bathhouse keeper said, referring to Will.

The keeper of the bathhouse had no ears and two top teeth protruded from his lipless mouth like fangs. His head was bald, and he had tiny black eyes. Adding to his reptilian appearance was the long tongue which he poked out again as he spoke.

"Whitewood Creek ain't gonna get no warmer 'til next summer, Mizz Crown. So richeern' now's a good time to getcher bath if'n you gotta notion to drown yer fleas and pick yer ticks."

Tansy frowned and shook her head. "They don't have fleas or ticks."

"But you might," the keeper stuck out his tongue as he leered at her. "If'n you let me watch, I'll letcha take yer bath fer free."

"No," Tansy mumbled, totally distracted by the knowledge Bolton had posted Will to keep her away from him. "Will, did Bolton say where he and Gimpy are headed later?"

"Well then, it's two bits fer a cold bath," the keeper interrupted, "and ten cents extry if'n ya want hot water."

"Blazes!" Tansy snapped at the keeper. "I'm not taking a bath!"

"Jo-fired jackals ta hell." The keeper's tongue darted out and he grumbled, "Dern tick 'n flea talk usual' works on uppity ladyfolk."

"Jigger, I don't know any more now than when Bolt sent me to the saloon for that bottle of wine you gave him," Will said.

"Be astaggerin' like zig-zag Virginie fences when they get outcheer," the keeper said.

"I doubt that," Tansy said to the keeper and turned

back to Will. "I'll wait right here and talk to Bolton when he and Gimpy come out."

"I's thinkin,' they ain't acomin' out 'til yer gone, little missy!" the keeper cackled. "But you kin stay 'n watch whilst I take a bath."

Will scowled at him and asked, "You do know that's Bolt Rivers in there, don't you?"

"Rivers?" The blood drained from the keeper's face. He stood and rubbed a hand over his mouth. "It's closin' time!" That stated, he slithered off toward the creek.

"So, he won't come out until I'm gone?" Tansy asked. Unable to meet her gaze, Will nodded. She dismounted and said, "Then I'll have to go in and talk to Bolton." She put her hand to Will's arm in an attempt to move him from blocking the door. But he didn't budge.

"No, Jigger." Will shook his head. "Bolt appointed me his right-hand man. How would it look if you got past me?"

"I guess it would look like you couldn't handle your job." Tansy sensed being Bolton's right-hand man was the most important work in the world to Will. Then she whispered, "Please help me keep track of him, Will."

"You go back to the saloon." With a conspiratorial wink, Will promised quietly, "I'll get word to you when I can."

Tansy was confused. Bolton had listened to her and made up with her. Hadn't he? Shoulders heavy with the weight of her many mistakes, she mounted Angel and headed toward the saloon. It was a busy day in Deadwood and before Bolton had come to town, she would have been accosted by the men passing her. Now, even at dusk, they afforded her a respectful berth. Many tipped their hats or waved, calling out their gratitude that Bolt Rivers had added a giant notch in his gun.

Riding down Main Street alone in the evening was just one of the ways Bolton had changed her life. For a short time, she'd had a passionate lover and best friend, a fearsome protector, and trustworthy confidante. If she could repay Bolton for all he'd done for her, mayhap he'd love her. But how could she repay him? Digging for that elusive treasure and not finding it, Tansy tethered Angel and dragged herself into the saloon.

"They're at the bathhouse," Tansy said hollowly to Lupe who was waiting on customers. "I don't know what's next."

"The Badlands."

"Why do you say that, Lupe?" Tansy asked, feeling sick to her stomach.

"I overheard *jefe* telling Gimpy that before he met you, he'd turn in his wanted man to the local law, get a bath and usually go to the nearest whorehouse."

Would Bolton do that again? Would Dolly tug his muscular body into her bed tonight and be showered with his fiery kisses? That image was a killing one.

"And since Will is with him," Lupe continued, "he'll lose his innocence to one of Dolly's doves instead of taking mine."

"No, Lupe. I don't think so," Tansy said, striving to regain her composure.

With a frown at Tansy, Lupe shrugged and said no more. Miserable that everyone she loved was angry with her, Tansy busied herself waiting on customers. Near closing time, she decided Will had either lied to her or Bolton had prevented him from getting word to her. She rode Angel to the livery, keeping an eye out for Bolton, Gimpy, and Will. By the time she returned to the saloon, Lupe had closed up and was sitting at Bolton's usual table. Tansy joined her and stared at the empty chair in front of the wall.

"They're at Deadwood Dolly's," Lupe said. "I know it."

No sooner had Lupe said that when galloping hooves sounded outside and footsteps hit the plank walk. A breathless Will swung into the saloon from the darkness.

"They left the bathhouse zig-zaggin' like Virginie fences, all right!" Will shook his head and laughed. "After the wine, they had me buy 'em a couple of bottles of red-eye. Now Bolt and Gimpy are corned! Walkin' like they had bricks in their hats!"

Tansy didn't know whether to laugh with relief knowing Bolton was still in town or cry in shame that she'd driven him to take a chance of being too intoxicated to defend himself should the need arise.

"Singing Little Brown Jug as loud as they could and they were terrible off key," Will continued. "You shoulda heard 'em."

"He's going to get himself shot and killed!" Tansy said. "Where did they go?"

"You're in a pickle there," Will said, shaking his head. "On accounta they went to Russel's Pool Hall."

"Russel's?" Tansy gasped. "No!"

Lupe put a hand on Tansy's arm. "I think maybe you do love him."

"Yes, I do. With all my heart." Tansy hugged Lupe and said to her and Will, "I love all of you. But everything I've said and done since Bolton left Deadwood to find Parker has been wrong!"

"That's not true," Will said. "You made friends with the Lakota. So instead of killing us, they took us to Parker's mines. And you got Bolt back to Deadwood."

"You got Bolton back here, Will, by admitting we couldn't find our way home."

"*Jefe's* still here because of you, Jigger."

"I doubt that's true." Tansy smiled at the support from Lupe and Will. "But I have a treasured piece of information I need to clarify with Bolton."

"What do you mean?" Will asked.

"I need to explain it to him first," Tansy said. "Of all the places he and Gimpy could have gone why did they go to the one establishment that doesn't allow women?"

"Because Bolt said he's through with women," Will replied. "Gimpy told him Russel's is the only place in town that's got no whiskey servin' bawds, no female card dealers, no dancehall doves, and no plain ol' whores." Will's face reddened a little. "Absolutely no ladies allowed!"

"Blazes!" Tansy said, stamping her foot.

BOLT WAS GOOD 'N DRUNK. For a bounty hunter that could mean suicide anywhere, but especially so in a raucous pool hall like this one. Several fights had already broken out over billiards, bets, and a faro card game. A heavy haze of tobacco smoke hung in the air and the sour smell of old beer suggested the floor hadn't seen a mop since Easter. Another scuffle erupted near the bar, with one man pulling his gun. The pool hall owner immediately threw the man out, but as the night had worn on customers became increasingly boisterous and rowdy.

No wonder Tansy closed her saloon right about now. The later the hour, the more liquor poured, and the most malicious side of Deadwood crawled out of the cracks. Bolt wondered if the marshal and sheriff ever got a full night's sleep.

A wanted man with a sharp eye and quick draw,

aiming to keep a bounty hunter from taking him in could end it all here and now. Only Tansy knew he had retired the second Harless Parker dropped dead.

"Hell, whaddo I care?" Bolt slurred.

"Whadja say?" Gimpy mumbled, eyes crossing.

Sitting with his back to the wall proved Bolt did care. Yeah, he cared about Tansy, damn her. He didn't want to leave town without her.

If it were a regular night at the Crown Saloon, he'd be in her corner instead of this one. She'd favor him with her sunny smile and, irresistibly drawn to her, he'd take the room in a few quick strides. Amidst their regular customers' good natured cat-calls and occasional lust-filled stares, he'd tug a laughing Tansy into the kitchen. He'd kick the kitchen door shut and pull her into his arms.

Honeysuckle would envelop him as he imprisoned her in his embrace. She'd twine her slender arms around his neck and thread gentle fingers through his hair. Molding her soft breasts to his chest she'd tilt her pretty chin up. Green eyes would close, and pink lips would part. He'd bury his hands in her curls and lower his mouth to hers. Her kisses were an adventure all their own and he wanted one more.

No, he wanted a lifetime.

It was taking a will of iron to keep from pressuring Tansy the way Rance had tried to force her affections. He'd leave this smoke-filled pool hall in a heartbeat if only he could believe she truly wanted him. He longed to sweep his beautiful angel up in his arms and carry her to bed, strip her magnificent body and love her all night long.

"I'm done!" He slammed his hand onto the table, making Gimpy jump.

Tansy's responses in bed were no more real than those he'd paid for in the past, his liquor-soaked brain reasoned. That's why he'd sworn off women. That's why he was in this all male rum-hole. No, rum-hole was what they called small saloons in New York.

"Where the hell are we, Gimpy?" Bolt asked.

Gimpy whooped, obviously thinking he was joking. Gimpy tried to slap him on the back, missed, and whacked his whiskey off the table. With a puzzled expression, Gimpy aimed a slap at his own knee and missed that, too. That would be damn funny under different circumstances. But Bolt was shaken. First, the lapse of memory about swearing off women, Tansy in particular, and now a second lapse as to his whereabouts. Bolt knew what it was to have a serious case of amnesia and he didn't like it.

"Two coffees!" Bolt bellowed to the burley barkeep, doubting they had any.

Amazingly it only took a couple of minutes for the owner himself to set cups of steaming black coffee in front of Bolt and Gimpy. The owner said their drinks were on the house and thanked Bolt for stopping by. He'd just taken a sip of coffee when the swinging doors of the pool hall slammed open.

The man wore a black slouch hat pulled low over the brow. A poncho covered his torso and baggy britches flopped around his legs. A heavy shadow of beard hid half his face and, in his bulging, left cheek was a plug of tobacco.

"Who the dickens is that?" Gimpy asked, squinting at the stranger.

CHAPTER 30

"I DON'T KNOW," BOLT SAID AS SHERIFF BULLOCK WALKED in behind the stranger who then tromped toward the bar. The sheriff frowned at the back of the stranger before making his way to Bolt's table.

"Been looking for you, Bolt," Bullock said, sitting down at their table. "I'd like to talk to you about Parker."

"What about him?" Bolt asked, signaling the owner to bring another cup of coffee.

"I want to apologize for not getting Isaac Brown's note to you sooner."

"Will told me you delivered the note as soon as you'd found it. I'm much obliged." Bolt said.

"The day you left Deadwood, Stapleton and I were expecting General Crook any minute. We felt we had to refuse Jigger's request to catch up with you and help you get Parker," Bullock explained.

"News to me." Bolt was touched that Tansy had sought out help on his behalf even though he'd said he didn't need it. He turned to Gimpy. "Thank her for me."

Gimpy merely sipped his coffee as the pool hall owner delivered a cup to the sheriff.

"When Crook didn't arrive, Marshal Stapleton and I had time to do some digging on Harless Parker," Bullock said. "We started with the box of stories your friend, Will, gave us. We checked dates and places against hatchet killings and missing folks with the Board of Health and jail records. We suspect Parker murdered at least two dozen people in and around the Black Hills."

"I found those bodies," Bolt said, noting Will hadn't taken any credit for that but instead told him of Tansy's determination and courage. "Parkers buried with them now."

"Thank God." Bullock nodded. "But Parker would have continued killing if not for you. To show the town's appreciation, the Board of Health would like to make a presentation to you tomorrow, Friday evening at the Grand Central Hotel."

"I'll be gone by tomorrow night," Bolt said, knowing his pride was backhanding a reason for him to stay. But the mention of the Grand Central Hotel where he'd planned to celebrate with Tansy made Bolt want another whiskey.

"We figured you'd ride out after getting Parker. Until I spotted you here, I was afraid I'd missed you," Bullock said. "Anyhow you stopped him from killing and we'd like to thank you."

"If Jigger hadn't saved me after I got shot and sick, I wouldn't have been alive to get Parker," Bolt said, giving credit where it was due.

Gimpy then recounted to Bullock, the story he'd heard from Will about how he and Jigger had met up with the Lakota Indians who'd led them to Parker.

"I hope that bunch of Indians escape General Crook's

troops," Bullock said. "As for the Crow, we think they're the ones who killed Preacher Smith. Anyway, we got definite word that Crook will arrive tomorrow. There'll be a ball in his honor at the Grand Central Hotel. That's when we plan to honor you, Bolt. Please bring Jigger and whoever else you would like as well."

Bolt grimaced at hearing the hotel mentioned again. "I don't think—"

"After we honor you for ridding this town of three killers," Bullock interrupted, seeming to sense Bolt was on the verge of declining completely, "Mayor Farnum will make a speech and General Crook will shake hands with the townsfolk. Reckon you could stay on another day or two?"

"He'll be there," Gimpy said and slapped the table. "Heck-fire! We'll all be there!"

Bolt frowned at Gimpy until a movement by the stranger at the bar grabbed his attention. The little man clutched his throat. How ironic since Bolt's own throat was raw with pain. Looking at the burly barkeep, the small fellow shook his head as though relaying he couldn't speak. The barkeep held up three fingers. The stranger nodded and tromped toward the piano.

"Good!" Bullock said. "Deadwood owes you, Bolt." The sheriff offered his hand and Bolt shook it. "I almost forgot; the bank manager was looking for you today."

"That's right, Bolt," a blurry-eyed Gimpy said. "He dropped in the saloon, too."

"All right." Bolt figured the manager had been contacted by the Sonoma bank. "I'll see the bank manager before I leave town."

As the stranger took a seat on a stool and plunked the piano keys, Bolton, Gimpy and Bullock drank their coffee. Though the saloon was noisy, the drinkers, gamblers, and billiards players recognized "Jim Cracked Corn." Bolt smiled, that's sure what he and Gimpy had done tonight. Those patrons, who were sober enough to make their hands meet, clapped. Others stomped lead feet trying to keep time to the lively tune. The crowd cheered and raised mugs of beer and shots of whiskey when they heard "Oh! Susanna." It was a favorite at the Crown Saloon and the pet song of the '49 gold miners who'd left behind loved ones in the pursuit of gold.

Bolt knew Tansy wouldn't cry for him when he was gone.

"That little feller plays piano 'most better'n Jigger," Gimpy slurred with a happy-go-lucky smile.

Bolt was thinking there was something familiar in the sound of "Little Brown Jug" and in the swing of the piano player's body. Bolt's heart skipped a beat as the stranger slowed the pace with "When Johnny Comes Marching Home Again." Perhaps thinking of loved ones, the rough crowd quieted. The men clapped almost reverently at the end of the song and then the haunting melody of "Beautiful Dreamer" floated across the room.

Bolt felt as if his heart had stopped. He knew only one person on earth would have selected these specific tunes.

"That doesn't sound like a tune a man would play," Sheriff Bullock observed. "I told Calamity Jane I was going to arrest her for impersonating a man if she didn't leave town. If that's her, I'll throw her in jail and keep her overnight."

"Nah, don't do that. Jane's a friend of mine," Bolt said, made eye contact with Gimpy, and mouthed *Jigger*.

If ever a drunk man instantly sobered it was Gimpy as he sat up straight and sputtered, "Sh-sheriff! Did you hear 'bout Arkansas Hank bein' at the Crown Saloon?"

Tansy wasn't sure what to do as she finished playing. If Bolton didn't know who she was by now she was sunk. She'd dressed as a man to get in and planned to go straight to Bolton until the sheriff entered the pool hall on her heels. Aware of the trouble with Calamity Jane and the sheriff, Tansy had suddenly feared being arrested. So, she'd bellied up to the bar in as manly a way as she knew how. The burly barkeep demanded to know what she wanted to drink. On the spur of the moment, she'd clutched her throat as if mute and mouthed the request to play the piano. The barkeep had said she could play three songs. She'd played five and knew she had to go now or be tossed out.

"Let's go," said a deep voice behind her.

For a split second, Tansy froze. Then his voice replayed in her mind. She whirled around on the piano stool and faced his gun belt. Her gaze worked its way up his clean flannel shirt to his sun-bronzed throat. Those sapphire eyes were a little red and his eyelids looked heavy.

No tables were closer than ten feet. Still, she was careful to cover her mouth as she swallowed the gooey tortilla she'd hoped looked like a plug of tobacco. Bolton frowned at the stubble on her face.

"Coffee grounds," Tansy said and stood.

"You gotta get out of here. Bullock thinks you might be Calamity Jane."

With the serenading over, the customers returned to their disruptive recklessness.

"I'm not going anywhere until you tell me why you are drinking the night away instead of spending it with me."

"I don't spend nights with *men*," he said with a smirk.

"Dammit! What the blazes is wrong with you?"

Both his brows shot up and he swayed. She didn't know if it was because she had cursed or because he was corned. Either way, he was adorably vulnerable and outrageously sexy.

"You said you'd done all you cared to do for me. You said for me to find a lady who wanted to share my dreams."

"We got past that on our way back home."

"Did we?" he growled.

"Or mayhap..." Tansy began as something occurred to her, "you thought you were rid of me at the cave, felt sorry for me in the forest, and then came to your senses in the light of day."

"What? No." He shook his head. "You just want me to free you of Rance."

Tentative hope fluttered in Tansy's heart as she stared up at him. Sober, this man was impossible to control. Tonight, he might a little more flexible. Tansy smiled and put her hands to his muscular chest.

"Don't touch me like that," he gritted, through his teeth. "This is an all-male pool hall."

Bolton took her arm and Tansy grasped the edge of the piano. No one had paid much attention to them up to this point. But now some heads turned. She was afraid that if Bolton deposited her outside, he'd go back in, leave by the rear door and she'd never lay eyes on him again.

"Bolt?" the sheriff called out. "Want help?"

"No!" Bolton barked and gave her a tug.

"Bolton, wait," Tansy whispered. "I lied when I said I'd done all I cared to do for you so you wouldn't be saddled with a saloon whore."

"What saloon whore?" Bolton asked and frowned.

"I'm not like Dolly's doves, but you'd come to think of

me as similar when compared to the ladies in Sonoma. That's why I said for you to find a lady who wanted to share your dreams."

"You don't know me very well."

"I know you want me to let you go." Tansy touched her fingers to his chest and then clasped her hands over her heart. "I just don't know how."

With her hands at her breast, and off the piano, Bolton grabbed her left wrist. He wrapped her left arm around his neck and swung his right arm around her waist. As her toes did her walking, she grabbed the back of the first chair in her path. Bolton was temporarily stopped in his attempt to throw her out. The seated bald man had no ears! From the corner of his mouth darted a long tongue. Tansy gasped. If the reptilian-like bathhouse keeper recognized her, Sheriff Bullock would surely arrest her for impersonating a man. The keeper studied her as another man at the table spoke up.

"I don't know who he is, Marshal Rivers, but cuff him and throw him in jail!"

"Yeah, I might," Bolton agreed.

"I want you to come home with me," Tansy said, trying to lower the pitch of her voice. All around them were the sounds of choking and spewed liquor. "Forget about Lewis Rance! I want you!"

"Let go of that chair or I'll drop you into the bath keeper's lap!" Bolton warned.

"Jo-fired jackals ta hell! I don't want no man in my lap!" the keeper hollered, scrambled to his feet, and backed away.

With a victorious grin, Bolton pulled Tansy and the empty chair toward the door. He had moved both mountains onto which she'd held.

"You are as slick as they come, Bolton Rivers!" Tansy

said.

"Stop talking!" Bolton barked.

All hell broke loose as customers, from every corner of the establishment, decided to help Bolton get rid of his admirer. Scraping chairs back and raising billiards sticks, they closed in quickly.

"We'll string 'im up for you, Marshal Rivers!" one cowboy yelled.

At that, Bolton hoisted Tansy off her feet and heaved her over his broad shoulder. Clyde Crown's hat fell off her head and her long blond hair tumbled out.

"Jigger Crown!" someone shouted, as they all laughed.

"Rivers is a lucky man!" summed up the consensus.

Seeing the last of the hat, the colorful poncho Lupe had lent her fell over her head. Tansy felt the britches she'd borrowed from Gimpy slipping down her hips and Bolton's old boots falling off her feet. She squirmed, trying to grasp the britches and wrinkle her toes inside the boots. Obviously thinking she was fighting him; Bolton smacked her fanny and the customers howled.

Will pulled open one of the saloon's swinging doors and Bolton carted her outside. Inside, a roar of hoots and hollers filled the air from the miners, cowboys, gamblers, merchants, and the whole assortment.

"Wish a lady like Jigger would come after me!" one man hollered out.

"Bed her twice, once for me!" another customer yelled after them.

With a thud, Bolton deposited Tansy on the plank walk, in the light of the pool hall.

Will stood tall and admitted, "I told her you were here."

"I gave her the poncho, *jefe*," Lupe said, standing next

to Will.

"Looks like we all helped her," Bolton muttered, taking in his old boots. "She's wearing my shirt."

Not only was it cold outside, but the shirt made Tansy feel closer to Bolton. A befuddled Gimpy joined them as Sheriff Bullock left the pool hall chuckling. When Lightning whinnied at the hitching post, Bolton walked to the horse and untethered him.

"Bolton, wait!" Tansy said, quickly brushing her hair out of her face. "I need to clarify something very important!"

Bolton squinted. "That you're not a man? Yeah, everybody got that."

"No," Tansy waved her hands in the air as if to erase her masquerade as she had waved them when trying to erase calling the Lakota healer a buffalo. "I figured out the wapiya told me to *take* you to the Valley of the Moon. For the longest time, I only tried to *send* you there. Let me repay you for all you've done for us, by *taking* you there!"

"I said we'd part even."

How quickly he had buried her treasure of how to repay him and perhaps give him time to love her. Despite the warm glow from the pool hall, there was that freezing chill in his blue eyes. A muscle flexed in his clenched jaw. She knew he was thinking she had no right to try and hold him to her, living without him was her problem, not his. Any second he would say she had to let him go because he didn't love her.

"When we find out where the Valley of the Moon is, I have to *take* you there," Tansy persisted. "And you can't go without me because...I...I..."

"Blazes!" Bolton barked. "Just spit it out!"

"I can't stop loving you, Bolton Rivers!"

CHAPTER 31

"I NEVER KNEW YOU'D *STARTED* LOVING ME," BOLT SAID IN response to Tansy's confession.

Because she hadn't. He was drunk and she'd come to his rescue just like she had when he was shot. The boots on her feet were a painful reminder.

Tansy's chin quivered as she stepped closer and placed her hand over his heart. "What turned your heart so cold and indifferent to me?"

Cold? Bolton thought a man would have to be cold in his grave to be indifferent to this unique package of angel and adventuress. Only she could be so adorable with coffee grounds smeared over half her beautiful face. Only she could tempt him so sorely with a poncho camouflaging her perfect breasts. Only she could swing her hips so saucily in a pair of baggy britches. Only Tansy would ever do. He swept her hand away from his chest.

"Look, I know it's part of your nature to take people under your wing, but I don't need that." Bolt said, wanting to get out of here before he accepted her charity instead of her love.

"Actually, Bolt, I'd still like to go to California with you," Will said.

"Will," Bolt replied. "After I'm done in Fort Laramie, I'm going back to New York."

"Bolton, you once told me to stop running from Rance," Tansy said. It was not or never, so she was blunt. "Let's forget about the trouble in my past and make our future in Sonoma."

Bolt was confused. Did she want him to get Rance or not? "You go someplace warm and set up your clinic. I'll make sure Rance doesn't follow you." As Bolt lifted Lightning's reins with his right hand, Tansy grabbed his left hand. He jerked it from her. Surely, she knew that even in his intoxicated state, especially in this state, he had to keep at least one hand free to draw his gun. But such hurt glimmered in her big emerald eyes he grasped the gun handle to keep from reaching out to her. "Go home, Jigger."

"Please don't yank the rug out from under her, Bolt," Gimpy said. He looked at Bolt with an expression that said he didn't understand and, shoulders slumped, quietly walked away.

"It never bothered me not having a last name 'til I saw how people respect yours," Will said. "If ever a judge comes to this ol' gulch I reckon I'll ask him to make Rivers my last name." Will smiled and shrugged. "That is if you have no objection."

Bolt was too stunned by what Gimpy and Will had said to answer. Tears in her eyes, Lupe shook her head at him now as she had done to Tansy before she'd tried to escape in Larson's ox cart. Lupe and Will turned then and caught up with Gimpy.

Two men, who minutes ago had been ready to string Tansy up, exited the pool hall. Declaring themselves his friends, one man stuck a full bottle of whiskey in Bolt's hand as the other one clapped him on the back. But Gimpy, Will, and Lupe were the best friends he'd made since Tom Smith died, and they'd just vanished around the corner. He opened the bottle and swallowed some red-eye. He'd liked being good and drunk better than sober.

"Bolton," Tansy said. "I don't want our farewell to be said on the street in front of a pool hall." The moonlight rimmed her head like a halo. Her eyes sparkled as brightly as the stars and her tousled hair looked like it did after their lovemaking had taken him to heaven. "Tell me goodbye tomorrow morning at the Grand Central Hotel."

"That was your plan all along, wasn't it?" Pain rammed through his whiskey-induced fog, striking Bolt as hard now as when this thought had first hit him. "You were going to tell me goodbye at the hotel. When I derailed your grand farewell by going after Parker, you told me goodbye early in your kitchen."

"No! I wanted to celebrate the best month of my entire life with you at the hotel! Can't you trust me like I trust you?" Tansy grabbed his upper arms and squeezed. "I think you were hunting Parker for so long you can't see yourself being happy, yet. Be happy with me. Give yourself time to love me back."

Bolt realized she was beginning to sound convincing. But even if she loved him like she did Gimpy, Lupe, and Will that didn't mean she was in love with him. Forget seeing the bank manager. If he stayed tonight, he'd want to stay forever. And what if the next needy soul she took under her wing took his place in her bed? The idea of

Tansy making love to another man was worse than a mortal wound.

"I'll give you a ride to your saloon on my way outa town," he said.

"Well," Tansy sighed, released him, and splayed her hands in a giving-up gesture, "at least I got you out of that dangerous pool hall."

Sure enough, now that she had rescued him, she was done with him. Bolt put the whiskey bottle to his mouth and guzzled. The red-eye burned his aching throat and rolled in his empty stomach, but he needed anesthesia. When he leaned over to set the bottle on the boardwalk before mounting Lightning, his head spun. Straightening up, he saw two sets of snapping green eyes and at least four pursed lips. He stepped sideways to regain his balance.

"Ladies first," he decided and extended a hand to help her.

"I have a horse and I know how to ride!" Tansy said. "I don't need you dumping me in the street."

"Fine. You ride. I'll walk."

Bolt tried to glower at her. Hell, just seeing one of her was a goal. He patted Lightning's neck and the horse let Tansy swing herself up in the saddle. Bolt grabbed the whiskey bottle and walked the horse and rider along Main Street. Knowing these were the last minutes he'd ever spend with Tansy, he swigged the red-eye.

"The deed to your saloon is at the Miners' and Mechanics' Bank," Bolt said. "When I get to New York, I'll send you the twenty-five thousand dollar bounty for keeping me alive so I could get Parker."

"We're here," Tansy said, way too soon.

"Where?" Bolt asked and stopped Lightening.

"Where I'm spending the night." Tansy dismounted and snatched the whiskey bottle from him.

"Awright," Bolt said. He wanted to kiss her goodbye but couldn't risk it. Holding the reins, he tried unsuccessfully to find the stirrup with his left foot.

"Can't mount?" There seemed to be a double meaning to Tansy's taunt.

"The hell I can't." Bolt grabbed the pommel on the saddle but missed the stirrup again. He staggered back a step. "Blazes!"

When he tried and missed a third time, he had to hop backward to keep his balance. Where had all the postholes in the ground come from? He landed on his backside with a thud. Lightning looked at him and snorted. Where was his bedroll? What the hell. Yawning, Bolt lay back and moved his hat over his face. He stacked his hands under his head and crossed one booted foot over the other.

"Is he sleeping in the street?" Will asked as he, Lupe, and Gimpy hurried over to them.

"Not for long," Tansy said.

TANSY ADDED another log to the fire and padded across the thick carpets. Burying her fingers in the burgundy velvet curtains, she looked outside. As cold rain pelted the window pane, the wind howled, bending sturdy trees to the breaking point.

It was pitch black outside, at least a couple of hours before dawn. Her breath fogged the glass and she shivered. She shut the drapes and tiptoed past the brightly crackling fire in the fireplace. Nearing the huge four poster bed, she smiled knowing who lay sprawled between the beautifully carved footboard and headboard. Above him was a burgundy velvet canopy and to the side of the plush bed was a polished mahogany stair. Tansy stepped onto the stair and enjoyed the view.

How at home Bolton looked sleeping in this big, fancy bed. Remembering how she had once said she was quite certain she would never crawl into bed with him Tansy crawled under the covers, facing him. He rolled to her, and a strong arm closed around her, pressing her to his warmth. Heartbeat to heartbeat, she slipped an arm around him, never wanting to let him go.

"Are we in the hotel?" he murmured sleepily.

"Yes," she whispered. "I brought you here last night with some help from Will while Gimpy took Lightning to the livery."

"I remember," he said, eyes closed.

"And when we were finally alone you said you wanted to be with me always and forever."

"Did I?" he asked, a smile tugging at his lips.

"Until the end of time."

"I do want that," he said softly, his fingers trailing a tad clumsily up her body to her cheek.

"My beard, poncho, and pants are gone."

"'bout damn time."

Tansy giggled as his fingers brushed her lacy camisole and then held her breath as his hand slid down her satin drawers. This is what she'd hoped would happen when she brought him to the hotel. She wanted it always and forever with him, too.

"Where's my knife?" he asked, pushing back the covers. "Hell, where're my pants?"

"I stripped you down to your underclothes. When your heel was hurt, I stuck a kitchen knife under the mattress to cut the pain. Last night, I put your knife under this mattress to help lessen the headache you're going to have."

Bolton rolled away and felt under the mattress. Eyes not yet open, he pulled out his knife and leaned over her. His thick black hair fell forward.

"Spread your legs, angel." He hooked her right ankle with his foot and pulled her legs apart, easing the knife between her thighs.

"Bolton!" she gasped. "I had confidence in you when you cut my clothing off the first time, but your eyes were open and—"

"Chatterboxing might throw off my precision," he said and sliced a strategic hole in the satin.

"Stop!" she said breathlessly as desire burst wide open inside her. "I want to feel every inch of your body against mine. I'll do the cutting."

In the light of the blazing fireplace, Bolton rolled to his back. A sexy, half grin quirked up a corner of his mouth. He opened his eyes as he handed her the knife. His dark blue gaze smoldered, sending red hot tingles racing up and down her spine.

"I'll watch," he said huskily.

CHAPTER 32

Knife in hand, Tansy moved between Bolton's spread legs. She grasped his undershirt, held it taut, and sliced it open from the bottom up.

"I thought you were cutting off your clothes, not mine," Bolton said with a lazy chuckle. When she blew on the blade of the knife as if it were hot, he cocked a brow. "I dare you to do that topless."

She acknowledged his challenge with a flirtatious nod of her head. Putting the knife aside she flattened her hands to his muscular chest. He grasped her lacy camisole and as she leaned forward, he pulled it off. He stacked another pillow behind his head and eyed her naked breasts.

"Even in the firelight, these tips look like harvest ripe grapes."

Though in the past thirty days this man had seen and touched every inch of her, his intimate observation beaded her nipples. Tansy picked up his knife again and touched the razor sharp blade to the top of his drawers, slicing open the waist where it buttoned. He widened his muscular legs and undulated his tapered hips.

"You are so bad, Bolton."

"Only with you."

His words moistened Tansy's most private part as his drawers grew tighter before her eyes. She folded back the opening of his underwear exposing inch after hard inch of his burgeoning arousal.

"I want you out of these," she said, raising her eyes to his.

"So, I gathered," he said with a smug grin. "I'll strip."

"I'll watch," she whispered.

When he was naked, he grabbed the knife and flipped it. The tip dug into the bedpost at the foot of the bed. Tansy's eyes widened as she looked from the bedpost back to Bolton.

"Might as well make sure they know we carved a notch or two in this bed," he said.

He then stretched in the big bed, and with the firelight flickering behind her, Tansy straddled him. Bolton looked to the vee between her legs where her drawers brushed his erection. Sitting up he slid his arms around her, slashing his mouth across hers as his tongue tasted her lips. He trailed a fiery path of kisses down her neck and lifting her to her knees, closed his lips over a nipple.

Tansy moaned, pleasure assailing her.

While his mouth suckled at her breast, his hand slipped between her thighs and she worked her legs farther apart, arching her back. His fingers found the slit in the satin and caressed her damp center as his tongue played with her beaded nipple. She rocked her hips as he stroked her. With a groan, his lips fastened on hers and his hands moved to her fanny, tenderly kneading her.

"We're gonna do something new, Tansy."

Bolton eased her to lie back with her head at the foot of the bed. She smiled up at him as his muscle-packed body moved over her. The firelight illuminated his handsome face just before his head lowered. But instead of kissing her lips or breasts he slowly planted his mouth where, only moments before, his fingers had played.

In the opening of her satin drawers, he kissed her! His lips and tongue were wildfires. Bolton slid his hands under her bottom, lifting her slightly up. Tansy clutched the sheets, writhed, and arched as his mouth bathed the fevered flesh between her thighs. He found a hidden button of pleasure and the center of her being ignited. As his warm tongue explored, she spiraled upward into a sky of rapture. Bolton gently held her to his heavenly sweet kisses and euphoria struck her like white hot lightning.

"Bolton!" she gasped, reaching for him. "Come here!"

Bolton pulled her drawers off, lay on top of her naked body, and fastened his mouth to hers. She reached between their bodies and curled her hand around his long, thick manhood. Hot, hard, and unrestrained he was ready.

"I want to do to you what you just did to me," Tansy whispered.

"Next time."

Bolt had never done to any woman what he'd just done to Tansy. He hadn't wanted to with anyone else. And though he'd let it be done to him, he knew it wouldn't compare to what he'd experience with Tansy. Gently she tightened her fingers around his arousal and guided him to her wet, velvety soft center. As he pressed into her womanhood, his tongue ravished her mouth.

"You're so tight," he whispered his erection fully inside. He raised his head, and she threaded her fingers through his hair. She was his siren's song. As he pulled out to sea, she waved him back to shore. The blood in his loins pounded and his climax coiled like a spring. Harder and faster, he thrust, Tansy meeting each plunge with an arch. He closed his eyes and impaled her. "I'm so deep inside you and so in love with you, I'm lost," he said softly.

If only he weren't intoxicated, Tansy thought. If only he'd said he was in love with her when their bodies weren't coupled. Surely there was no lapse of memory as to whom...

"How lost are you, Bolton?"

"Tansy, wrap your legs around me and love me back."

Tansy locked her legs around his waist. Come to think of it, he'd called her Tansy when he'd said they were going to do something new. She smiled as Bolton moved erotically, thrusting deeply, spreading boundless pleasure and happiness throughout her soul. Her lower body vibrated with her climax as she felt the hard pulsing of his release. When their heartbeats slowed, she whispered in his ear.

"I pray you gave me your baby to love."

Not a smidgen of firelight flickered between their bodies. Just when the silence could be cut with his knife, Tansy sucked her lips between her teeth as if that could yank her prayer back into her mouth.

"When was your last monthly visit?"

A thrill shot through her at having this gorgeous man ask her such an intimate question with his manhood still inside her. She concentrated on his question. She had first slept with him on August twentieth. It was nearing the end of September now. Her last visit had ended the day Hickok was shot. The day she met Bolton. Should she tell him? No, she didn't want him to feel trapped.

"I'm due."

"Yeah, late next spring."

Giving her no time to ponder that future, he gently rolled over on his back, tugging her on top of him. She kissed his lips before nibbling her way down his chest, stomach, and lower. With abandonment, she loved all that made Bolton male, desiring him always to remember the adventure of this first new kiss.

BOLT WOKE, wondering if his wildest fantasies had actually come true. He reached for Tansy, but the bed was cold and empty. So, it had all been a dream.

Then his fingers brushed paper. Groggily, he rubbed his eyes and read. A note from Tansy said Marshal Stapleton had stopped by the saloon looking for him the previous evening and told her about the ball. His change of clothing was in the armoire. She hoped he stayed to accept the mayor's presentation that evening. She wished him good luck and...goodbye.

"Dammit to hell!"

Bolt rolled out of bed, yanked on his pants, and went to the window. He opened the curtains and squinted as the sun streamed in. He'd been asleep for hours. It was probably ten o'clock. His stomach growled and then it rolled. Hell, he should have stuck his knife back under the mattress to cut this pain.

He grinned, recalling how Tansy had used the knife. He pulled on his clothes and boots. After what he and Tansy had done in that damn fine bed, what was she up to now?

Hell-bent on finding out, he tore out of their room. As Bolt left the hotel, Marshal Stapleton stopped him and introduced him to Mayor Farnum.

"I understand you've been on the road for weeks at a time like General Crook and his troops. Anything I should be prepared for?" the mayor asked Bolt.

"Send 'em to the bathhouse," Bolt replied, chafing to take off down Main Street. "And they'll want women."

"Let's make that known to the right establishments," Mayor Farnum said to Stapleton and turned back to Bolt. "Since you're still in town I'm hoping you've decided to accept the Board of Health's presentation, Marshal Rivers. I will have a table reserved for you at the ball later this evening."

Bolt smiled noncommittally, bid the mayor and marshal farewell, and took off toward the Crown. Passing the Miners' and Mechanics' Bank, the manager hailed Bolt into the bank and handed him a letter. Bolt made himself take the time to scan it. Finally, he hurried on and burst through the swinging doors of the saloon. Gimpy and Will grinned at seeing him.

"Where the hell is she?"

Simultaneously, they jerked their thumbs toward the kitchen door. As Bolt stormed across the saloon, regular customers nodded respectfully at him. A few, who knew him by reputation only looked ready to run. Bolt shoved the kitchen door open and stopped in his tracks.

Tansy and Lupe stood with their backs to him as Lupe held Tansy's hair away from her face. Bent over a dish pan on top of a counter, Tansy retched as Lupe glanced over her shoulder at him.

"Mi Dios!" Lupe wailed. "Jigger is so poorly. She doesn't know why she has the dry heaves."

Tansy straightened and pressed a cloth to her mouth. Bolt slowly walked to her and looked into her pasty-white face. Gently, he took her arm and seated her in a chair. Bolt gave Lupe a nod, so she scurried out of the kitchen and closed the door.

Grabbing a chair, Bolt pulled it in front of Tansy and sat down. In a quiet voice, he said, "I can identify with feeling a little under the weather today. But mine's from drinking too much. I think you know exactly why you're queasy. Don't you?"

"Yes," she said, her gaze falling below his gun belt to the masculine bulge between his spread legs. She rolled her eyes toward the counter and Bolt grabbed the empty dish pan. After another dry heave, Tansy shoved the pan away. "I thought you'd still be in bed resting up for the presentation and ball."

"I'm not going to any ball without you. And you can forget telling me goodbye because you're taking me to the Valley of the Moon."

Tansy hung her head. "I can't now."

"Yes, you can." Bolt placed a finger under his chin and tipped up her head. "The bank manager gave me a letter from the California bank. In it are details about my property in Sonoma. But I'll only go if you come with me."

"Do you own a great big house and acres of vineyards?"

Bolt grinned. "And then some."

"How would it look for you to drag an unwed, expectant barkeep into town?"

Bolt took her hands and held them. "It would look like I couldn't keep my hands off you or leave you behind."

"Society would be so scandalized they wouldn't purchase your wine."

"My wine is distributed all over the country." He grinned when her eyes widened. "The label on the bottle of wine you gave me wasn't intact," he said, and she nodded as if remembering that. "While I was at the Deadwood bathhouse, I studied the small portion that was there. If we had another bottle, we'd see the name Rivers at the top of the label."

Tansy's mouth dropped open. "No wonder you knew how to make this saloon turn a profit so fast! In addition to everything else, you're a businessman!"

"Who says you'd be going to California unwed?" Bolt gently squeezed her dainty hands. She was so adorable, and he loved her so much his headache vanished. "I want this baby to have my name."

"Well, slapping the name Rivers on a bottle of wine is a lot easier than slapping it on a baby."

"Whose last name will the baby have, Tansy?"

"Mine."

CHAPTER 33

"No!" Bolton shook his head like an angry lion and let go of her hands. "I fathered this baby and I'm going to raise it." As he scowled at her, his fists clenched atop his thighs. "We'll get married and move to California."

"No!" Tansy said, wanting exactly that. She'd had this man between her own thighs just hours ago and been so happy. "I'm not trapping you into marriage with a baby! No more mail orders or bullwhips!" She pointed an accusing finger at Bolton. "And no bounty hunter marshal who breezed into town stole my virginity and planned to leave me until finding out I'm carrying his child."

"Stole your...Hell! You found me in the Number Ten Saloon," Bolton said with a growl. "You were on top of me that first time and I told you not to sit down." He pointed his finger at her now. "And you're the one who told me not to come back."

Tansy seethed at the absolute accuracy of his words and smacked his hand away. He'd said once there were too many secrets between them. Well, she was no longer the frightened woman on the run that she was when he met her. Her wishbone was a strong backbone these days and she would bravely confront him with her last secret concern.

"You're the one who decided Emma was good enough to be your wife, but I was only good enough to be your barkeep."

"Stop it, Tansy."

"No, I won't stop it." Truth was, she couldn't stop now that she'd started. "The next man I marry will be wildly in love with me! Never again will I be any man's platonic companion or imprisoned nursemaid! And I will not be a broodmare to a man who'll always compare me to a ghost!"

Bolton stood up and kicked his chair across the kitchen. He paced across the room then pivoted. His hair whipped to his back, and he settled his hands on his gun belt.

"All right, let's compare!" His voice was steady as his brow cocked. "Emma never made me mad like you do. I'm as angry now as I was the day you went after Skinny."

Tansy shrugged, raised her chin, and stared him in the eye.

"Emma prayed for the homeless. You take in the homeless. Emma had her family's maid make chicken soup for me when I was sick. You slept in a rocking chair at my bedside until you saved me from dying. Emma dressed up and invited me to ice cream socials. You dressed up and got me out of Russel's Pool Hall before what happened to Hickok, happened to me."

"Emma was a lady."

"Not the right one for me," Bolton said. After a moment he walked to Tansy and spoke less harshly.

"When I called to her on that riverbank, she ran the other way. When I called to you at the jail, you ran straight to me. My gut told me then and there you were the one and only woman for me. You make me laugh, you've made me cry and you make me burn in bed."

Bolton made her laugh, too. His sense of humor had always been one of the qualities that attracted her to him. Tansy remembered his eyes misting as they'd sat near the campfire in the forest.

"But any woman can make a man burn in bed," she said.

"I never kissed any woman the way I kissed you just before dawn," he said boldly, making her cheeks grow hot. "I have no children because I only lost control with you."

And just like that, the lingering ghost was banished. Tansy took his hand and tugged. Standing in front of her, Bolton squatted down on his haunches.

"Tansy, do you remember what you said to me," he tilted his head toward the saloon and took both of her hands in his, "out there on the bar?"

"I don't know," she fibbed and smiled.

"You said unless you had my baby, you'd have no one's."

"Because I love you and no other man could measure up to you, Bolton."

"No other woman can measure up to you, angel. I've met my match." He cocked a brow and then said, "If anyone deserves to be honored with a presentation, it's you. All that I have just said is my presentation of how honored I am to be the father of this baby and how in love with you I am."

"Wildly?" she asked.

"Wildly." His voice raspy with emotion, he said, "You're the queen of my heart."

Tansy smiled, envisioning the queen of hearts card she'd pulled out of Angel's saddlebag.

"Bolton, you are my best friend. No man could make a better father for our baby. It would be my dream come true to bear you all the children your heart desires. You're the king of my heart. I will love you always and forever. Until the end of time."

"I suppose our baby will be a little chatterbox, like you."

"Mayhap." Tansy slipped off her chair and kneeling in front of him brought his hands to her heart.

"Will you marry me?"

A fleeting expression of surprise touched his handsome face. "I swore I wouldn't pressure you into marrying me. But I never thought you'd propose to me."

"Is that a yes?"

"Yes, ma'am."

Tansy twined her arms around his neck and his sinewy embrace molded her to him. Bolton's mouth came down on hers, searing her lips with a fiery kiss. When the kitchen door squeaked, they ignored it.

"Why are they on their knees?" Will whispered.

"Ya think ever'thing's awright?" Gimpy asked.

"Shh!" Lupe ordered.

"We're getting married," Bolton announced, rising to his feet.

Gimpy, Lupe, and Will spilled into the kitchen then, congratulating them and asking questions. Bolton helped Tansy stand and wrapped his left arm around her.

"Quiet now or you'll scare the baby!" Bolton said with a grin, splaying his right hand on Tansy's flat tummy.

"Mi Dios, this is a blessing from above," Lupe said, tears in her eyes.

"Yes," Tansy said, having prayed just that morning for a baby.

Congratulations began all afresh from their family of friends.

"Tell them about California, Bolton," Tansy said.

Bolton filled them in and then asked, "Did I mention my letter from the California banker referred to Sonoma by the name the Indians gave it?"

"Tell us," Tansy breathed.

"The Valley of the Moon," Bolton replied with a broad smile.

Will smacked a hand over his heart and Lupe crossed herself as Gimpy scratched his bald head.

"I knew it," Tansy whispered, hugging the father of her baby.

"Are these three part of the deal?" Bolton asked with a nod to the three friends he and Tansy cared so much for.

"Yeah!" Will whooped, then asked, "Aren't we, Jigger?"

"Por favor!" Lupe said, clasping her hands under his chin.

"Who'll run the saloon?" Gimpy asked, tugging on his mustache.

"We'll sell the saloon," Tansy said.

"Gimpy, think you could take care of the customers who visit the California winery?" Bolton asked, placing a hand on Gimpy's shoulder.

"Well-sir, you betcha I can!" Gimpy grinned from ear to ear, seeming to grow an inch taller.

"Will you help me in the clinic, Lupe?" Tansy asked.

"Sí! Sí!" Lupe said happily, clapping her hands.

"Does Sonoma have a newspaper or something?" Will asked, shifting back and forth.

"Yes," Bolton replied. "But I'd like you to start a company newspaper for the winery and be my right-hand man, Will."

"So, you're all part of the de—"

Tansy got no farther because she was cut off as she and Bolton were showered by handshakes, hugs, and kisses.

"Gimpy, go tend bar," Bolton said as he shooed them back and chuckled. "Lupe, go wait on customers. Will, go put an ad in the newspaper offering the saloon for sale."

All talking to each other at once, Gimpy, Lupe, and Will left the kitchen.

"I have a job for you, Bolton," Tansy said after the others were gone.

"Name it."

"Take me to the ball this evening."

"I will if you'll let me replace the dress you tore in the forest with a dress fit for a ball."

When Bolt left the kitchen alone, Lupe was walking Will toward the swinging doors.

"Where's Jigger?" Gimpy asked, picking up an empty coffee cup.

"She disagrees that I owe her a dress for the ball, so she's thinking it over in the kitchen."

"She is?" Lupe asked with amazement in her eyes and voice.

"Yeah." Bolt chuckled as he crossed the saloon. "Lupe, let's go to Boughton's Dress Shop." He tossed the key to the handcuffs toward Gimpy. "Uncuff her when she promises to behave."

Gimpy cackled as the key landed in the coffee cup. With a grinning Will and a giggling Lupe hot on his heels, Bolt left the saloon.

. . .

TANSY HAD NEVER BEEN in the quaint shop belonging to Mr. Vondey, a master watchmaker and jeweler. But that's where she and Bolton were when General Crook and his troops marched into Deadwood.

"That's Black Hills Gold," Mr. Vondey said.

"I've never seen anything like it," Tansy said, staring at the wedding band. "Bolton, there's a grape leaf design carved into this band. The wapiya would say it's a sign of his vision coming true. I love it!"

Bolton nodded. "Is that the ring you want?"

Tansy said yes. Bolton paid for and pocketed her wedding band. Tansy pointed to a gold pocket watch in the jeweler's case. On the front was a beautifully carved image of the Black Hills.

"I'll take that watch, Mr. Vondey," she said. "He tends to look out the window and guess at the time." She pulled some of her reward money for Skinny out of her pocket and handed it to the jeweler. Outside the shop, she took Bolton's hand. "This is my wedding gift to you. I want you to always remember our *time* in the Black Hills," she said placing the watch in Bolton's hand.

"I'll always remember." He looked at the watch and said, "My father had a pocket watch and when the noon whistle at the shipyard blew, he'd always check his watch. It was broken that final day, so I thought it only right to bury it with him. Thank you."

"You're so welcome." Tansy smiled, even happier to have bought the watch for him as he slipped it into his vest pocket.

"My folks owned that shipyard in New York. They left behind a fortune in cash and property."

Bolton took her hand, placed it in the crook of his arm and they strolled down the boardwalk.

Tansy was speechless for a long moment. "But I

thought you became a bounty hunter because it was the only way you could make a living while hunting Parker. And being a marshal let you cross state and territory lines in pursuit of him."

"True," he agreed. "My father always told me to invest in the land of my choice. He didn't say finance a manhunt with it. The bounties I collected let me keep raising the one on Parker and the bonus was getting other killers off the street."

Tansy looked up at him and said, "The presentation for you tonight is long overdue."

"I sold the New York holdings and began investing in California. The vineyard's been managed by an overseer. We won't be starting from scratch. The letter from Sonoma said the overseer is ready to retire, so I really do need Gimpy and Will. We'll hire whatever help we need to manage our household and to assist you and Lupe with your clinic. Money won't be an issue."

"Oh, Bolton," Tansy said. "I'm so happy and at the same time so afraid that something will prevent our beautiful dreams from coming true."

"I won't let anything happen," he said, smiling. "Do you want to know my latest dream?"

"Always."

"You're expecting and surrounded by grapevines. Your toes are buried in the rich soil of our land and," he grinned, "our son will be at your feet eating harvest-ripe grapes."

"So," Tansy drawled as if having to consider the perfect picture he'd painted, "do you mean you're dreaming of me carrying your second baby?"

"Yes. I mean to keep you happy in and out of bed," he said and winked at her.

"Promise me it will all come true."

"I promise you it will."

"Preacher Smith is dead and there's no judge in the gulch to marry us," Tansy said, "But I suppose we could ask Mayor Farnum if he can perform the ceremony."

"For now, buy shoes to go with your new dress. I've got things to do."

"I don't need new shoes," she said as they paused outside the cobbler's shop. "I'll stay with you."

"Some of my business is private." Bolton shook his head and said, "Tansy, I will treat you like the queen of my heart, if you'll let me." He took her hand and dropped several double eagles into it. "I hope to see satin and lace tonight instead of my shirt and boots."

"Mayhap you will and mayhap you won't!" Tansy flirted with love and longing hardly believing the dashing and dangerous man would soon be all hers. "I have a private business, too."

CHAPTER 34

"I HAD YOUR DRESS DELIVERED TO THE HOTEL, SO MEET ME there when you're done," Bolton said and grinned. "We can have supper in our room and then attend the ball." He draped one arm around her, placed a hand on her belly, and whispered, "Go now, little girl, but none of your adventures. You have my baby in there."

"I love you!" she said.

"I love you, too."

Bolton gave her a nudge into the cobbler's shop. After selecting shoes for herself and Lupe, she stopped by Annie Dunne's shop for satin and lace. In both places, she heard customers saying tonight's ball would be the finest and fanciest Deadwood had ever seen.

Finally, Tansy returned to the saloon where many of General Crook's troops were carousing. Since they probably didn't have much money, she told Gimpy to charge them half price. In the kitchen, she put together a special recipe and while it baked, she went to her room and packed her carpet bag.

An hour later, Tansy took a pie tin out of the oven

and placed it in a basket. Bag and basket in hand, she went into the saloon and smiled at Will who was back. They would close for the evening soon, and General Crook's troops would have to patronize one of the other twenty-five saloons in Deadwood.

"Like Bolt told me, I put the ad in the newspaper to sell the saloon," Will said to Tansy and Lupe. "And" he glanced at Lupe, "I also gave Mr. Merrick notice."

Lupe threw her arms around Will and kissed him. Tansy grinned at Gimpy who rolled his eyes.

Waving goodbye, Tansy headed for the hotel. Some of the troops were marching south while others headed north. The bathhouse keeper and the badlands madam would be busy.

At the Grand Central Hotel, Mr. Wagner, the proprietor, snapped his fingers as Tansy entered. Instantly, two bellhops were at her service. One took her bag and the other her basket. Mr. Wagner offered his arm. The three men escorted her to the hotel's finest room on the second floor. There the bellhop carrying her bag also took the basket, setting her bag on the bed and placing the basket on the marble top table between two large wing backed chairs. The other bellhop efficiently added logs to the fire making it flare up and crackle. At the far side of the fireplace was a bathtub. Tansy smiled; it was big enough for two. Four maids arrived toting eight kettles of steaming water which they poured into the half-filled tin tub. Mr. Wagner then asked Tansy if she needed anything else.

"No, thank you. I think Mr. Rivers has thought of everything," Tansy said, needing only the man himself. Where was he?

After she was alone, she looked around the room. On both bedside tables and the fireplace mantel sat crystal vases filled with flowers of every color. The yellow ones, discretely blended in with the others, were tansies that bloomed from July through September in the Black Hills. In the middle of the canopied bed was a crystal bowl spilling over with red grapes.

On the marble top table, between the two overstuffed chairs, a copper cooler of water set next to her basket. She took a bottle of red wine out of the water so cold it had to be straight out of Whitewood Creek. The wine label made her heart thump.

"Bottled by the Rivers Family Vineyard in the Valley of the Moon," she read aloud sinking down into one of the big, comfortable chairs.

Above the words was a sketch similar to the one drawn by the Lakota healer. A mansion, two stories tall had left and right wings, a tiled roof, six chimneys, and a covered porch with ten enormous white pillars. Surrounding the house was a valley of grapevines. Even the full moon, the wapiya had pointed to in the forest, was hanging in the sky above the house and vineyard.

"The word family in the label was out of respect for my folks and now it includes you and our baby," Bolton said, standing in the open doorway.

"Bolton," she said, so engrossed in the wine label she hadn't heard his footsteps. As he closed the door, she carefully put the bottle on the table, then stood and flung herself into his arms. "The beautiful dreams you talked about when you were so sick, are right there on your wine label."

"Yeah. Let's not go to the presentation, Tansy."

"Yes, please," she insisted. "You deserve to be honored."

"I don't care about it," he said. "Let's at least skip the ball."

"But you bought the prettiest gown in Deadwood for me to wear."

"Let's just eat supper up here and go to bed."

"Why, Bolton Rivers, you're nervous about being honored!" she said, hands on her hips.

He didn't respond as he moved to the window and looked down at the street. Turning around there was a fleeting glimpse of the bounty hunter and marshal in his eyes.

"If you're set on these blamed festivities, I'm taking a bath."

Tansy nodded and unbuttoned his shirt. She pulled the shirttails out of his pants and ran her fingers up his bare chest. Removing his gun belt, he shrugged out of his shirt, the muscles in his upper arms and chest flexing as his stomach muscles rippled. She took hold of his silver belt buckle and unfastened it. He rested his hands on her shoulders as she unbuttoned his pants. She smiled up at him, but he was looking over her head and out the window.

"Bolton, what's wrong?"

He didn't answer as he sat down on the bed and yanked off his boots. His pants followed. Tansy shed her dress as Bolton lowered himself into the hot water. In her camisole and drawers, Tansy picked up a cake of soap off the stack of towels on the dresser. Dipping her hands into the water, she rubbed the soap into foam, lathered his hair, cupped her hands full of water, and rinsed it.

When Bolton started to get out of the tub, Tansy stopped him by dropping her underclothes on the floor. She eased into the tub with him and, facing Bolton, giggled as the hot water sloshed around them. As they'd often done, since their first escapade of falling into a tub together, she straddled his lap. With his hands at her waist, she leaned back dipping her hair into the water. She lathered it, swished the soap out, and felt for Bolton under the water. He was ready for her.

Bolt groaned and gripped the sides of the tub as Tansy positioned him. Impaling her, he took her ripe nipple into his mouth and suckled. She tossed her pretty head back, moaned his name, and ground against him. She raised and lowered. He placed his lips on her other nipple and Tansy's beautiful body shivered with her climax. When her lips met his, he thrust himself more deeply inside her and spent himself within her warm tightness. When their heartbeats slowed, Bolt leaned back.

"You had your way with me." Bolt cocked an eyebrow. "We're getting dressed now."

He stepped out of the tub and wrapped a towel around his waist. He helped her out of the bath and gave her a towel. Wrapping her hair in it, she swiveled to face him dripping wet and naked. As he boldly looked her up and down, she threw a delicate hand to her throat as if terribly scandalized. Tantalizing Tansy, as sizzling hot as the fire raging behind her. She batted her eyes at him.

"I believe my bodaciously good looking fiancé just had his way with *me!*"

Bolt chuckled as he dried himself off. "It's difficult to look maligned when you're naked, already expecting my baby and literally daring me for more. So be careful, little girl."

"Oh? Do you have your handcuffs, Marshal Rivers?"

"You know I wouldn't need 'em," he said. "By tomorrow morning you wouldn't be able to walk out of here."

Provocatively, Tansy swayed to him and wrapped her

arms around his neck. Possessively, Bolt wrapped his towel around Tansy and held her to his heart wanting to protect her and their unborn baby from every war in life, every battle in the world.

"Tansy, let's leave town tonight and get married in Sonoma."

"No, I want to wear my new dress."

"It can be your wedding dress."

"Bolton," she said looking up at him. "I asked you earlier and I'll ask again, what's wrong?"

"I don't want to go to that damn ball."

"If we skip it, we'll miss the chance to ask Mayor Farnum if he's qualified to marry us."

Bolt grumbled, "We'll eat supper and go."

"Well now. That's more like it," she said, smiling up at him.

Without another word, Bolt yanked on his change of clothes along with a new shirt and vest Tansy had purchased for him. Tansy began donning her many layers. Silk stockings showed under the hem of her white silk drawers. A white lace camisole was followed by a white satin petticoat or two.

"I'll never get all that peeled off you tonight," Bolt said with more of a growl than he'd intended.

"You said you wanted to see satin and lace," she said and giggled.

Standing at the dresser he used Tansy's brush to smooth back his damp hair. Tansy picked up the pants he'd worn before the bath and folded them. Slipping out of the front pocket was a handkerchief wrapped around a piece of paper.

"Who does the initial 'D' represent?" she asked, looking down at the letter embroidered on the hand-kerchief.

"Give me that," he said, taking the handkerchief and paper from her and jamming them into his pants pocket. Bolt said nothing more as he picked up a rawhide strip and tied his hair back. But he knew he must look the villain to this angel in white lace and satin.

"There was a day when I might have thought that was a secret love letter."

Bolt turned to the delicate woman. Gently, he took her face in his hands and was about to kiss her when she dug in his pocket and yanked out the handkerchief.

"Bolton, who does the 'D' represent?"

"Dolly."

"I know Dolly was not part of your private business," Tansy said with confidence.

"You're right. My private business was getting the flowers, wine, grapes, and bath put in here for you. I ran into Dolly at the bank. Luckily, she doesn't hold a grudge."

"Lucky for you!" Tansy said with a small laugh. "She bid me good riddance."

"She called me a sorry son-of-a-mule," he said and chuckled before sobering. "Secrets between us are done. I didn't want to upset you with this tonight but go ahead and look."

Tansy unfolded the handkerchief and then the piece of paper.

"Oh please, God, no," Tansy said as she dropped the handkerchief and paper on the floor.

CHAPTER 35

"DON'T PANIC," BOLT SAID, LEADING TANSY TO A CHAIR. He picked up the piece of paper and sat down across from her. "It's not good for you or the baby."

"Don't panic?" Tansy stared at him. "I take a wanted poster for Tansy Wiley out of your pocket, and you say not to panic?"

"I already talked to Stapleton about the poster."

"Does he know it's me?" Her emerald eyes widened. "Is he going to take me into custody?"

"Stapleton and Bullock would never cross me by trying to put you into that jail. Secondly, they had no idea who Tansy Wiley was until I told them."

"You told them?" Her brows shot up and her eyes widened.

"Yes. A few days before I went after Parker, Con Stapleton introduced me to Charlie Utter, the man running the Pioneer Pony Express from Deadwood to Fort Laramie. Charlie said he'd heard about me from Hickok." Tansy nodded and he went on, "I gave Charlie a message asking the Fort Laramie marshal to telegraph

Texas authorities as to any charges against you. They'll be back here next Wednesday. I expect with official word clearing you."

"I don't how you figure out what to do or how to do it, but I'm so thankful you know." She smiled, making his every breath worthwhile. "I'm lucky the poster doesn't look much like me."

"As far as the general public goes, that's true," Bolt said and glanced at the poster. "Stapleton and Bullock are good men. They'd have to be dishonest to take you into custody because of the way the poster's worded."

"Let me see the poster again and tell me what you mean," she asked and was given the poster. "Wanted for murder in the poisoning deaths of Mrs. Lewis Rance and Dr. Walter Wiley. Five thousand dollars will be paid by Lewis Rance for the live capture and return of Tansy Wiley," Tansy read out loud. She looked Bolt in the eyes and whispered, "Papa was stabbed by Sanchez. I took good care of Mrs. Rance, but she just kept getting sicker. Do you think Rance poisoned her?"

"I suspected when you first told me about Rance that he had something to do with her death. That's why he's offering the reward and not the United States Marshals or the government. On Parker's wanted poster the Governor of New York was asking for his capture, not me."

"Yes, I remember that." She nodded. "What about your bounty on Parker?"

"I left ten thousand dollars with Governor Fenton's office before I started tracking Parker. If he had been captured alive, I would have traveled to where the authorities were holding him and confronted him. I'd have sent for the balance due to the person or people responsible for bringing him in."

Tansy looked at the crystal vases overflowing with flowers. "Tansies are only poisonous to..."

"Worms like Rance," Bolt finished for her.

Bolt swore to himself that Rance would rue the days he had kept Tansy a prisoner and marred her pretty back. When Tansy reached across the table, Bolt took her hand and gently squeezed. Her brows knitted in concern.

"Surely Dolly didn't get this poster at the newspaper office before Will could tear it down."

"No, Will wouldn't have let that happen," Bolt said. "Dolly said she owed me a favor for making sure Crazy Earl didn't kill any more of her girls and she owed both of us for getting Skinny out of her house. She got the poster from a would-be customer."

"Would-be?"

"Would-be because Dolly turned him away. Says she's trying to be more careful since her run-ins with Crazy Earl and Skinny. Anyhow, she took it from that Indian corpse maker, Arkansas Hank."

Tansy didn't move. She didn't even blink. Bolt was fairly certain she wasn't breathing. He gave her hand a gentle shake to make her stir.

"He knows!" Tansy yanked her hand from him and pressed her fingers to her temples. "Arkansas Hank will be coming for me!" she predicted, terror in her eyes.

"For God's sake, I'll handle it," Bolt said.

A knock on the door caused Tansy to jump and gasp.

"Just a minute!" Bolt barked and nodded to the bed. "You get under the covers, and I'll get the door." When Tansy was up to her neck in quilts, Bolt asked, "Who is it?"

"Mr. Wagner, the proprietor. I'm delivering your supper in person."

"Come in," Bolt said, a Colt .45 cocked and aimed, just in case.

Mr. Wagner quickly set two steak suppers on the marble top table between the chairs. Bolt thanked Mr. Wagner, who departed a shade paler than when he'd arrived.

"Let's eat." Bolt tossed back the quilts and scooped Tansy up in his arms. She seemed to weigh nothing yet meant everything to him. After seating Tansy in a chair, Bolt picked up the bottle of chilled wine, opened it, and after pouring a small amount of the crimson liquid into a glass, handed it to Tansy before filling his own glass. "I'm not sure you should drink since you're expecting, but I'd like you to have one small taste of my...*our* wine." Sitting across from her again, he held his glass toward hers and toasted, "To us, our baby, our family, and the Valley of the Moon."

Tansy took a sip. "It's just as delicious as I knew it would be," she said, her sunny smile melting Bolt's heart. Her hair had dried and was cascading in curls around the low-cut camisole which revealed the alluring swell of her breasts. Then she set her glass on the table and her lovely smile faded. "But if we go to Sonoma, Arkansas Hank will track us there."

"Dolly said she suspected you were the woman on the poster because she lived in Texas and recognized your accent. Arkansas Hank has no way of proving who you are. Besides, he hunts Indians."

"Yes, we had words about that."

"Gimpy told me you threw a glass at him."

"I missed." Tansy shrugged. "Arkansas Hank obviously comes from Arkansas and Texarkana is between Texas and Arkansas. He must have run across my poster down south along with a good description. He's found me and he expects to turn me in and collect the bounty!"

"I won't say your fears are completely unfounded. I'm just suggesting we deal with them calmly. Now, let's eat supper."

As they ate, Tansy had little to say. After they had finished, Tansy uncovered the brown betty in her pie tin. Bolt asked if she'd made it and she said baking it was the private business she'd had earlier. Then she fell silent once more.

"Ya know," Bolt grinned, shaking his fork at her, "the last time we had brown betty you got quiet like this. Are you thinking of your father again?"

"No, I'm thinking if Arkansas Hank drags me back to Texarkana, Rance will kill me and that means our baby will die."

"That Arkansas headhunter will never drag you anywhere. And I would send Rance straight to hell before I'd let him kill you and our child."

"Rance will kill you first."

"Blazes!" Bolt smacked a fist against the table, making the dishes rattle. "He's not going to kill us!"

"Papa said I wouldn't have to marry Rance and that everything would be all right. Then Papa was stabbed to death," Tansy said and placed her hand on his fist.

"Tansy." Bolt took her hand in his. "I'm sure your father was a fine man and meant what he said. But he was a doctor, not a marshal and a bounty hunter. The fact I'm alive today is because I've held my own against every gunman I've ever gone up against."

"Gimpy always says the baddest of the bad are afraid of Bolt Rivers."

"Then have some faith in me."

"But with that bounty on my head, it's only a matter

of time before posters will be everywhere. I'll be hanging in places with the likes of the James-Younger Gang!"

"No, you won't." Bolt forced a smile. "The only thing Rance can do is distribute his posters to sheriffs or bounty hunters willing to work outside the law to bring you to him."

"And if you remember, owning sheriffs is Rance's forte and a bounty hunter who works outside the law is Arkansas Hank."

Bolt knew that was too damn true. Arkansas Hank was lingering too far north for some reason.

"We happen to have a couple of friends in California now who are marshals. I'll let them know we're coming. Fort Laramie's on our way to Sonoma. I'll wire Rance, but send you on ahead of me with Will, Gimpy, and Lupe."

"No!" she gasped. "Promise me you'll forget about Fort Laramie."

"Settle down." Bolt got up, gently pulled Tansy out of her chair, and wrapped his arms around her. He whispered, "If you don't want me to wire Rance from Fort Laramie, I won't. But sooner or later, I'm going to deal with him because you're not living the rest of your life in fear."

"I want you to live the life of a vineyard owner and hang up your guns."

"I will and you'll be safe with me in a mansion surrounded by thousands of acres of land in the Valley of the Moon. Now how about I do my job of taking you to the ball?"

. . .

"I THINK everyone here has heard by now that Marshal Rivers ridded the Black Hills of three murdering outlaws in a matter of weeks," Mayor Farnum announced.

Bolton, flanked by Mayor Farnum and General Crook on one side and Sheriff Bullock and Marshal Stapleton on the other side, was standing on the board-walk in front of the Grand Central Hotel.

Tansy smiled up at Bolton, knowing he'd rather be anywhere but where he was at the moment. She stood between Will and Gimpy who had bought suits for this special occasion. Lupe was at Will's side wearing her birthday shawl and new shoes which went perfectly with the yellow evening dress Bolton had bought her when he'd purchased Tansy's gown.

An enthusiastic group of the Board of Health members, town officials, merchants, General Crook, and his troops were all attending the fancy ball. In addition, at least two thousand townsfolk, miners, prospectors, cowboys, and others had gathered in the street to be a part of the appreciation being shown to Marshal Rivers as well as General Crook and his men.

Mayor Farnum continued, "One of the outlaws Marshal Rivers stopped was a marauding murderer who'd been slaughtering people around the country for at least ten years. We estimate he killed another twenty-five folks in and around the Black Hills."

Tansy nervously scanned the crowd for Arkansas Hank. There were so many people everywhere she could easily be overlooking him. She'd told the head hunter that Bolton deserved a medal. How ironic that as Bolton was honored as the hero he was, she stood in fear of Arkansas Hank.

"Some folks say that Deadwood is dear, delightful, and dev'lish," the mayor continued. "Others say it's the wildest, the most flamboyant, and the wickedest mining town on the American frontier. What matters to the Board of Health and to me is that Deadwood is safer today, because of United States Marshal, Bolton Rivers."

As people clapped and cheered for Bolton, Tansy thought how he was a combination of these descriptions of Deadwood, dear, dev'lish, wild, and wickedly handsome. Perfect for the American frontier. Beautiful California, the last frontier.

Tonight, he was resplendent. With his black suit, black tie, and black boots, he wore a crisp white shirt and a dark green vest. His Stetson was pulled low, his hair tied back with a leather strip. The pearl handled Colt .45s, slung low on his waist, added danger to his dashing appearance. Tonight, for the first time, he wore his United States Marshal's badge pinned on his coat.

"Thank you, Marshal Rivers," the mayor said, as Bolton accepted an envelope.

The mayor, sheriff, and marshal shook his hand. Then General Crook congratulated him and shook his hand as well, while the crowd roared and clapped. Tansy wiped a tear of happiness from her cheek and clapped along with Lupe, as Will and Gimpy whooped and hollered.

Bolton stepped off the boardwalk and wrapped his arm around Tansy as the mayor moved aside for Sheriff Bullock.

"Folks, I just got a report someone spotted that one-eyed, killer bear at the outskirts of Deadwood this morning," Bullock said as people nodded, having seen, or at least heard of the bear. "Anyhow, looks like it's been bitten by something and is rabid now. So, if you see it, stay clear or shoot it."

Finally, Crook addressed the townsfolk, telling them about trying to catch up with Sitting Bull.

"Mizz Crown?" the mayor asked, coming up to her and Bolton after Crook's speech.

"What may I do for you, Mayor Farnum?" Tansy asked.

"It's what I can't do for you that troubles me," he said and splayed his hands. "I'm not a justice of the peace. I can't join you and Marshal Rivers in holy matrimony."

"Oh, I was afraid of that." Tansy sighed with regret.

"But he has some good news," Bolton said.

"Yes, I do," Mayor Farnum agreed. "There is a stage-coach that is supposed to be bringing a new preacher and his wife to Deadwood."

"But Deadwood doesn't have stage service," Tansy said, a little confused.

"We will as of Monday," the mayor replied. "The Cheyenne and Black Hills Stage, Mail and Express Line left Cheyenne a few days ago. By midday Monday, it will arrive in Deadwood."

"That's wonderful," Tansy said, thinking this was a sign of dreams coming true.

"Marshal Rivers told me this belongs to you." The mayor handed Tansy the envelope he'd given to Bolton during the presentation. "It's the five thousand dollar bounty on Hatchet Harless Parker the Board of Health presented to Marshal Rivers on behalf of the United States Government. The marshal here told me he'd have died from Hickok's bullet if not for you. He says you made it possible for Deadwood to be free of all three cold blooded killers."

"That she did." Bolton smiled at Tansy.

Stunned, Tansy looked at Bolton. "You never told me

there was an additional five thousand dollar bounty on Parker along with the reward you offered."

"You never asked." Bolton grinned down at her and winked.

Shaking her head in wonder at Bolton, Tansy said, "Thank you, Mayor Farnum."

"You're welcome and now I'd like you to meet General George Crook."

What she could see of his face through a bushy mustache, beard and sideburns was creased and weathered. His thin lips were made even thinner by his smile. Something disturbed her about this man that went deeper than her outrage at his treatment of the Lakota.

"Mizz Crown, it's a rare pleasure to meet someone as brave and beautiful as you are," General Crook said with a courteous tilt of his head.

"Thank you," Tansy replied as politely as possible.

"Please consider George Crook to be at your service. My troops will stay in the area for the next couple of months to rest and to protect Deadwood against the Sioux," the general added. "We diverted Crazy Horse and his people away from here. But Sitting Bull and his people could come through Dakota Territory. We've heard they're on the run to Canada."

"Canada?" The word resounded in Tansy's head. "Yes, running to Canada makes sense."

General Crook nodded his agreement and left with his troops. The mayor asked Bolton if, before the hotel ball, he would accompany them to Jack Langrishe's Theater. There, the marshal and the general would shake hands with the grateful townspeople.

Not one to seek out such attention, Bolton declined. Even so, people gathered around him on Main Street to express their appreciation or make his acquaintance.

Gimpy, Lupe, and Will were nearby, mingling with the throng in front of the Grand Central Hotel. From the badlands to the bathhouse, from the Bella Union where fine shows were performed to the Gem Theater notorious for its risqué acts, excitement filled the air.

"In case you're thinking about masquerading as a Lakota Indian and making a run to Canada with Sitting Bull," Bolton cocked his brow, "don't."

CHAPTER 36

"I CERTAINLY WON'T, MARSHAL RIVERS," TANSY SAID. "AS you once warned me, I would not want to deal with you when you caught me."

"Tansy, are you all right?"

"Yes, but meeting the general was unnerving."

"Because of the Indians?"

"Yes, in part." Tansy realized what had upset her. "General Crook looks very much like Rance."

"Bolt!" came a woman's husky voice. Swaying up the middle of the street was Dolly. "I ain't been invited to the ball!" she complained. "But I had to catch George to thank him for the business his troops'er bringin' me. In return, I been sendin' most of 'em to the Gem Saloon or the Cricket Saloon and a few to the Bella Union."

"To keep them out of trouble until the ball?" Bolton asked.

"That's exactly what the general asked me when I told him," Dolly said with a throaty laugh. Then she looked over at Tansy. "My, my," she sighed. "Them's gotta be the biggest emerald eardrops and matchin' emerald pendant I ever did see."

"They're Bolton's wedding gifts." Tansy touched the large emerald suspended on the yellow gold chain that brushed the crease of her cleavage. They had been part of his private business and Dolly didn't seem surprised to hear they were getting married. "He bought them to go with my emerald green dress."

"I'll bet he bought them to go with his fiancée's emerald green eyes." Dolly's shrewd gaze didn't miss the dark green vest Tansy had bought for Bolton. "You look beautiful as always, Jigger."

Tansy was taken aback. She also noted Dolly could have used her real name and hadn't.

"Why, Dolly, thank you." Tansy added sincerely, but softly, "I'm so grateful you gave Bolton that poster. I don't know how to thank you."

"You already have," Dolly said. "You was the only decent woman in all of Deadwood to ever talk nice to me."

With a quick glance over his shoulder, a man sidled up to Dolly and muttered frantically in her ear. All the while his eyes took in Tansy, lingering on the bodice of her gown. Bolton slipped an arm around Tansy's waist and pulled her closer.

"The neckline of your dress is lower than I expected and it's driving me crazy," Bolton whispered.

The scooped velvet décolletage showed more cleavage than Tansy had ever displayed on her own. The rest of the gown was demure with long velvet sleeves cuffing her wrists in green satin. Her still small waist was trimmed with a green satin bow and the velvet skirt puffed out over her new petticoats.

An instant later, an irate, red-faced woman grabbed

the man talking to Dolly, cursed the madam, and dragged the man down the street.

Unruffled, Dolly said to Tansy, "I'd take Bolt away from you in a heartbeat if I could. And don't think I ain't tried." Dolly smiled at Bolton. "He's the first man who ever turned me down and I was mad for a spell." She shrugged. "He wants a lady and I always knowed you was one, Jigger. Get away from this lonely ol' gulch and marry Bolt while he's in the mood."

"We're leaving soon," Bolton said.

"I won't ask where yer goin' cause I don't need to know and you wouldn't tell me nohow," Dolly said to Bolton then turned to Tansy. "Jigger, you make this handsome devil the happiest man on earth. Cause if you don't, there'll be no shortage of purdy, upstandin' women who will. Take care of him."

"I will," Tansy said and smiled up at Bolton.

"Bolt, yer probably the closest I'll ever have to a man friend. So, as yer friend, I'm tellin' you to treat Jigger right."

Will overheard and piped up. "Jigger's a huckleberry above a persimmon if ever there was one!"

"Oh, my gawd!" Dolly hooted. "Please tell me yer takin' Wilber Hector with you!"

"We are," Tansy said, laughing.

"Good!" Dolly replied with a sharp nod. She then leaned forward and pecked Bolton's cheek. "Goodbye, gorgeous." She opened her parasol, raised it above her head, and with a look of envy at Tansy, said, "Goodbye, Mrs. Rivers."

As Dolly strolled down Main Street, women shunned her, one going so far as to pucker her lips and spit. Dolly used her parasol to deflect the hate.

. . .

286 | LYNN ELDRIDGE

INSIDE THE GRAND CENTRAL HOTEL, as a string quartet began to play, women hinted at wanting to dance with Bolt, but he politely changed the subject. Perhaps due to his reputation, none of the men were bold enough to ask for a dance with Tansy. When Bolt whisked her onto the dance floor, a woman in the arms of the general, crooked her finger at him. Bolt closed his eyes as his refusal and breathed in Tansy's honeysuckle scent. The evening wore on and as he swept her into his embrace for a waltz, Tansy thanked him for taking her to the ball.

"You're welcome, angel," he whispered. "But I'm tired of all the men ogling you like you were a steak they'd like to devour."

"Like Dolly, they're just in awe of the beautiful emeralds you gave me."

Bolt held Tansy to his heart, not blaming the men. The other women present couldn't compare to Tansy. Tonight, her green eyes were luminous with a special sparkle and an innocent vulnerability touched her sunny smile. The velvet beneath his hands was soft and Tansy's body even softer. He wanted her all to himself. After their waltz, he pulled out his pocket watch and looked at the time.

"Let's go up to our room, Bolton."

Saying goodnight to Gimpy, Lupe, and Will then quietly left the grand affair.

"Tansy," Bolton said as he unlocked the door to their room. "Even though you were in my arms tonight, you were miles away." He tugged her into the room and after shutting the door, said, "Never will I forget you're an adventuress who knows how to disappear." Sweeping the sides of his coat back, he put his hands to his hips. "My gut's telling me that poster has you so scared you're still wanting to run."

"I promise you..." Tansy smiled up at him and unbuttoned his vest, "all I am wanting is for you to make love to me until I can't walk."

"I WOULDN'T WALK AWAY from this offer, Bolton," Tansy said on Monday as they sat at Bolt's corner table across from the highest bidder yet for the Crown Saloon.

"No, the offer's fifteen hundred dollars less than we're asking," Bolt replied.

"He drives a hard bargain," Tansy said to the potential buyer. When Bolt felt Tansy rub her foot along his leg, under the table, he knew she was flirting with him and winked at her.

"Look, I know this saloon does the most business in town these days. Awright, I'll pay your full price, Marshal Rivers," the man said.

"Sold," Bolt agreed. "Jigger, you're in charge of the money."

The buyer counted out the money and Bolt signed over the deed. One problem solved Bolt thought. As the men shook hands, Tansy seemed edgy and scooted back her chair.

"If you gentlemen will excuse me, I'm going upstairs," Tansy said politely and left the table.

Bolt walked the new owner out, saying the saloon would be his on Friday.

"The saloon's sold and the stage is due in today," Bolt said to Gimpy and Lupe when he came back. "I'll reserve the coach just for us, so we can head to California at dawn on Friday. The two of you and Jigger will ride in the coach. Will and I'll ride alongside and tie Angel behind Lightning."

"Hot diggety!" Gimpy exclaimed.

"I'll tell Will!" Lupe said excitedly.

Bolt took off upstairs and found Tansy staring out of the window, eating the last bunch of grapes.

Leaning against the closed door he asked, "What's upsetting your applecart? Carrying the baby, selling the saloon, or leaving Deadwood?"

With a word from Bolt, Bullock and Stapleton had run Arkansas Hank out of town. Another problem solved. Tansy turned to him with a smile that wasn't sunny enough to reach her eyes.

"I need to stop worrying about the past and future. In the moment is where one has some control," she said. "Tell me about your vineyard."

Tansy walked across the room and held out her hand. Bolt took it, sat down in the rocking chair, and pulled her onto his lap. She popped the last grape in her mouth and grinned.

"The first time I saw it was years ago when tracking Parker led me west," he said, gently rocking. "I rode over a rise and before me lay a majestic valley covered in grapevines. Realizing I was trespassing I skirted around the vineyard and when I reached the opposite hill I stared across at the largest, most impressive mansion I'd ever seen. The green valley looked like ripples in a flying carpet and above the tile roof gleamed a full moon."

"Your wine label," Tansy whispered.

"Exactly," he said and patted her hip. "I hadn't felt such peace in a long time."

"How did you know it was for sale?"

"I didn't. But I rode up a wide, circular carriage path and decided to ask. I lifted a large brass door knocker on one of the double doors and an elderly lady answered the door. Turned out she was looking to sell the house and property because her husband had just died. I offered her a fair price and I owned a house and vine-yard." Bolt hugged Tansy closer. "I want you to turn that mansion into our home."

"Turns out," Tansy's sunny smile was back, and she kissed his cheek, "I recently collected a bounty here in the Black Hill that was more money than I expected to have in a lifetime. I'll start by decorating our baby's nursery. The first thing I'll put in that room will be the tansies my mother painted for me."

"You asked me once if I could have any bounty in the Black Hills what it would be," Bolt said. "It's you. Tantalizing Tansy is my Black Hills bounty," he said softly. "You keep your money for your clinic, and I'll give you whatever you need to decorate our home."

"Does our property have a name?"

"The lady I bought it from was French and said the house was known as Le Chateau. She told me chateau means castle."

"Le Chateau Rivers."

"I like that."

Bolt smiled and kissed her. He tasted a happy tear that ran down her cheek to their lips. When he looked into her emerald eyes, he saw the love and trust he had hoped would be there by the time he had dealt with Parker and was free to leave.

"You'll be king of the Valley of the Moon, Bolton."

"And you'll be my queen."

"Your baby and I love you so much."

"Let's go see history made as the first stage rolls into town. If the preacher doesn't look too tired, we'll ask him about marrying us."

· · ·

A SHORT TIME LATER, Tansy, Bolton, Will, and Lupe along with hundreds of enthusiastic locals, welcomed the stagecoach. Six huge, snorting, lathered horses pulled The Cheyenne and Black Hills Stage, Mail and Express Line coach to a stop near Red Clark's Livery.

"I'm David Dicky!" the stagecoach driver announced, waving his cowboy hat in hello as the townsfolk cheered. When the man riding shotgun, jumped to the ground and opened the stagecoach door, Mr. Dicky said, "And here are your first arrivers!"

"There's the preacher!" Tansy said and pointed to a man with a white collar and Bible. The preacher then helped his wife out of the stage. Tansy squeezed Bolton's hand with both of hers. "See?"

"Yes." Bolton looked down at her and chuckled.

The next passenger struck terror in Tansy's heart.

CHAPTER 37

"WILL, TAKE JIGGER AND GO STRAIGHT TO THE NEWSPAPER office," Bolton ordered, before Tansy could say a word and steered her into Will's hands. "Lock the door and don't let her out of your sight."

"Bolton?" Tansy gasped. "How did you—"

In his deep blue eyes was the steely glint of the infamous and notorious bounty hunter. In the clenching of a chiseled jaw and tension in his powerful body, the respected United States Marshal prepared for war.

"Lupe do not run but go tell Gimpy that Rance is here," Bolton said. When she only stared, he clasped her shoulder and turned her toward the saloon. "Close the saloon and tell Gimpy to load the shotgun I put in his room. Will, remember what I said when I gave you your shotgun, just aim the barrel in his direction and pull the trigger."

"Yes, sir!" Will said as Bolton and Lupe took off in two different directions.

"What shotguns?" Tansy asked Will who didn't answer but tugged her forward. Her only relief was seeing Bolton heading away from the stagecoach instead of toward it.

"Don't let Rance see your face!" Will barked, sounding a lot like Bolton. Tansy turned away from the stage and tried to speed up, but Will held her at a steady pace. "Never draw attention when you don't want to be seen."

"Did Bolton teach you that?" Tansy asked and Will nodded. "Will, we have to help him!"

"We are," Will replied, heading straight for the office of the Black Hills Weekly Pioneer.

"Why is he sending us to the newspaper office?"

"Because Rance won't know to look for you there."

Out on the street they blended in with the townsfolk, still in a flutter over the first stage into the gulch, like the tansies had blended in with the other colorful flowers. From the opposite side of Main Street, as they neared the Crown Saloon, Lupe suddenly hopped away from the crowd to the boardwalk.

"That's my *novia*," Will said, as Lupe grabbed the saloon doors and closed them.

"CLOSE THE BACK DOOR, RED," Bolt said to the livery owner. He loosened a board in Lightning's stall and took out the new rifle he'd bought from the McAusland Brothers. The rifle he'd used to kill Parker was at the saloon. Not taking any chances, he'd bought this second rifle and the two shotguns for just such a confrontation involving Rance.

"Who're you after, Bolt?" Red asked.

Bolt stood, patted Lightning's flank, and replied, "The man who looked enough like General Crook to be his brother, the Mexican missing his index finger and the man wearing a badge."

Red nodded. "That's what I reckoned."

"Stapleton was in the crowd when the stage arrived. I already caught up with him and he'll notify Bullock that there are three Texans in town looking for Jigger."

"Do you think they'll come here? They don't have horses for me to keep."

"Yeah." Loading the Winchester rifle, Bolt said, "They'll try to get information out of folks, like you, who know all the regulars in town."

"I understand."

"Bolt?" Seth Bullock called from outside.

Bolt answered, "In here, Sheriff."

Bullock pulled the door open and closed it behind him. "Last Stapleton saw, the killer missing a finger is looking for her in the badlands. Rance is checked in at the IXL Hotel and the so-called sheriff is up here on north Main Street circulating a portrait of Jigger and some man."

"That man in the portrait is her father, Dr. Wiley," Bolt said, knowing now why Tansy couldn't find the portrait when she'd fled Texarkana.

"Stapleton wants to run them outa town, Bolt. Hell, General Crook would be only too happy to have his troops get 'em outa the gulch," Bullock said.

"That would be temporary," Bolt replied. "I want Rance stopped permanently."

"I'll have Crook post men twenty-four hours a day at the front and back doors of the hotel for your protection," Bullock said.

Bolt held up his hand for silence.

"I don't hear anything," Bullock whispered, moving to Bolt's left side.

"The latch on the back door moved," Bolt explained quietly.

Rance's sheriff threw open the back door and there, brawny, and compact stood a man with a small forehead and flat face. His brow protruded over black eyes that darted like an animal's. His shoulders were stooped, and hairy hands hung long at his sides. The word ape sprang to Bolt's mind.

"Bullock!" the monkey-man blared. "I ain't found nobody in this gulch who's got the guts to identify Tansy Wiley as Jigger Crown. But that's the alias Arkansas Hank swore she's usin'."

"Arkansas Hank was run outa town," Bullock replied.

"My party and me come a long way to get this gal. Are ya'll gonna help Señor Sanchez and me flush her out in the open'er ain't ya?"

"I'm goin' home," Red Clark said, heading for the back door.

"Wait! I'm Sheriff Mullins. Take a look at this here portrait." He held it out for Red. "Tell Sheriff Bullock who she is."

"Whoever she is, she's too pretty to be here in Deadwood." With that, Clark exited the livery.

"Let me take a look," Bolt said.

He was handed the photograph of beautiful Tansy. Her father, a dignified looking gentleman, sat in a chair, Tansy standing beside him with her hand on his shoulder. Bolt flipped the photograph over and on the back in Tansy's feminine hand, was written; *Papa and me ~ 1874.*

"Seen her?" Mullins demanded.

"If Arkansas Hank found her, why'd you come all the way to Deadwood for her?" Bolt asked. "Why didn't you let him haul her to you?"

"On accounta my boss, Mr. Rance—"

"Since when does a sheriff, who's elected by the people, have a boss?" Bolt asked.

"That ain't none o' yer business!" Mullins sneered. "Mr. Lewis Rance of Texarkana ain't fixin' to let this bitch slip through his fingers, so he come after her hisself."

It took all of Bolt's willpower, not to shoot this ugly ape on the spot. Looking at Tansy's likeness, he said, "She *is* pretty. Mind if I keep this?"

"I sure as shit do!" Mullins said, eyes darting. "Give it back!"

"Nah." Bolt slipped the portrait into his coat pocket. "I'm keeping her."

"I represent the law in Texarkana and—" Mullins shouted.

"And you're out of your territory," Con Stapleton said, coming up on Bolt's right. "Maybe you should start claiming you're a United States Marshal."

Mullins' expression puckered into a gorilla-faced frown as he realized all three men facing him down wore badges. "All I know is Mr. Rance wants Tansy back real bad!"

"Why do you care what Rance wants?" Bolt asked. "Aren't you supposed to have a town to protect somewhere?"

"I care on accounta Whip says I can umm—" Mullins wiped drool off his lips with the back of his hand. "Uh, that I can umm..."

"Have her if you help him find her?" Bolt said, clenching his jaw.

"She poisoned his wife!" Mullins said. "If Arkansas Hank's done been run off, then when I find Tansy Wiley, I'll collect her bounty."

"You'll die first," Bolt said firmly.

Mullins glowered at Bolt. "You heard him threaten me, Marshal Stapleton!"

"Warned, not threatened," Stapleton replied.

"If ya'll know where she is, I want Tansy Wiley put into my custody!" Mullins said.

"No." Bolt raised the rifle and leveled it at his side, pointing the barrel of the gun at Mullins' crotch. "Tansy Wiley is my Black Hills bounty."

"I seem to recollect we're waiting on Colorado Charlie's pony express telegram from the Texas authorities. Isn't that correct?" Stapleton asked.

"Yeah," Bolt said. "They'll tell us if the United States wants Tansy Wiley for murder. If not, then it's Rance who wants her."

"We'll know on Wednesday," Bullock said to Bolt, then turned to Mullins. "Speaking of Colorado Charlie Utter, did you know he came to Deadwood with Wild Bill Hickok?"

Frowning, Mullins didn't answer, obviously unsure what that had to do with Tansy.

"This man," Bullock jerked a thumb at Bolt, "strolled into the Number Ten Saloon and came within a few feet of Wild Bill. Then Hickok took a bullet to the back of his skull that exited his cheek."

Mullins eyed Bolt warily as if interpreting that to mean he'd murdered Hickok and been allowed to get away with it. Bolt knew Bullock was further intimidating Mullins by suggesting they were crooked like he and Rance.

"We heard Hickok was dead, but we didn't hear no details," Mullins mumbled, taking a step back. "Why didn't ya'll arrest him?"

"Isaac Brown was the sheriff then, but somebody killed him, too," Bullock said and shrugged.

"We're the law now," Stapleton said in a gruff voice. "Some people leave Deadwood alive, and some don't."

Mullins grimaced and turned to Bolt. "If you got Tansy Wiley, just give her to me and I'll getcha yer five thousand dollars, sir."

"Yeah, I'll do that," Bolt began, his grin glacial, "when hell freezes over. In the meantime, I'll wait for Charlie Utter to bring me the telegram from Fort Laramie clearing Tansy Wiley."

"I GAVE Will and Gimpy shotguns instead of rifles because they won't need precise aim. The shot will spread out and hit its mark," Bolt said to Tansy after she'd asked about the guns.

"Will kept his shotgun pointed at the door and made me sit in a dark corner," Tansy said as they sat in front of the snapping fire in their room at the Grand Central Hotel. "He wouldn't even let me look out the window."

"I'm impressed he accomplished that without my handcuffs," Bolton said, shaking his head.

"When I begged Will to help me find the sheriff and the marshal, he threatened to tie me up!"

Bolton laughed heartily. "Will is a huckleberry above a persimmon."

"Bolton, we've been locked up in this room for twenty-four hours," Tansy pouted flirtingly, clad only in a satin and lace petticoat as she sat across the marble top table from him.

Bolton shuffled a deck of cards. "Rance knows I sent the telegram to Texas and it's scaring the hell out of him. He'll make a fatal mistake before we can get the telegram clearing you tomorrow."

"I don't want to miss the stage on Friday," Tansy said.

"We won't," Bolton said looking across the table at her.

"I'm glad Gimpy, Lupe and Will are in the hotel now," Tansy replied and shivered. "Bolton, if you weren't here in Deadwood as the marshal and bounty hunter everybody knows you to be, Rance would have already killed our friends and I'd be at his mercy for as long as he let me live." She got up, stepped out of her petticoat, and straddled Bolton's lap.

"I tend to lose my self-control when you sit on me." Bolton laid the cards aside and locked his fingers behind his head. "So, get off."

"I just lost another hand of strip poker and my petticoat." Clad in her camisole and with only her drawers and his pants between them she pressed against the bulge between his legs. "Let's make love."

"Hell." Bolton groaned and closed his eyes. "I've lost my shirt and vest trying to keep your clothes on you, but you can't bluff worth a damn. I know when you're playing a bad hand."

Tansy felt him hardening beneath her. She unbuttoned her camisole and pressed her nakedness to his bare chest. "I have on the drawers that you slit open with your knife. So, you could just—"

Bolton slid his hands under her arms and lifted her off his lap. He stood and towering over her raked his fingers through his long hair. His eyes straying to her breasts, he pulled a rawhide strip out of his pocket and tied his hair back.

"Please put your dress on, so I don't get caught with my pants down when Rance comes knocking."

"Blazes!" Tansy said and flounced saucily to the bed. There she grabbed her dress, stuck her tongue out, and then licked her lips invitingly.

"Later, bad girl," he promised with a cocky grin. He didn't bother with his shirt but put on his black leather vest. "Supper should be here soon."

Tansy reluctantly donned her dress, went over to the fireplace, and from the mantel, she picked up the portrait she thought never to see again. Next to it was the feather the Lakota healer had stuck in Bolton's hair. She looked at her father's likeness and then smiled at Bolton. Like a magnet, Bolton drew her. Reaching him, Tansy slipped the end of the feather under the rawhide strip, letting the feather fall down his back along with his hair. Bolton had told her while playing cards that during their meeting with the Lakota Indians in the forest, he had remembered he had Indian blood.

"The wapiya sensed your Indian blood and that's why he called you brother," Tansy said.

"Yeah." Bolton nodded in agreement as a knock sounded on the door.

"Supper," Tansy recalled Bolton telling her to always ask who was at the door before she opened it. Winking at him, she said, "Who's—"

"Bolt!" came a voice followed by a muffled yelp.

With cat-like grace, Bolton grabbed Tansy and his gun belt. He slid to the left of the door and pressed Tansy safely behind him.

"Come on in, Will," Bolt said calmly.

CHAPTER 38

"DROP THE GUN, RIVERS!" SANCHEZ SHOUTED, BURSTING through the door to face a Colt .45. Greasy hair stringing from under his sombrero, Sanchez held a knife at Will's throat. Sanchez's grimy chipped teeth showed as he sneered, "Or this kid'll get my knife."

"Will!" Tansy cried. In addition to a cut on his lip, it appeared Will was going to have a black eye. He'd put up a good fight.

Blocking Tansy and training his gun on Sanchez, Bolton asked Will, "Who do they have?"

"Both Lupe and Gimpy," Will mumbled, sounding dazed. "The so-called sheriff said he was taking 'em to the saloon through—"

At that, Sanchez backhanded Will across the face.

"Will," was all Bolton said sternly and lifted his chin a notch.

Will's eyes narrowed, as he squared his shoulders and spat out a mouthful of blood onto Sanchez's boot before finishing his sentence. "The hotel's back door where they took out Crook's men."

"You give me Tansy and I'll let 'im go Rivers," Sanchez said.

"Hell no." Bolton's snarl was deep and spine chilling. "You release Will and I'll go with you to see Rance."

"Gringo bounty hunter can only shoot his gun, can't handle a knife?"

Bolton pulled the knife out of the sheath strapped to his muscular thigh and holstered his gun. Tansy's eyes flicked to the bed as she remembered how Bolton had casually flipped his Bowie knife at the narrow bedpost leaving a deep notch in it.

"Can't handle your knife without a human shield?" Bolton taunted, motioning with both hands for Sanchez to come at him.

Sanchez pushed Will away and he went straight to Tansy's side. As Bolton squared off with Sanchez, Tansy recognized the Mexican's knife was the Missouri toothpick used to kill her father.

"No!" Tansy cried and tried to take a step, but Will moved in front of her.

Sanchez lunged forward and slashed at Bolton's abdomen. Bolton deftly side-stepped him and laid open Sanchez's cheek to the bone. Sanchez screamed, smearing the blood over his face.

"Yer dead, gringo!" Sanchez shouted.

Sanchez slashed at Bolton again and missed, stumbling forward as Bolton sliced a deep gash across his jugular vein. Sanchez dropped his knife and grabbed his bleeding neck. He staggered backward and reached behind his back.

"He's going for a gun!" Will yelled.

With deadly aim, Bolton flipped his knife. Hitting between the ribs, it sunk into Sanchez's chest. Sanchez grunted and wrapped his hand, missing the index finger, around the knife handle and for a moment stared at Bolton in shock. A second later the killer fell. Dead before he hit the floor.

Tansy flung herself at Bolton and hugged him. "Are you all right?"

"Yes," he replied, wrapping an arm around her.

"This is my fault, Bolt," Will said, the awe and hero worship clear in his brown eyes as he swiped at his bloodied face. "I was visiting Lupe and let my guard down."

"You lived to learn from it." Bolton put a hand on Will's shoulder. "That makes you stronger. Did they get your shotguns?"

"No, sir." Will smiled then. "Like you said, we kept them handy but out of sight."

"I feel dizzy," Tansy said.

"Tansy, sit down and rest." Bolton walked her to the chair. "Will, find Bullock and Stapleton. I'll drag Sanchez out of here."

When Bolton and Will were gone, Tansy finally ran.

SLIVERS OF LIGHT streamed around the edges of the drawn shade in the front window of the Crown Saloon. Of the two heavy doors made to close over the swinging doors, one was shut completely and the other was slightly ajar.

Sitting at a table in the middle of the empty saloon were Lupe, Mullins, and Lewis Whip Rance. Gimpy sat tied up at the bottom of the staircase. Rance was guzzling red-eye. Mullins held Lupe prisoner on his lap as he squeezed her breast. She slapped at him, Rance threw his head back and howled with laughter.

"Here I am," Tansy said as she pushed the door open.

Swinging his head toward her, the grin faded on Rance's face. He snapped his fingers at Mullins, shoved his chair away from the table, and stood up at Mullins' side.

Tansy slowly walked toward them, biting the insides of her cheeks. *Be calm.* Bolton would be calm and in control.

Lewis Rance was a hyena about to get the laugh kicked out of him. From under bushy brows, Rance's close-set eyes glinted. As he peered down his nose at her she could sense his evil nature rearing its vicious head. This was a brutal, merciless murderer. The sideburns and beard made him appear older than his age, but she wasn't fooled. There was strength in his wiry body. Under his gray cowboy hat and inside his head lurked a snake.

Taking her stand, Tansy stopped just out of Rance's striking distance.

"Well...hello, Tansy," drawled Rance, sweet as molasses as he lay his hand to the bullwhip coiled like a rattler on his gun belt. "It's mighty hospitable of ya'll to come callin'."

"I'm not going back to Texarkana with you, Lewis," Tansy said coolly.

"Where's Rivers and Sanchez?" Mullins demanded.

"At the hotel with the young man you had beaten," Tansy replied.

"Is Will dead?" Lupe cried, struggling against Mullins.

"Smarter and stronger than ever, Lupe," Tansy said.

Rance glanced at Lupe. "I think you should take the little Mexican dove back to Texarkana with us, Mullins," Rance said. "I'll bet this soiled senorita has pleasured every miner in this gulch."

"You're not taking Lupe anywhere," Tansy said in a steady voice.

Rance rounded a table and walked toward her, but Tansy stood her ground. Rance clamped both his hands to her arms and with his fingers digging into her flesh he stuck his face close to hers.

"Saloon gals are soiled doves. Are you soiled now, Tansy?" Rance asked. Twitches contorted Rance's face. She'd forgotten that hideous trait, but how quickly she remembered it. "Answer me, damn you!" Rance demanded, ripping her right sleeve.

"Get your hands off me," Tansy ordered, clenching her fists, and staring Rance down. He let go, making a dramatic show of releasing her as he backed up a couple of feet. Thanks to Bolton's explanation about Rance's impotency, Tansy confronted him with confidence and a clear conscience. "The question is not if I'm soiled, but if you could enjoy my charms."

"Want me to find out if she's soiled?" Mullins said, shoving Lupe to one knee as he rubbed the heel of his hand over a lump in the front of his pants.

"Shut up, Mullins!" Rance blared.

"We traveled all this way to get her, you ain't gonna change your mind about it now, are ya, Whip?" Mullins asked.

"I'll tell you when," Rance replied. "I asked if you were a soiled dove, Tansy."

"Well, Whip," Tansy drawled as she called him Whip for the first time. "I'm not a dove."

Rance's twitches noticeably intensified. "But you're soiled?"

"Mullins will have to let Lupe go before I answer any more questions," Tansy said.

"Do it, Mullins! I want her to answer me," Rance said.

At the rage in Rance's eyes, Mullins let Lupe go. She started for Tansy, But Tansy nodded for her to see about Gimpy. Standing alone, Tansy faced the Texans. Bolton had taught her that unleashing her temper was one thing. Losing it was not an option. She squared her shoulders and lifted her chin, holding her head high.

"Somebody put starch in your spine, Tansy," Rance said, sensing a game change. He clutched the handle of the bullwhip and gnashed his teeth. "Who?"

"I'd say that bounty hunter marshal put it in her," Mullins said.

"Your dress is buttoned up wrong and you're bare-foot," Rance said, scowling at Tansy. "Were you in bed with Rivers when Sanchez arrived at the hotel?"

"Not when Sanchez arrived," Tansy replied with an ice cold smile.

"Shouldn't Sanchez be here by now, Whip?" Mullins asked, coming over to Rance.

"Your hired killer, who stabbed my father to death, is dead," Tansy said.

"How the hell did Sanchez wind up on the little end of the horn with Rivers?" Rance asked, glowering at Mullins as they stood in the middle of the saloon.

"You ain't seen how damn big 'n mean that sono-fabitch Rivers is," Mullins replied.

"Leave town now before you see for yourself," Tansy said, hoping to get rid of her enemy so that Bolton wouldn't have to deal with him.

Instead of leaving, Rance grabbed Tansy's wrist and removed the bullwhip from his gun belt.

"Of all the men you coulda met, I don't know why the hell it had to be him, you scheming, lying little slut!" Rance shouted as he shook the coiled bullwhip loose.

"Do not strike her," a menacing growl warned.

Rance snaked the bullwhip around Tansy's arms and waist.

Just coming up beside the bar, strode a warrior ready for battle. Long hair tied back, the tip of the Lakota feather touching his shoulder. His open black vest bared his muscular chest. A gun belt rode low on his hips and the still bloody Bowie knife showed in the scabbard tied to his thigh. Draped over his left shoulder hung a Winchester rifle and a belt loaded with cartridges. He stared down the barrel of his Colt .45 trained on Lewis Whip Rance.

"Rivers," Rance said, with none of the contempt he'd just used on Tansy.

Finding Tansy gone, Bolt realized she could bluff and was playing out a bad hand. He knew that just as he couldn't be swayed from catching Parker, she was determined to protect him from Rance. To that end, the brave adventuress had run toward Rance instead of from him. Out of the corner of his eye, Bolt noticed Lupe had managed to untie Gimpy. But to their credit, they weren't giving that away.

"Let her go," Bolt said.

CHAPTER 39

"WE'VE HEARD OF YOU DOWN SOUTH," RANCE SAID, holding Tansy prisoner with the bullwhip. "Hell, no wonder you're feared far and wide. You're a damn savage!"

"A quarter Mohawk," Bolt said. With his Indian blood exposed, the fear Rance spoke of mingled with hatred across the Texan's face.

"Rivers ain't no Injun name."

Striding within a dozen feet of Tansy and Rance, Bolt said, "Hiawatha, which is Ojibwa for He Makes Rivers, is an ancestor. Mohawk Indians love danger. Probably scalp you for the sheer hell of it."

"Can I shoot him, Whip?" Mullins asked, wiping sweat off his brow.

"He'd blow your damn head off before you could draw your gun," Rance replied and looked at Bolt. "You're stupid for wanting Tansy Wiley," he said. "She's as poisonous as her name implies."

"Then why are you so obsessed with her?" Bolt asked, keeping his gun on Rance.

"None of your friggin' business, Rivers," Rance said.

"Could it be she embarrassed you when she left Texarkana? People are saying you weren't man enough to make a young woman happy."

"Shut up, Rivers!" Rance sputtered, turning red.

"The only way to keep face is to drag her back and say she returned on her own," Bolt shot back.

"I'm gonna marry her and in nine months she'll give birth to my child," Rance said.

"That won't happen."

"Sure it will."

"How?" Bolt asked and when Rance's eyes darted to Mullins, Bolt knew what was going on. "You must be a very desperate man to have Mullins father a child you'd pass off as yours."

Tansy struggled against the bullwhip around her stomach. "Bolton, I'm going to tell—"

"No." Bolt wasn't sure what Rance would do if he knew Tansy was pregnant. Earlier, Bolt had taken the pins out of her hair, and it cascaded in curls down her back now. Lamplight reflected in her glistening emerald eyes, and he saw the heightened pink in her pretty cheeks. Bolt also detected the tremble beneath her torn dress and saw the angry red handprints on both of her arms.

"Tell me what?" Rance demanded.

Protectiveness raced through Bolt's veins with possessiveness on its heels. Tansy was beautiful, pregnant and as Rance was about to find out; all his.

"Why Tansy?" Bolt asked instead of answering. "She can't be the only pretty filly in Texarkana."

"Look at her!" Rance's features convulsed into disbelief. "She isn't just a pretty filly, she's the prettiest! Heads turn when she walks by, and I want her walking with me. She claims she's a healer. She's going home with me and prove it."

"She healed me," Bolt said casually.

Rance's glance dipped to Bolt's crotch.

"A bullet wound in my foot," Bolt said. "But we know where your problem is."

Rance's face turned redder, spittle coating the corners of his mouth. At that moment, Tansy worked her hand into her dress pocket. Bolt figured she had her derringer with her.

Mullins squinted at Bolt. "He's got that Colt .45 in his left hand, Whip. Ya think Sanchez hurt his right hand? I can't recollect which hand he held the rifle with yesterd'y, but it'll make a difference on how fast he is."

"You sound like an old woman, Mullins." Bolt's laugh was harsh.

Humiliated, Mullins pulled his gun at the same time Tansy yanked out her derringer. Evidently convinced he could outshoot Bolt; Mullins raised the gun in his direction. Tansy squeezed the trigger.

Lupe screamed as Mullins took a .22 caliber bullet in his right thigh. He staggered sideways hollering in pain as Rance knocked the derringer out of Tansy's hand.

Mullins managed to shoot, but not as fast as Bolt. Mullins took a .45 caliber bullet in the middle of his forehead before the bullet meant for Bolt buried itself in the floor. Mullins slammed into the wall and slid down dead.

"Two down. One to go," Bolt said evenly.

"This isn't your fight, Rivers!" Rance hollered and pulled his gun. "See that tin on the table? In it's your bounty. Take it and leave."

"Lupe, go get the tin," Bolt said.

"*Sí, jefe.*" Lupe ran and picked up the tin.

"What's in it?" Bolt asked.

"Mucho silver dollars."

"Smellin' money now, you're coming to your senses, huh Rivers?" Rance said.

"Lupe, the silver is yours. Go find Will," Bolt ordered.

"That was five hundred dollars!" Rance screamed as Lupe escaped through the front door.

"Supposed to be five thousand," Bolt said. "Five hundred is chicken feed."

"That's more money than you'll see in your life!" Rance replied.

"Stop hiding behind a woman and face me like a man, Rance."

"I'm twice the man you think you are, Rivers," Rance said, still behind Tansy.

"I think the Texas toad has a limp rope in his pants," Tansy said boldly, "I prefer your battle gun, Marshal Rivers."

Flaming scarlet crawled up Rance's leathery neck, past his beard to his eye sockets. A twitch at his left eye nearly shut it. With the bullwhip still around Tansy's waist, Rance drew his gun. Jamming the barrel of the gun in Tansy's ribs was the only thing keeping Bolt from putting a bullet through Rance's head. With his back to Gimpy, Rance stared at Tansy with obsession and madness.

"You whore." Rance's voice oozed with venom.

Gimpy silently came up behind Rance and knocked the gun out of his hand. In trying to recover the weapon, which Gimpy then kicked away, Rance lost his grip on Tansy. Gimpy had fulfilled his vow to get even with Rance.

"Tansy," Bolt said.

Instantly, Tansy ran straight to him. Never taking the

Colt.45 off Rance, Bolt hugged Tansy to his side. Together, they faced Lewis Rance in a long awaited showdown.

"You're gonna pay for whipping her, Rance."

Running the whip through his hands, Rance glared at Tansy as though he didn't know what Bolt was talking about. "I never whipped her."

"I've seen the mark."

"After my wife died," Rance looked from Tansy to Bolt, "I proposed to her, that's all."

"You'd marry a woman who supposedly poisoned your wife?" Bolt asked,

"Yes!" There was a maniacal glint in Rance's eyes. "It's common knowledge in Texarkana that Tansy wouldn't let any man touch her and they all wanted her. I want 'em to think I got to her first."

"Bolton was my first and only!"

"I don't want to hear how far you spread your legs for him! I poisoned my wife to be with you!" Rance shouted. "When your father suspected it, I had him killed! You owe me!"

"I despise you for killing my father and Mrs. Rance!" Tansy said.

"Tansy, let's go back to Texarkana." Rance twitched and fingered the whip.

"When hell freezes over!" she spat, with a glance at Bolt.

"I'll forgive you for crawling into Rivers' bed and you can forget about him," Rance bargained.

"I took Bolton to *my* bed!" Tansy informed him hotly. "I'd never forget about Bolton, and you'd be reminded of him daily when I give birth to his baby next spring."

"His baby?" Rance said incredulously and stared at

them. "You're gonna die tonight and the best part of killing you is killing Rivers' kid!"

"You're insane," Bolt said.

"You wanna fight a crazy man, Rivers?" Rance laughed maniacally, dropping his gun belt on the floor. He held the whip in one hand and ran it through the other. "Without guns?"

Bolt holstered his Colt .45, laid his gun belt on the bar, and placed the Winchester rifle next to his pistols. Rance grinned until Bolt pulled the bloody Bowie knife from the sheath tied to his thigh.

"I can slap that knife outa your hand with my eyes closed, Rivers."

"Do it."

Tansy was yanked behind Bolton's back a second before the explosion tore through the air. But Bolton's guns lay on the bar, and no one fell. From behind him, Tansy saw the bloody stripe across Bolton's right upper arm. The noise had been the crack of Rance's bullwhip. Like a snake, Rance's insanity had uncoiled its forked tongue, lashing out across Bolton's naked arm, shoulder, and partially bared chest. Tansy let out a bloodcurdling scream, knowing firsthand how wickedly that hurt. Baring her teeth, she curled her fingers into talons and charged Rance.

"Tansy!" Bolton roared as Rance reared the whip into the air. "Get outa the way!"

Tansy veered toward the stairs and met up with Gimpy who wrapped his arms around her.

As Rance brought his arm forward again Bolton caught the bullwhip, wound it around his right hand, and jerked it so hard, Rance stumbled forward. When Bolton yanked the whip a second time Rance lost his grip on it and reached toward the floor for his gun belt.

When the sound of the whip exploded in the air this time it bit into Rance's hand. He shook off the whip and fumbled with the gun belt. Bolt raised his arm again and laid the whip across Rance's face. Rance shrieked.

"Once for Tansy, once for me," Bolton said.

"Damn her and damn you to hell, Rivers!" Rance freed the gun from the belt and stood.

"Shut up," Bolton said an instant before his knife found a home in Rance's throat, causing him to drop the gun.

Choking, spitting blood, and grasping at the knife, Rance stumbled and fell not far from Mullins' body. Tansy rushed to Bolton's side. As Rance glowered up at them, Bolton jerked his knife out of Rance's throat. He wiped the blade clean on Rance's shirt and that was the last thing Rance saw before his eyes glazed and his head rolled to the side. Bolton dropped the bullwhip on Rance's chest.

"Mr. Beasley would say that's as dead as dead gets," Tansy said softly. Her eyes misted as she looked at the whip mark dripping blood on Bolton's chest, shoulder, and arm. "It's over, Bolton."

"Another problem solved."

Stapleton pushed through the swinging doors as Gimpy joined them in the middle of the saloon.

"The Texas marshals will be obliged to you for saving them the trouble of hauling Rance back for trial," Stapleton said.

"Bolt!" Will shouted from outside. "Watch out in there!"

Above the swinging doors appeared the fat, square head of Arkansas Hank. Tansy had seen him like this once before and couldn't believe she was faced with him again. She now knew his evil secret was alerting Rance to her whereabouts.

"I thought we ran your sorry ass outa town!" Stapleton barked.

"Ya sure done did that. But I got myself back to the gulch. Then Rance double-crossed me, the Mexican knifed me, and they left me fer dead." Arkansas Hank grabbed the top of the swinging door to steady himself and blood from the wound dripped off his hand. He looked at the marshal and pointed a bloody finger at Tansy. "Now I got me a hankerin 'fer the five thousand dollar bounty on her!"

"The killer bear's behind him!" Will yelled.

The head that raised alongside Arkansas Hank's was not mounted on a stick this time. It was mounted on a seven foot tall black bear, foaming at the mouth.

Tansy screamed in horror.

"I ain't fallin' fer that ol' trick," Arkansas Hank said.

Bolt's guns were on the bar, but his gut said Will had his shotgun. He grabbed Tansy and whisked her toward the staircase. Gimpy took off after them. Stapleton fired off a shot at the bear which missed before following Gimpy.

The rabid bear opened its mouth and closed it on the back of Arkansas Hank's neck. The head hunter's eyes bulged in disbelief. Paralyzed physically, mentally, or both, Arkansas Hank put up no struggle. The bear swung his massive head, lifting the killer off the ground.

"Will!" Bolt yelled. "Shoot!"

Will fired and the bear roared. The animal dropped Arkansas Hank on his back and fell to all fours on top of him. Knocking open the saloon's swinging doors the sick bear was wounded but not dead. The headhunter appeared to watch as the bear's vice-like jaws opened, baring razor sharp teeth which sunk into his throat and neck several quick bone crunching, skin severing times.

Will fired the shotgun a second time.

The bear dropped dead atop Arkansas Hank's corpse. Will and Lupe jumped onto the boardwalk as Bolt, Tansy, Gimpy, and Stapleton met them on the other side of the one-eyed bear and headless headhunter.

"Will, you stopped the bear that killed my folks. Gracias," Lupe whispered.

Will hugged her as Bolt felt Tansy slip her arm around his waist. When Bolt looked down at her, there were tears of relief and happiness glittering in her emerald eyes.

Will, Lupe, Bullock, General Crook, and the troops, who'd been guarding the hotel's entrances, spilled into the saloon. Doc Pierce was in tow as one of the troops had what appeared to be a bandaged stab wound in his side and the other man had a huge bump on his head. Bolt figured Mullins hadn't shot the guards so as not to alert anyone to his and Sanchez's arrival.

"Now it's over," Bolt said quietly.

"THANK YOU, MR. UTTER," Tansy said Thursday afternoon to the rugged man clad in buckskin. Bad weather had held up the delivery of the telegram for a day. Colorado Charlie had brought it to them personally along with his apology for the delay.

The saloon was closed, the bodies of the corrupt men and the rabid bear were long gone. Along with Mr. Utter, she and Bolton were sitting at Bolton's favorite table for one last time. Tansy read the telegram from Fort Laramie again. Then she smiled at Bolton.

"I was never suspected of any murders, but Rance was."

Bolton winked at her. "We're both free." He held out a payment for the good news to Mr. Utter, but the man who'd been Hickok's best friend refused it. Bolton then offered him a bottle of his wine which Utter accepted. The men stood then and shook hands. "Thanks, Charlie."

"My pleasure, Bolt," Charlie said, tipping his hat in farewell.

Deadwood's new preacher opened a swinging door for Charlie Utter and then stepped inside.

"Hello folks," he said, carrying his Bible. "Now that all the buryin's done, are you two ready for marryin'?"

EPILOGUE

Valley of the Moon
September 1879

"THE CABERNET SAUVIGNON OF THE RIVERS FAMILY Vineyard is among the world's most highly prized red-wine grapes," Tansy read in the company newspaper that was enclosed in each case of wine.

She was sitting on a whitewashed bench beneath an eight foot high, trellised grape arbor. The branching canes, planted on the large front lawn, formed a lush canopy over her head.

Tansy smiled at the king of her heart as he faced away from her studying some grapes hanging on the vine. To her delight he often shed his shirt on hot days, exposing his healed, sun-bronzed skin. He snapped off a bunch of grapes, the muscles in his back rippling from his broad shoulders down to the snug pants riding low around his waist.

These days there was no gun belt.

No one who met Bolton today would guess he'd tracked and stopped killers for ten years, Tansy thought with loving pride. Those who knew, like a couple of marshals, respected him all the more. Sonoma and the wine country had embraced the Rivers family as one of their own.

"Bolton, your wine is the best in the world," Tansy said.

"Schooling just improved Will's flair for reporting," he said, referring to the newspaper item as he turned to her. "One thing's for sure, my wife has a flair for beauty."

Bolt smiled, thinking how her emerald eardrops and pendant she had on today were as green as their vineyards. Her wedding band mirrored the grape arbor and on her right hand she wore her first anniversary present; a sapphire ring she'd picked out to match his eyes. The scooped neck of her white sundress tempted him with a hint of her sun-gold cleavage and her lips were as crimson as the grapes in his hand. Tansy's long blond hair cascaded in silky curls toward her waist.

She'd made Le Chateau Rivers their castle and she was his queen. Bolt loved to watch her regally glide through the twenty-two large, high-ceilinged rooms which she'd decorated with such exquisite taste. And when she would drawl his name on her way into his office in the right wing, his heart soared.

"Read what else Will wrote," he said.

"The Rivers Family Vineyard's cabernet has been judged as fine as the claret produced in the Bordeaux region of France. Here in the Valley of the Moon, summer temperatures range between eighty-five and one hundred, and in winter hover between fifty and seventy-five. Thus, there is little wonder why our vineyard is in the midst of harvesting yet another bumper crop."

Bolt nodded and checked his Black Hills Gold pocket watch before peering at the double front doors of the elegant mansion. He was anxious to see a certain someone come bounding toward him. Using his knife, he sliced grapes in half and removed the seeds, dropping the halves into a crystal bowl on the bench.

Tansy smiled and continued, "In eighteen seventy-seven and eighteen seventy-eight, we farmed four hundred acres and produced fifty thousand cases of wine. This year we will produce seventy-five thousand cases. We have acquired an extra one hundred acres of the most beautiful green valley on Earth. Planting on that land will begin soon and we expect to top one hundred thousand cases of wine by the year eighteen eighty. To your health, Will H. Rivers."

"Papa!"

Bolton's sapphire blue eyes lit up. Sheathing the knife, he took off to meet the little boy just coming onto the huge, stone porch. The child ran to meet him and with their beloved toddler in his strong arms, Bolton returned to Tansy.

"Did you have a good nap?" Bolton asked.

"Dood," the child replied and nodded.

"Very good," Mrs. Percy called from the porch.

They had hired Mrs. Percy as their housekeeper and Annie, as their cook. Both were loving nannies, as well. Annie, a widow, had quite the crush on Gimpy.

Before the baby was born, the Rivers Family Clinic was built on their land using the bounty from the demise of a murderer. Tansy knew that would have pleased Papa. She had finished training Lupe in midwifery and together they had trained two more women. The clinic was open five days a week and they made house calls. As of late, Lupe had blossomed in taking charge.

After Mrs. Percy went back into the house, Lupe came out.

"Is my husband back from the South Forty Print Shop, yet?"

No sooner had she asked, than Will rode into view from the direction of the print shop on what he had dubbed the south forty. Next to the shop was a new four bedroom house where Will and Lupe lived. Gimpy, by choice, enjoyed having his living quarters at the winery.

Will was strapping now at a couple hundred pounds and six foot two. Not since Tom Smith, had there ever been a more loyal and devoted best friend, not just to Bolton, but to Tansy as well. Lupe waved and rushed to meet him. The family always had Sunday supper together.

"Hey!" Will called to Lupe and brought Bill to a stop near the mansion. Sliding out of the saddle, he hugged Lupe and waved at Bolton, Tansy, and their son.

"Will!" The little boy clapped his hands.

"Howdy pardner," Will shouted to him. "Bolt, I've got the latest edition of our newspaper printed."

As Will and Lupe headed to the left wing of the mansion, Lupe called out, "Annie says to tell you that she has our supper almost ready, and it's fit for royalty!"

"Gimpy go?" the child asked.

"Gimpy Goe is at the winery, but he'll be here soon," Bolton answered, holding the toddler. He put a half-grape into the child's chubby hand. Their son popped it in his mouth and Bolton chuckled.

"Chew, chew, chew," Tansy said.

"Love Papa," the child said, wrapping an arm around

Bolton's neck and pressing tiny lips to his father's clean shaven face.

Tansy's heart beat with love as Bolton told the little boy he loved him, too, and kissed a petal-soft cheek. Then he ruffled the baby's mop of solid black curls.

"Love Mama," the toddler said, looking at her with eyes, the same sapphire blue as Bolton's.

"I love you, too, angel." Tansy put the winery's newspaper aside and Bolton handed their child into her waiting arms.

"Mama doesn't have much room left on her lap for you to sit, does she, Wiley?" Bolton asked the little boy, who was almost two and a half years old.

Wiley put his hand to Tansy's tummy.

"I will again soon," Tansy smiled. "The baby is due any day now, Wiley," Tansy whispered.

"I want at least four." Bolton gave her a sexy wink. "After all, this valley was named by the Indians. I should do my best to add some more."

"Yes." Tansy laughed. "As many as your heart desires."

Wiley hugged her and then wiggled out of her arms. Chewing another grape, he sat at her feet playing one of his favorite games, burying her toes in the rich soil of the Rivers Family Vineyard. Tansy gazed up at Bolton and laid her hand to her rounded stomach.

"Your baby just kicked me, Mr. Rivers."

Sitting down beside her Bolton wrapped an arm around her shoulders and splayed a sun-brown hand on her tummy. The baby he'd fathered kicked again and they grinned simultaneously.

Bolton kissed her and whispered, "Today reminds me of the way I once promised you it would be, Mrs. Rivers."

"Once a beautiful dreamer always a beautiful dreamer." Tansy put her hand to his cheek and said, "I love you, Bolton. Always and forever."

"You once said my claim to fame was being a bounty hunter." Bolton shook his head. "It's loving you, Tansy. Until the end of time."

HISTORICAL BACKGROUND

Bolton Rivers' gunshot wound and poultice treatment were common in Deadwood in 1876. The use of ether and chloroform began a few years before the Civil War, however in a place so isolated and violent as Deadwood it was unlikely, they would have had either available.

Bolton's best friend, Tom Smith, was a real United States Marshal whose fierce reputation and untimely death were accurately depicted. Tom's horse was named Silverheels.

Tansy Wiley's 1,200 mile journey from Texarkana to Deadwood, often on foot, was as courageous, daunting, and risky for a young woman alone and without resources in 1876, as it would be today.

Tansy's choice of Jigger as an alias comes from the measure for an alcoholic drink. Cowboys would often trade a bullet for a jigger of whiskey and that's how the term a shot of whiskey originated.

James Butler Hickok and Martha Jane Cannary met while traveling to Deadwood in Charlie Utter's wagon train. By some accounts, Hickok and Cannary became lovers, married, and had a daughter together in 1873. At the very least they were good friends and Calamity Jane readily admitted her great admiration of and infatuation with Wild Bill.

Deadwood Dolly was loosely patterned after Dora DuFran, the Black Hills' leading madam. The badlands bordello with numerous outside doors and painted inside doors is based on a true story.

Hatchet Harless Parker was a serial killer, a term not invented until the 1970s by FBI agent and profiler, Robert Ressler. Lewis Whip Rance was a narcissistic sociopath. Arkansas Hank was modeled after the horrific practices of bounty hunters who killed Native Americans.

Crooked Nose Jack McCall, California Joe, Mr. Merrick, Carl Mann, Charles Rich, William Massey, Doc Youngblood, Preacher Smith, Swill Barrel Johnny, Mr. Robinson, Isaac Brown, Seth Bullock, Con Stapleton, Mr. Deetkin, Red Clark, Laughing Sam, Al Swearigen, Sitting Bull, Crazy Horse, General Crook, General Custer, Mayor Farnum, and David Dickey made appearances in and around the Black Hills in 1876.

The Number 10 Saloon, Black Hills Weekly Pioneer newspaper, Pioneer Drug Store, Grand Central Hotel, IXL Hotel, Gem Saloon, Cricket Saloon, McDaniels/Langrishe Theater, Boughton's Dress Store, Bella Union, McAusland Brothers' Gunsmith store, pest house, and cave jail all existed and contributed to making Deadwood itself a devilish and delightful character.

Jesse James and Cole Younger's gang attempted to rob a Northfield, Minnesota bank on September 7, 1876. They netted $26.70. This failed raid was the end of the James-Younger gang.

Sonoma, California famous for its wines and vineyards is still known as the Valley of the Moon.

Bolton's Bowie knife is in tribute to my next book titled Remember the Passion featuring handsome frontiersman Blaze Bowie and fiery beauty Noelle Charbonnez.

A LOOK AT: TAME THE WILD

BY LYNN ELDRIDGE

On New Year's Eve 1905, Genevieve Morgan attends a ball at
the elaborate Palace Hotel in San Francisco hosted by Seth
Comstock, the newest, most eligible bachelor in town.
Desperate to escape the infamous bordello she inherited,
Genevieve hopes to charm and marry Comstock. Easier said
than done for a nobody fish in a little pond who cannot waltz.
As Seth catches her eye, Genevieve prays he has a warm
personality to take the chill off his cold smile. If only there was
someone to give her a few lessons not only in dancing but in
the art of seduction.

Seth warns his twin sister, Selma, to distract Harriett Peak, a
local journalist who wrote about the Nob Hill house he claims
he's building, so that he can make Genevieve his teammate for a
midnight scavenger hunt. Genevieve is not to suspect this ball
is for her benefit. Enter Luke Harper, a riverboat gambler who
is staying at the hotel while he unloads a horse ranch he won in
a high stakes poker game. One glance at the beautiful siren with
lilac cat eyes and Luke goes on his own kind of hunt.

As the music stops and dancers switch partners, Genevieve
finds herself in the arms of this man, so gorgeous he rivals
Adonis. The thought crosses Luke's mind to never let her go as
she stomps his feet. No, he's leaving soon. But finding out she
wants to marry the host, Luke's gut warns him that Genevieve
is headed for serious trouble. Will Luke vanish into the wild or
strike a deal with Genevieve, who is anything but tame?

AVAILABLE NOW!

ABOUT THE AUTHOR

Lynn Eldridge is a former president of the West Virginia Chapter of Romance Writers of America and earned an honorable mention in their Golden Heart Contest. Lynn is the author of several historical and contemporary romance novels including, Desire in Deadwood, Remember the Passion, and Tame the Wild. Her next book, soon to be released, is Skyrocket to Surrender, and she is currently working on another historical romance titled Hearts and Mountains. In addition to her writing career, Lynn is a licensed clinical therapist and dedicates one day a week in an outpatient behavioral health facility in Charleston, West Virginia.

www.ingramcontent.com/pod-product-compliance
Lightning Source LLC
Chambersburg PA
CBHW010824250626

47169CB00010B/2939